Teresa Hunter emerges from the factual world of financial services, to enthral us with her first novel, Dead Money. She brings to her story the rare combination of a close knowledge of finance, gained through her time as an award-winning consumer and personal finance journalist, and an ability to create characters, motivations, and situations with which we can all identify.

Teresa is currently a regular contributor to the Telegraph Group, Sunday Times and Corporate Adviser, as well as a member of the Chartered Insurance Institute's Professional Standards Board.

She began writing about financial matters in 1985, as a senior editor of a small team which launched MoneyMarketing, one of the industry's premier publications. She is a former personal finance editor of Scotland on Sunday and the Sunday Herald in Glasgow, and spent many years as deputy personal finance editor of the Guardian. She has also worked in television for BBC1's Watchdog and news output.

Teresa, who has an MA in Critical and Creative Writing from Southampton University, divides her time between her home in South Warwickshire, where she lives with her husband Paul, and London, Edinburgh and Cornwall. She has three children, Simon, Edward and Katy, and a cat called Willow.

With special thanks to Strathclyde police for allowing the use of their name, even though they bear no resemblance to the fictitious force in the novel and merely have the misfortune to be the force local to the region where some of the story is located.

To the good guys …

This story is dedicated to many friends in the financial services world, who taught me so much, and who, I know, work hard trying to do the right thing.

PROLOGUE

Midnight Wednesday, October 3, Bearsden, Glasgow

"Stand back, stand back," a paramedic shouts at the crowd of photographers, television crews and ghoulish onlookers, gathering in the rain outside a modest semi in a town called Bearsden. By breakfast, this respectable home will be immortalised in the minds of the nation as a 'House of Horrors'. The family who live here, no longer mother, father, son, daughter, but copy fodder for headline writers.

The mob parts to let the stretcher out. Inspector Poitu of the Met waits while the doors of the ambulance slam shut. Lights pump in the darkness as the vehicle departs.

Feet crunch on the gravel path, as he steps towards the entrance.

"Hope you had your tea early," says the officer guarding the front door, giving the inspector's ID no more than a cursory glance. He is expected.

Poitu enters the hall. Scenes of crime officers, already working in the lounge, do not stop to acknowledge the outsider. Three men kneel around the rim of a pool of blood, soaking its way through a beige carpet. Another is zipping up a body bag.

Poitu steps out through the open patio doors into the garden. Sleet rain is draining blood into tiny rivulets, glowing red under the police incident lighting. He has an uncontrollable urge to spit.

"The fourth?" he asks, as he steps back into the lounge. He means body, of course.

Without looking up, an officer taking samples from the carpet points back to the hall. "Second on the left," he says.

Poitu finds the study. More police are working there, silently, apart from the swinging 'clack-clack' of an office ball game someone has accidentally knocked. He doesn't notice the immaculate decor. He doesn't open the three filing cabinets, so cannot admire their wonder of order and efficiency. Only later will he remember not a single piece of paper is out of place on the desk.

His eyes are drawn straight to the wall behind it, splattered red.

"Blew his brains out, bastard," says one of the officers. Poitu stares at the sticky, sickly substance, clinging to the wall.

"Wish I'd got there first," the officer adds.

Midnight Wednesday, October 3, Edinburgh

Fifty miles to the east, the stillness of an office is broken by the shrill ring of a telephone. Alexander Ross starts, and rubs his eyes. He flicks his wrist to check the time.

"Midnight …" he hadn't realised it was so late. Closing a buff file on his desk, he reaches for the receiver.

"Who can this be?" He wrinkles his handsome, intelligent face into an irritable scowl.

He knows the voice at the other end. As he listens, his heart begins to race, quietly at first, then louder, until it thumps against his rib cage.

The line goes dead. He lets the receiver drop, cradling it in the crook of his neck.

"No, no, dear God, no. It was only money, Ken," he says, slumping down in his chair.

"Dear God," he repeats over and over.

Midnight Wednesday, October 3, Black Top, Glasgow

The room is cold and dark, but the child is too afraid to switch on the naked bulb. The dark is infinitely preferable to what the light might bring. A tear slides down her cheek. He had promised to help them. To set them free.

"Just a couple more days," he promised.

How she had dreamed of it … and then the nightmare began …

2

Chapter One

9.30am Friday, September 28, Whitechapel, London

"Bad news, I'm afraid, Jules," Omar Khan greeted me with what just about passed for a smile. "They won't drop the case."

I was disappointed, but not exactly surprised. I had always doubted that getting me sacked would satisfy Kane National Savings Bank. No, I had to be permanently ruined.

"We had hoped that now ..."

"Now they've dropped the action against the Examiner ..." I finished for him.

"We understand they've withdrawn the libel writ against the newspaper ..."

"But not against me personally?"

He shook his head slowly. "The Examiner are such cowards. They would have walked it in court. Victor Kane didn't have a leg to stand on."

"It's my fault, me and my sharp tongue. When will I learn?"

Omar smiled despite himself. "What was it you wrote? Kane but not able."

"It was a joke."

"Not everyone shares your sense of humour."

He was right, of course, and so was the Examiner.

"The legal bills would have crippled them. There were a thousand jobs at stake," I said.

"Which bullyboy Kane knew full well... straightforward thuggery." For a lawyer, Omar could be endearingly injudicious, but, try as hard as I did, I couldn't bring myself to hate my former employer for giving in to the bank's blackmail.

"And it worked," I said, which was the hardest bit for both of us. "It always works. The deepest pocket always wins."

Our eyes met across the desk of my office in Whitechapel.

"Don't you ever get tired of it all, Omar? All the slippery

characters, the crooks who get out with their millions just before the whistle blows."

"It's your millions I'm more worried about right now."

"Millions?" I laughed. "You can't get blood out of a stone."

It was laughable. Only a few short months ago, I was the proud possessor of an office overlooking the Bank of England, a senior editor with the City Examiner. Then I tweaked the nose of KNS's Victor Kane, forgetting he had learnt his business survival strategies in the playgrounds of Glasgow's East End.

"Come on," Omar wasn't having any of it. "You'll live to fight another day."

I shook my head.

"It's over."

"Not at all. It'll never get to court. There's no case to answer. Kane's lawyers aren't idiots. They know they'd be slaughtered, and hammered with costs for wasting court time."

"I wish I had your confidence."

"It's a simple game of who blinks first. And it won't be us."

I knew he meant well, but the time had come to walk away.

"I can't fund a fight," I pleaded. "I need all my money to pay my bills while I crank start my career."

"Money's no problem," he said deadpan. "We do loans. We can mortgage your flat."

He threw back his head and laughed, "Your face … a picture."

But when his chuckles subsided, he turned serious. "Dad says our family owes you, so you're not to worry about a thing."

My spirits had improved by the time he left, but not for long. My next visitors were two trade unionists, convinced they had been robbed by their employer.

I felt sorry for them. Truly, I did. They had never asked anyone for anything, and now they were asking me. But there was nothing I could do to help them.

"You're our last hope, Julia," said the Glaswegian. "We've been to the polis and the fraud office. We've even been to government, but nobody wants to know."

I'd known Ken Strachan for years. He was a good man, a good trade unionist, and a good friend to me. Given me some cracking leads in the past; indeed, my first big break. He was straight and he was sound. But my mind was made up. I had to stay out of trouble until this court case was settled.

"I'm sorry Ken. Truly sorry. But there's nothing I can do. You'll never prove fraud. Even if we did, it won't get your members their money back."

"Maybe. But I'd be happy seeing somebody behind bars."

"Sure," I agreed. "That won't happen either."

"It might." He slammed a newspaper cutting on the desk and stabbed at the picture of a dark-suited man, wearing a trilby hat on top of iron grey hair.

"Here's a good place to start. We need you. We can't do this ourselves." He spoke in short sharp bursts, agitation rising along with his frustration. "You got the folk at English Life their money back. Helped those mugs, who bought dodgy bonds. You've helped tons of people, whose savings vanished. This thing's bigger than all that. Bigger than you ken. Why will you no help us now?"

I looked Ken straight in the eyes. "We can't win, we can't beat them."

"Nay, lassie, nay," defeatism was not in his vocabulary.

"We never have. Not really."

He flinched.

"It can't be right. You graft all your life, put a wee bit by for when you're old, then just as you're ready to hang up your boots you're told your pensions been lost."

Of course, it wasn't right. It had nothing to do with right or wrong. It was business.

"Lost, they say," Yorkshireman Jim Sugden joined in. "Lost, like you were careless, or summat. Somehow mislaid a fortune." His thumbs twitched erratically across his palms. "I paid my money in every week for 40 years. That was my money. It isn't lost. It's been stolen."

Ken had warned me about the breakdown, when he called to arrange the appointment. Sugden's nerves were shot to pieces. I had tried ever-so-gently to put them off, but they wouldn't be waylaid.

"It came as a terrible shock," Sugden continued. "'Don't worry,' we were told, 'At least, your pension's safe. They can't touch that.' It was all lies. At nearly 58, I was out of work without a penny to live on. I had a nervous breakdown with the shock. Under psychiatrist for three months. Then I had to find work …"

"What work can you get at 58? Tell me that?" Strachan interrupted.

"Ended up as a baggage handler at an airport, humping heavy cases," Sugden's lips were trembling.

"First his back went," Ken was angry. "Then his knee. He was told by the doctor to use one of those metal frames."

"Couldn't," Sugden's voice quivered. "Had to keep working. Nothing to live on. Had to keep doing the lifting job."

Ken leaned across my desk and took my hand pleading.

"Help us Julia and I'll give you the best story you've ever printed."

But he was asking for the impossible. I had just been sacked in humiliating circumstances, and had a writ for a million pounds hanging over my head. There was no way I could start heading into more trouble right now. Even if I did investigate and come up with a decent story, who would print it?

He dropped my hand, and slammed a tight fist hard onto the desk.

"How come nobody listens?" he shouted furiously. "Tell us, Julia, just tell us. How do we get folk to listen?"

Sugden had one more try. "You will help us, won't you?"

I did not respond.

Chapter Two

1pm Friday, September 28, Whitechapel, London

When they had gone, I switched on the television to catch the 1 o'clock headlines. Another teenager stabbed in London; an engineering firm had collapsed with the loss of 500 jobs; students were drowning in debts; and the stock market was down a further 20 points. Not much joy there. I killed the screen.

Meanwhile, I had to get on with my life, and my first priority was finding work. I had an office, a desk, a TV, a telephone and a PC; everything I needed to embark on a new career as a freelance journalist. There was only one ingredient missing … commissions.

I had spent weeks trying, ever since Marsha offered me office space in the community project she ran on the Whitechapel Road.

There was nothing for it. I began calling and emailing every contact I could think of.

"Josh, it's Julia Lighthorn, how are you?" I bubbled down the line to the financial editor of the Weekly City News. I'd known Joshua Bailey for 20 years.

"Jules, how good to hear from you," he responded, before cursing, unconvincingly, "Oh, damn …"

How did I know this was coming?

"My other line's going. Can I come back to you?"

"Sure," my heart sank.

"Email me your number, I'll get back soonest," and he was gone.

He wasn't the first old friend to cut me dead and he wouldn't be the last.

But I wouldn't give up. I would never concede defeat. If I allowed Kane to destroy me, his victory would be absolute. Evil would emerge triumphant. I couldn't let that happen. So I kept calling, as the weak autumn sun seeped out of a darkening sky. Call after call was either cut short on some lame excuse, or simply tolerated in non-committal silence. My inbox was empty. Emails unanswered.

At 5pm I decided to call it a day. Mina, Marsha's reluctant receptionist, put her head round the door, and plonked a coffee in front of me, announcing her departure for the evening.

"Tell her ladyship, if she wants anything tonight, she can get it herself." Quomina, to give the former bag-lady her full title, pronounced the 'her' with a huff. She had never quite forgiven Marsha for rescuing her from Waterloo's cardboard city, and making her respectable.

I stood sipping coffee for a while at the window, watching the busy world go by below. The offices, above a Bangladeshi supermarket, were squeezed between silks and spice outlets, discount stores and betting shops; the stalls of the Whitechapel market a wash of colour opposite the severe Victorian hospital across the road.

Traffic, both human and petrol-driven, poured ceaselessly by, twenty-four-seven. This tiny corner of London was a beacon and sponge for all the world's weary; the dispossessed and the outcast. Its capacity to absorb, integrate, and expunge refugees through the centuries knew no limits. They came and they went, but the market lived on, vital and vibrant.

As soon as there was a London, they had come. Those persecuted by religious wars had found a safe haven in its filthy streets; the Huguenots, Irish and Jews. After them, Asians, fleeing tyranny, came in search of asylum. Many, like Omar's family, the Khans, flourished. Three Khan brothers fled a war-torn Kashmir in the 1940s in the hope of a better life. An uncle encouraged them towards the law, and paid for their studies, even though he could ill afford it. They each held a two-foot by one-foot brown attaché case, into which were neatly packed all their belongings, when they emerged out of Whitechapel tube station, looking for that uncle's house. Each Khan brother had three sons, and those three sons spawned dozens of sons and daughters, almost all of whom became lawyers.

Now Khans had grown to become one of London's most powerful law firms. They moved out of Whitechapel long ago, into prestigious offices in Docklands. Not quite the City, but no longer the East End either. A bridge, maybe, between the two.

Now, it was the time of the Afghans and the Kurds, the Romanians and Somalis. They scuttled by on the street below; children, who never seemed to be at school; women in their yashmaks; the elderly, tired and crumpled by their experiences, old beyond their years. The young stallholders, mobiles glued to ears, exuded energy, hope and enterprise. Soon, they too would be gone, in search of their first million.

Next came the student nurses and doctors, jogging towards the pelican crossing, heading back to their rooms at the Royal London for a quick bite and change before the night shift.

The phone rang. I seized it hopefully, but it was a wrong number. So I returned to the window, where I saw Marsha running in haste to get back to the office. She was returning from a meeting with the probation service. Marsha exuded everything that was good about London. Born and bred in Tower Hamlets, just like her parents, and their parents, she loved every smell and brick, every hope and disappointment of this deprived borough.

I knew she would begin badgering me the minute she arrived. "Jules, how do we get the banks to agree to offer ex-cons banking services?" she would ask. Tricky one that, reconciling bank robbers and bank accounts.

I was rehearsing the words with which I would try to explain the banks' anathema to armed villains, when the phone rang again.

"Julia speaking."

"Julia," came a dark voice at the other end. "This is Andrew Ludgate. I am …"

I knew perfectly well who Ludgate was; commissioning editor of the Square Mile Journal, one of Britain's foremost daily financial publications. It was one title I hadn't approached. I thought they wouldn't touch me with my current baggage.

"I've long been a fan of your writing and wondered if you might pop in for a chat."

He sounded friendly, not the ogre of repute.

"Yes, it would be good to meet," I tried to sound willing, but not desperate.

"Good. I'll be out of town for the next few days. Come and see me on Thursday. Let's make it 2pm. You know where our offices are?"

"Of course, near the Bank."

"Good, I'll see you then."

The line went dead, as Marsha came crashing through the door.

"Doll, don't you look like the cat that's got the cream," she said.

I couldn't help it. I leapt to my feet and punched the air.

"Yippeeeeeeeee," I squealed, running to her and throwing my arms around her leather-clad, short-skirted, little body. We awkwardly jigged a celebratory bop, before Marsha pushed me away.

"Leave it out," she said, wriggling the tight skirt back into place.

"That was the Square Mile Journal. They want to offer me work."

"Jules, that's triffic. What did I tell you?" Marsha was one of the few people, who never stopped believing in me.

But I never made it to the interview.

Chapter Three

7.30am Thursday, October 4, Southwark, London

I rose on Thursday, hope riding high, convinced my luck was about to turn. I picked the newspaper up off the door mat, glancing at the headlines above the fold. Nothing much. Political row over hospital waiting lists made it to the lead, with Israeli tank incursion into Gaza the main picture story.

I tucked the newspaper under my arm, and shuffled into the kitchen to make that first coffee of the day. This ritual had underpinned my life for years. I liked to concentrate on the little tasks. It was always the small things which mattered. It was the same with work. I had never gone looking for big scandals. I had learnt early on the job, if you chip away at small stories, more often than not you find the one cracked brick that brings the whole house down.

The kettle bubbled as I carefully measured the first spoon of coffee. Next, I filled the pot with boiling water, and waited three minutes precisely, before pushing the plunger.

It tasted delicious. Keep to the rules and the coffee never disappoints. The morning was starting well. All the omens were good. I returned with coffee tray and paper to bed. This was my favourite time of the day. Tucked up between the sheets, I would peruse yesterday's news, in anticipation of the new cycle about to begin.

I was scanning the front page for anything that would give me smart one-liners for the interview, when a headline in the 'News in Brief' column caught my eye. Blazoned in 14 point was 'Union Leader shot dead - turn to page seven'.

Don't ask me how I knew what these words foreshadowed, but my pulse started to race.

"Jesus God … please God no," I repeated, as I rapidly turned to page seven, dreading to find what I feared would be spread across the page; a picture of Jim Sugden, the man I had callously refused to help just a few days ago.

But when I got to the story, there was no picture. I began to read, but the words didn't make any sense. I couldn't seem to grasp, what they were trying to say. This had nothing at all to do with Jim.

Gradually, the mist began to clear and as it did so, a cold sinking feeling crept through me. I gasped, as the shock hit home, a hand lifting automatically to my mouth to gag any further sound. It was starting to make sense, yet it made no sense at all. The picture, the headline, and the story were falling into place. I understood everything, and yet I understood nothing. How could I have been so blind?

'Shooting tragedy near Glasgow

The close-knit community of Bearsden was last night reeling with shock after a shooting at the home of trade unionist Ken Strachan.

Four bodies were found at the house in Station Road. Strachan was known to have been depressed because of the collapse of Kelly's Brewery.

Police are still investigating, but believe Mr Strachan may have shot his family before turning the gun on himself.

Neighbours paid tribute to Strachan's life-time service to workers in the distilling and brewing industries throughout the UK, but in particular to those working at the Glasgow plant.

He had recently been campaigning for compensation for employees who ...'

... and so the story went on, but I didn't read any more.

Chapter Four

10am Tuesday, October 9, Glasgow

I don't know what took me to the funeral. Guilt I suppose. I had flown up the night before and booked into a city centre hotel. I couldn't face walking to the graveyard alone, so I caught a taxi outside Queen Street Station.

It was almost a dry day for Glasgow, a charcoal sky giving way to drizzle. People continued about their business unperturbed, no strangers to rain. I was forced to abandon the cab a few hundred yards from St Mungo's Cathedral, where the service was to be held. His parish church was thought too small to accommodate the numbers wanting to pay their respects. They were right. The traffic was gridlocked with mourners, so I joined an army of silent marchers heading for the funeral on foot.

They were coming in droves to respect the dead man; iron men with iron grey hair atop crisp black suits. Women came too, smaller in number, dressed with the chic austerity of Scotland in mourning. So many, the police cordoned off the arterials leading to the precinct. They had refused to listen to him in life. Now death had silenced him, they would come.

The pageant of the Strachan family funeral wasn't so much sad, as surreal. Multiple funerals, with the line up of different-sized coffins, are always a torture. Who can look on child-sized coffins, without wanting to rage at some higher being?

So we didn't look, stealing instead surreptitious glances at each other. Few of the faces meant much to me, but the heavy police presence and road blocks said it all. The congregation was pitted with the great and the good, as well, no doubt, as a smattering of the not so good. Who many were, I could only guess at. Certainly union leaders, politicians, and top brass from some big local employers would be present.

It seemed the eulogies were never going to end. Ken had plenty of enemies. In fighting for his members, he had never hesitated to strike with a poisoned knife. Now, one by one, his former adversaries stood up and sang his praises.

Ronnie Raeburn, national boss of the Brewery Workers Union was the first to the altar, and spoke of a man who always put others first, a fearless fighter.

"I've lost a dear friend and brother," he said. But he left me cold, something was lacking.

He was followed by the local MP David Ragland, also a senior cabinet minister. He had a ruthless reputation for assassination, which I had cause to know was justified. He spoke of his 30-year friendship with Ken, whom he described as one of the few people he could trust to tell him the truth.

"He could never see a small man in trouble and walk by on the other side of the street," he finished tamely. Not like your Government, I couldn't help thinking.

But what right did I have to criticise? I had been no better a friend.

Next, a junior minister, Richard Crippledown, who had repeatedly stonewalled Ken's letters, stood up to pay his respects.

"He worked tirelessly for the common cause."

I didn't think I could take much more of this. So I let my thoughts wander to the day I had spent on the phone last Thursday, after I had shoved the newspaper aside on the bed clothes. No one had been able to tell me what had happened; not the police; not the hospital; local hacks on the spot; not the union; none of his close colleagues or professional associates.

A gun had gone off sometime late that day. The police found four bodies when they entered the house. The news of the shooting had broken early enough to make it down to London for the next morning's last edition.

People were reluctant to pass comment, but the consensus seemed to be that strain had brought on some kind of psychotic break. He had lost his mind and killed his family, before turning his gun on himself. They even had a technical term for it, these days. He was called a 'family annihilator'.

Next, the business community lined up to give thanks for Ken's professionalism, pragmatism, and fair play in all their dealings across the negotiating table. They were followed by Stephen Russell, headmaster at Clydebank School, where Ken had coached football training. He spoke of Ken's great love of children. There was even a short thank you from Sister Robert, who ran the drop-in centre for asylum seekers. He had helped her with language classes. From Kelly's Brewery, though, there was silence.

Finally, the archbishop, leading a team of four priests, spoke of the great love the Strachan family had shared, and how they had gone to a better place, where they could be happy together. I wanted to scream at this cant and hypocrisy. Two children and an innocent woman lay dead in front of us. Yet, no one mentioned the 'M' word. No one said, we are gathered here together to celebrate the murder of three innocent people, and the death of a fourth, also an innocent.

I was not alone in these thoughts. A frail figure in the front pew raised a skeletal arm and began to gesticulate, stopping the cleric mid-sentence. An assistant priest descended the altar steps and walked towards her. It was an elderly woman, who looked as though she was collapsing in on herself. She wore a black mourning coat. White hair, like delicate silk threads, peeped out from below a shiny black hat, the sort Mexican bandits wear in westerns, but with a narrower brim. I had never seen anyone wear such a hat.

The hat was respectable enough though, which could not be said of what threatened to follow.

"Please dear God, don't do this," I thought.

God wasn't listening. The figure in mourning wobbled on a walking stick towards the altar, climbed its steps unsteadily, and made her way to the lectern.

But there was nothing frail about the way she turned to address the congregation, her eyes blazing with a look of deranged anger.

"My son never killed naebody," she whispered into the microphone. Then she raised her voice. "You killed them." Her words echoed around the ancient columns.

"It was you," she pointed straight into the body of the church, drawing a circle from left to right, shouting over and again, "All of you … All of you."

Ordinarily it would have taken a heart of stone not to laugh at such a spectacle. No one laughed. No one breathed. A chill crept through the pews. She lowered her arm, and walked back to her seat, as calmly and with all the dignity her frail figure could muster. She didn't shed a tear.

It was a relief to hear the music strike up, and watch the bearers hoist the coffins on to their shoulders. I spotted some of Ken's union friends among those who carried the family to their graves. Jim Sugden was with them. The clergy led the procession. A union banner, woven in black silks for such occasions, was carried ahead of the coffins.

The path to the top of the hill was slow and rocky, and the faces that marched upwards were frozen masks. The Victorian graveyard, overshadowing the cathedral, had been built for slave merchants. What would Ken have thought, I wondered, at spending eternity among such company. A Strachan ancestor had been a bishop, so it was decided, I don't know by whom, that they should all be buried in the family vault.

The climb to the top was tortuous. The steep path too narrow for the nigh on two-thousand mourners stumbling up it, many, like Mrs Strachan, hobbling with walking sticks. The numbers at least brought some comfort, along with the singing of the choir, as we marched in the grey drizzle, past hideous effigies of those long dead; monstrous symbols of egos, which still had power to haunt. Mausoleums, the size of small chapels, baroque statues and carvings, repellent in their extravagance. There were row after row of monolithic obelisks, like stone needles to pierce cloud storms and disperse evil spirits, a cruel reminder of how much those lying here had to fear from the afterlife.

A mist was descending as we made it to the summit. The column of mourners gathered into a crowd, as the coffins were laid outside the

16

mausoleum, in preparation for internment. The singing stopped. The archbishop mumbled the final prayers of farewell.

Yet his words were drowned out by the cawing sound of four huge gulls, flying inland from the Clyde, escaping from a gathering storm.

My eyes followed them, as they glided across the skyline, heading away from the sea and into the safety of the hills. And then I saw him. Jack Kelly. Standing in a black suit, and trilby, his face partly obscured by a dark shadow of cloud. So he had come after all. Jack Kelly, the man who killed Ken.

Chapter Five

12.45pm Tuesday, October 9, Glasgow

My attention was distracted by a police siren below. I looked down to see if I could distinguish whether it was a fire or car accident. But I couldn't, not from that distance.

When I raised my eyes again to the burial party, Jack Kelly had disappeared; vanished like a ghost into the mist. The praying stopped and mourners turned away from the grave to begin their descent home. For the Strachan family, the journey was over.

We started in silence, but mourners soon began muttering among themselves the platitudes one exchanges as one walks away from death.

There was time to kill before my flight home. I had a few good contacts in the city, who I knew would be happy to stand me lunch, but I couldn't face company. Across the cathedral precinct, Glasgow's famous Museum of Religious Art advertised an exhibition, 'Women and War'. I couldn't face that either, but I had to do something, anything to keep busy. I had to block out the image of that tiny black figure, in that strange little hat, kneeling in front of the mausoleum, back, straight as ramrod, dry-eyed, weeping those silent tears of the utterly bereft. So dignified, yet so alone.

I set off at a quick pace to beat the other mourners to a cab, when I felt a hand on my elbow, drawing me up sharply. I turned to see a strange-looking character, dressed in formal morning suit, complete with top hat. At first, I thought it was the lead undertaker, calling me back to the grave.

"C..C..Carlton C..C..Crabb, solicitor for the deceased," he stuttered. My heart went out to him. What an unfortunate name for someone so afflicted.

He got my name in one, though. "Ms Lighthorn, I am here to invite you to attend my ch..ch..chambers. Matter of a bequest."

At that moment, a cawing gull swooped down towards us. We both ducked, sensing it was about to release its bowels. I got lucky. Mortar grey motion splattered Crabb's top hat, and slid down the front of his frock coat.

Crabb pulled out a monster white cotton handkerchief, and began scrubbing furiously at his coat. I strangled an urge to laugh.

"Your hat," I pointed to his topper.

"My hat?"

"Your hat," I repeated.

He took it off, and saw what I was getting at.

"Dear me, what a mess," he began rubbing furiously, mashing the sides in the process.

"Perhaps he was a legal eagle?" I couldn't resist.

He gave me a dry look, and continued scrubbing, until, having removed most of the excrement, he replaced the stained and slightly battered hat back on his head and returned to business.

"Mr Strachan's bequest ... 106, George Square. I have a luncheon appointment, but 3pm would be c..c..convenient."

"You want me to come to your office for three? What for?"

"I am an agent of others. I c..c..carry out instructions. I am servant to my hourly fee. I will see you at three, then?"

With these words, he turned on his heels. I watched him disappear across the precinct, his misshapen silk hat balancing precariously. I wondered if his hourly fee covered his funeral expenses, because that hat was ruined.

Yet I was intrigued. He knew my name. If I interpreted correctly, he had something for me. It had to be worth half-an-hour of my life. I looked at my watch. A quick spot of lunch, and I'd still have an hour before I needed to set off for George Square. I looked again at the poster promoting the 'Women and War' exhibition. Maybe it was worth a twirl.

Chapter Six

3pm Tuesday, October 9, George Square Glasgow

In the 19th century George Square had been the finest plaza, in the second richest city, of the greatest empire on earth. In today's fashionable, edgy Glasgow it seemed unsure of itself, like an elderly uncle at a rave.

Crabb's offices had a foot in both worlds, new and old, conservative yet convincing, with a few delinquent floor boards that creaked in all the right places. I arrived at the dot of three, and was led through modern high-tech offices. In Crabb's office, though, there was no computer screen, no glass, no plastic, just a grandfather clock, ticking noisily beside the wooden coat stand. How Bill Gates would eat his heart out.

Crabb was waiting for me behind a solid oak desk, the size of a dining-room table and embossed with gold. He had changed out of morning suit and into a dark pinstriped outfit.

"My c..c..client engaged me to c..c..convey this," he paused to catch his breath, "article to you."

With these words, he pushed a padded brown envelope in my direction. The clock struck the quarter of an hour. He looked at his watch, checking its accuracy. It was slow, I supposed, because he began fiddling with the wind-up mechanism.

"Your client?" I asked.

"Mr Strachan."

I was not surprised. I knew Ken had collected a mountain of paperwork to support his case against Kelly. I opened the package carefully. Crabb looked at his watch again, as if making the point that his time was money and he couldn't be late for his next meeting.

"It's a diary," I said, turning the purple book over in my hands.

"Indeed."

"Did you know he had left me his diary?"

"Mr Strachan's Will won't be read for a week, but he gave specific instructions that you were to be handed this package discreetly immediately after his funeral."

This didn't make any sense.

"When did he give you these instructions, and the package?"

"A fortnight ago."

"But that's impossible. How could he have known …?"

"I never mistake a client's instructions, Ms Lighthorn."

"Well, you have this time. He must have deposited the diary with you for safekeeping for his family. You are confusing it with other papers he wished me to have."

Crabb looked shocked.

"Ms Lighthorn, I never confuse my client's instructions."

"This time you have," my voice was firm. "Ken Strachan was in robust health. He could see me any time he wished. Indeed, he did last week. A diary is a private document for posterity, for future generations."

He stood. "Ms Lighthorn, I have another appointment. Trust me, Mr Strachan wanted you to have his diary. It is not my business to know why. I merely suggest it is natural to wish to put matters in order before one dies."

"He wasn't facing death, he was in robust health," I repeated.

"Fear death, then."

"No, that's not possible," I shook my head. "That means …"

"It means he wanted you to have his diary."

I continued shaking my head in disbelief. "It's not possible. He couldn't have. There must be another explanation."

Crabb sat again. Maybe Strachan's hourly fee wasn't quite used up. He cleared his throat noisily several times. When he spoke again, his voice was softer.

"In our jobs, we both see much which is …" but there he stopped. I don't think his heart was in it.

"Will you tell them? The police?"

"My instructions were to hand this package to you. I have fulfilled the obligation for which I was paid."

He stood again. My time was up. As I walked down the stairs, I wondered how Ken could have used the services of such a man. But then, I seemed to know so little of the real Ken any more.

The plane was in the air, before I opened the book. I had spent the time in the airport lounge catching up with the news. Suicide bomber in Algiers, a shooting on Moss Side; the market had closed, after a day of falling prices. The slide was looking unstoppable. Fear beginning to take hold.

Purple was not a colour I would have associated with Strachan. In my mind, he had already ceased to be Ken. I turned first to the final entry, only to be disappointed. It offered little clue to his state of mind before he died.

Monday October 1
'Janey left me a fish pie for tea. Can't wait. My favourite.'

These didn't sound like the words of a man on the verge of blowing his family away.

The plane would touch down at City airport in 45 minutes, so there was only time for a quick skim of the diary. I turned back to the beginning, scanning the opening pages. Like many of his age, his grammar and spelling were meticulous. It began two years earlier, on October 3rd 2000, his 50th birthday and two years to the day before he died. The diary was a present from his beloved Emma, his daughter.

The first entry read:
'I must have done a good deed to someone sometime, dear lord, how you rewarded me. Life hasn't always been easy. We struggled when we were young. But you gave me the best wife and family any man had a right to. And work which has paid for a good life for us.'

How easy it could be to believe in a jealous God. Ken got his reward from heaven all right. Less than eighteen months later, Kelly's

Brewery called in the liquidators. He was about to lose his job and his pension. I skimmed on. Soon after that, he was in full swing, campaigning for compensation for his members, after they had discovered the pension kitty was empty.

In April he wrote:
'Interview with Radio Scotland went well. The more we do to highlight the cause the better. Jim says we should write again to the prime minister.'

But it wasn't all good news. The entries logged the times when his spirits flagged, and strain told on his marriage.

Last July 24 he wrote:
'Came home to find Janey in tears. "What'll we do, What'll we do," she kept crying. I had no answer.'

My name cropped up from time to time. My heart sank as I read the entry for September 28, when we had last met.

'Very successful meeting with Julia. I know she'll take up the cudgels on our behalf. She is very good and knows all the right cages to rattle.'

Well, if he thought our meeting had been a success, he must have been losing his marbles. The next sentence was puzzling though.

'Couldn't tell her the half, of course. In good time. Then we'll crack both birds with one stone.'

What couldn't he tell me? I read on. Two days later on Sunday he wrote:
'Hoping to see R tomorrow. Then the game will be up.'

Who was R, and what game was he talking about?

I flicked through the pages, scanning entry after entry; meetings with other trade unionists, some I recognised, while other names were unfamiliar. Little snippets of news. It seemed that on that weekend Janey and the kids had gone to visit her sister in Inverness for a few days, which explained why the fish pie had been 'left'. They must have returned on Tuesday or Wednesday.

I reread the penultimate entry.
'Hoping to see R tomorrow. Then the game will be up.'

Who was R?

I thought back to the funeral. Could it be Raeburn from the union or that dangerous Bearsden MP Ragland? What about Crippledown, the junior minister? His first name was Richard. Had Ken finally secured a meeting?

I looked out the window. The plane had begun its descent; the lights of London twinkled below. It was impossible. The pages were littered with people whose names began with 'R'.

I turned back to the book, and all of a sudden, on the page before me, his face appeared. And I saw him all over again, in my office, banging his fist on the desk.

And he was shouting, all over again, "This thing's bigger than all that. Bigger than you ken."

A chill crept through me. What did he mean, 'bigger than you ken'? And who was R? Had something at that meeting tipped him over the edge? Or was R the man who had sold him the gun?

Chapter Seven

8am Wednesday, October 10, City of London

The next day began with breakfast with Andrew Ludgate. We had postponed our meeting until after the funeral. I so needed this to go well. I was desperate for a fresh start, a distraction.

It was dark when I emerged from Bank tube station and made my way down Pope's Head Alley. Within minutes, I left the shadows of old London, and arrived at a glass tower. The lift whizzed me to the top floor. The view was magical. Lights flickered across the city. They never dimmed. Workers traded London during the day, New York all evening, and Tokyo through the night.

I was directed to a glass bubble at the end of a vast open-plan office. It was good to be back in a newspaper office. A few bleary-eyed hacks were making their way to their desks, slowed by the excesses of the previous night. Sounds were muted and hushed. Later the office would erupt into energy; phones would ring incessantly, editors shout instructions to their underlings, and at each other, amid the rows and power struggles of the day. Then, I would be glad to be gone.

Andrew was an interesting specimen. He had that easy charm which all journalists can switch on and off. Right now it was on.

"Julia, it's good to finally meet," he signalled for me to sit on a red sofa. He sat on a white one opposite.

"We're looking to refresh our team of writers and wanted to discuss possible assignments with you. We like your work."

"That's kind."

"What are you working on right now? "

"There's a firm of brokers in Guildford, churning investments; ripping off clients for commissions …" It was a rumour I'd picked up.

"The FSA?" he referred to the city police.

"Are on to them, that's why we need to do it soon."

"Can we, without being sued?" I determined not to blanch at the word 'sued', even though it hit a raw nerve.

"If we're careful, yes. A little bird tells me the FSA's going public next week. We need to get it away before this weekend."

"See if you can."

"I've been wanting to take a look at Estuary Bank," I continued.

"Creighton's a friend of the chairman," Andrew said, killing that idea, because of the friendship between the two boards.

"Also we need to look at the magic circle."

He shook his head. "It's in hand. That reminds me …"

"What about price fixing in the housing market," I was beginning to panic. This wasn't going well.

He cut me dead. Raising a hand, he shouted through the open door to his secretary.

"Helen, ask Dan Newall to come and see me in five."

My windpipe tightened. He had lost interest already. I was about to be dismissed.

He turned his gaze back to me and spoke the words I least wanted to hear. "The pensions story. We need to stay on top of it." He paused. "How was the funeral?"

Was it my imagination, or did his tone soften?

"Awful."

"Good. We'll have a colour piece for Saturday, and a full analysis of how we got here."

He stood and walked to a filing cabinet, opening the top drawer and rattling inside for a few moments. He returned clutching a wad of papers.

"I've had a contract drawn up. Our standard terms. Not ungenerous, I think you'll find."

My heart leapt as I flicked through the package. Not ungenerous was an understatement. I had to stop myself snatching the pen out of his hand and signing as fast as I could before he could change his mind. Play it cool, a little voice whispered.

"So, can I welcome you aboard?"

I smiled and bent to sign, but something made me hesitate.

"Andrew, have you heard?" I could have pulled my tongue out, but, too late, the words slipped through my lips. He cut me short.

"We know about the court case. I've read the story. So has the editor. It was a fine piece. We're both convinced you're the kind of writer we're after."

I smiled, perhaps a little too gratefully, and signed. Then I stood and we shook hands.

"I won't disappoint you," I promised.

"I hope not. By the way, do you know the Kellys?" he asked, still holding my hand firmly in his.

"Only from Ken."

"I followed them closely at one stage. I was covering the drinks industry for the Financial Times. Must be ten years ago."

"Were they legit?"

"As far as I could see. But I never liked them; had several run-ins with Jack Kelly; constantly had his lawyers on my back."

His voice trailed off, as if he were lost in thought.

"There was something about the business that didn't add up, but I could never quite put my finger on it."

His secretary entered with Mr Newall, and began to usher me out.

Ludgate came back from his memories.

"All steam ahead then!"

"All steam ahead," I replied, walking backwards towards the door.

His attention diverted to Mr Newall. I was forgotten.

"Oh Julia, one more thing," he suddenly turned back to me, before I disappeared out the door. "Watch the language. Tone it down. At least until the court case is settled."

I blushed, but he was grinning, so I grinned back. There was a spring in my step and a smile on my lips all the way back to Whitechapel. I had my first assignment in a long while, and it tasted sweet.

Chapter Eight

10.30am Wednesday, October 10, Whitechapel

Call it second sight, but I had known she would come, though I was surprised she had come so soon.

Omar and Marsha were waiting for me. They emerged from Marsha's office, the instant they heard my footstep on the stair.

"You've got visitors, doll," Marsha's face wasn't as relaxed as her tone.

The frail little lady in funeral black, still with that strange hat on, sat at my desk, back ramrod straight, with Jim Sugden at her side. She didn't turn when I entered, although Sugden rose to greet me.

"Jim," I grasped his hand, before moving towards Ken's mother.

I stretched out a hand to her, but she didn't respond.

"Mrs Strachan, can I say how saddened I was …"

Still, she didn't respond, so I sat at my desk, opposite her. She didn't look at me.

Jim began for her, "Mrs Strachan wanted to meet you," he paused. "Ken spoke of you so often. I told her you were at the funeral yesterday."

"I'm sorry I didn't … I didn't want to intrude …"

"On private grief …" She turned her eyes on me, and I could see the sockets were black with tears. "How can you know what grief is, you slip of a girl? One day you'll lose the thing you love. Then, you'll know pain."

I said nothing. Her bitterness could be forgiven, so raw was her loss. But she was wrong to say I didn't know grief.

"Julia, we're here because of Ken, and what he would have wanted," Jim said.

I nodded, listening.

"You said you'd investigate Kelly's Brewery."

"I … I …" I had said no such thing, but that was hardly the point.

In the vacuum of my hesitation, Mrs Kelly stood and banged the

28

table with her tiny fist, just as her son had done. It made quite an impact, for such a frail body.

"My son never killed naebody."

I stood up to face her.

"Mrs Strachan, I really am very sorry about your loss, all our loss. I was very fond of Ken. But this is a matter for the coroner."

"Idiots and crooks," she wheezed.

I sent Jim an imploring look. He had to make her see. I had watched too many loving relatives destroy their lives because they refused to bury their ghosts.

Sugden failed me. "The pensions ... if we could find someone to blame ... then it would make all this ..." he said.

I shook my head. I wanted to scream at them. "No it won't. No, it won't make all this better. It won't make it right. It won't bring them back."

But I was too big a coward. I nodded gently instead, when Jim made one last plea for me to investigate. And I looked with shame at the tears of gratitude which sprang into his eyes.

The tiny crow-like creature with him leant across the desk and grasped both my hands in a vice-like grip. All her grief, stress and love for her family surged like an electric current through those frail fingers. I looked into her face, and the shadow of Ken Strachan stared back at me. I hadn't seen the likeness before. But it was there. Mother and son linked by more than family commitments. Theirs was an atavistic bond. They shared the same genetic code, the same blood. I could see her grief more fully. That day in Bearsden, her own blood had been spilled, not just the blood of those she loved most in this world. She only released my hand when Jim said it was time to go. She left without another word.

After they were gone, I sat for a moment with my head in my hands. Why was life so goddamn awful?

When I looked up, Omar was standing in front of me, watching silently.

"Tell me you have some good news."

He shrugged, grinning apologetically.

"The court papers have come," he threw them casually across the desk. "You need to look at them."

"Let's settle. Ring Kane's lawyers tomorrow and say we'll settle. Let him bankrupt me." Suddenly, a row over a few loose words didn't seem to matter any more.

"No," Omar's voice was calm, but determined. "We're not settling. Someone has to stand up to the likes of Kane."

"But not me … I can't do everything on my own."

"You are not on your own." His face was a mask.

Chapter Nine

11.15 am Wednesday, October 10, Whitechapel

Shortly after 11am, an email from Ludgate pinged its way into my inbox, confirming this week's commission.

It read:

'1,500 backgrounder on the pensions story, plus 700 colour piece on funeral. Deliver by 9am Friday. And get digging. We want to stay on top of this story.'

So I started work, the anxiety of financial insecurity now replaced by that equally sickening fear of failure to deliver. Oh, not the backgrounder, that would be easy enough. The colour piece I would do against my better judgment, but occasionally the need to pay the rent drowned out the inner voice of integrity. The funeral was a story. It would be written by someone. Better me, from the Strachans' perspective, than someone else.

Beyond that, where was the story going? My mind flashed back to the numerous times Ken had sat in my office, thumping the desk, "They stole our money. It's not right."

He was convinced that Kelly had stolen money out of the fund, but was there any evidence? Sure, Kelly's scheme had collapsed with a shortfall, rumoured to be around £2 billion. Plenty of funds had gone down. It didn't mean the management were crooks. People were living longer; stock markets had failed to perform. Companies couldn't afford promises they had made 20 or 30 years ago. It was terribly sad, but, as for criminal negligence, or wilful theft, that was another matter.

On the other hand, the scale of the Kelly's black hole was unusually large for a scheme of its size, compared with other collapses. Certainly, eyebrows had been raised in other cases over last minute transfers of cash into directors' accounts just before schemes imploded. Companies were strictly prohibited from withdrawing cash from pension funds, unless there was enough money in the kitty to pay all the pensions promised, and there was a well-padded safety cushion besides.

Then again, you could play with the numbers and it was an open secret a few disreputable firms had. Pension professionals tut-tutted behind closed doors and shook their heads disapprovingly. Not a case had yet come to court.

Actuaries, unlike lawyers and accountants, had no legal duty to 'blow the whistle' on their fellow professionals. So it wasn't out of the question that Ken was on to something. But if Kelly did take out money, others must have colluded, such as the scheme's actuaries and trustees. Was that likely?

I reached across for my A4 pad, and began to draw a family tree of the main suspects. Art was never my subject, so it was a scruffy affair, but it helped me to focus.

It was an inverse tree, with the central character Jack Kelly at the bottom. He was the root and trunk from which all branches grew. From him stemmed his two sons and a daughter. The sons, Tom and Richard, were both directors, with daughter, Kirsty, a non-exec member of the board. I knew the old matriarch Mary Kelly hovered somewhere in the background, but I could never remember if she was on the board or not.

A quick tap on the internet filled in that gap. She had been, but resigned three years ago, before the company ran into trouble. And the same applied to the daughter Kirsty.

According to the last set of accounts filed, Jack took home £2 million in salary and bonuses, with Tom pocketing £1.2 million. There was no mention of Richard.

I searched his name and found an old newspaper article dating back four years. He had sold out of the business, among rumours of a falling out, and emigrated to Western Australia, Perth.

Ah, Perth, where Mum, Dad, Peter, Helen and the children lived. My parents had retired over there, to be near Peter and his family, after giving up on me ever providing them with grandchildren. I was glad of the space.

A quick click into the company's pension scheme and I had details of its legal advisers, Duncan & Aitcheson in Edinburgh. Actuarial advisers were Sherlock, often referred to in the trade as 'Shylocks'.

I scrolled down the trustees. No surprises there. Jack and Tom Kelly, two shop floor workers and a pensioner. Blinding the latter three with numbers would have been easy.

One name jumped out of the screen at me. Banker to the scheme: David Black. He was a director of Kane National Savings Bank. Of course, Kane was Kelly's banker.

I told Omar about Black, when I met him at the Savoy theatre that evening. He had invited me to a performance of 'HMS Pinafore' to take my mind off the funeral. He loved Gilbert and Sullivan.

"Kane's a ruthless bastard, but he's not a crook," he said, as we sat in our seats and waited for curtain up.

"Really?"

"You're prejudiced. I've met Black. He's OK."

"Maybe."

"If you want my advice, don't get involved. OK, so they lost their pensions. So've plenty of people. Bad luck. You've more than enough to worry about right now."

"It's just."

The orchestra burst into full swing, and the curtain was rising.

"Forget Ken," Omar's voice was suddenly sharp. "He's not your problem. And anyway he was probably wrong."

Voices behind shushed us quiet, and I relaxed as the performance got underway. It had been a good choice, with humour that lifted my spirits, and razor wit that warmed.

The Admiral's song had long been a favourite, particularly the lines:

'... and when the winds blow I generally go below, and so does his sisters and his cousins and his aunts, his sisters and his cousins, who he measures up in dozens, and his aunts ...'

It was an object lesson in staying out of trouble.

At the interval, we went to the bar for a drink.

"Andrew wants me to keep chasing," I said, as Omar handed me a glass. "I think there may be some history there."

"Old scores?" Omar shook his head thoughtfully. "Be careful. Bad idea, fighting other people's battles."

"I know," I nodded, sipping my drink. "And d'you know, for once I don't feel it, here, in my guts. I didn't when Ken kept badgering me and I don't, now. It's such a huge sum of money to have 'disappeared'. The rules and safeguards may not be perfect, but there are some. I can't see how they could have got away with it."

"There you are then."

"What if I'm wrong? Surely I should at least carry out some preliminary checks. Surely I owe that to Ken … and the others?"

Omar sipped his drink thoughtfully, but did not reply until we were back in our seats.

"You don't owe them anything, Julia. If they're unhappy, tell them to write to their MP. It's not your problem."

The orchestra was beginning the rhythmic opening of the second half.

"It's all just playing with numbers anyway," Omar shifted in this seat.

"Yes it is, unless it's your pension that disappears."

Renewed shushing from behind brought any further discussion to a halt as the curtain rose for the second half.

We were in a taxi and crossing the river in the direction of my flat before our conversation resumed.

"I just can't stop thinking …"

Omar took both my hands in his, and looked me straight in the eyes. "Don't do this to yourself."

"Do you really think Ken killed his family? What made him do it, Omar? What could have made him do such a thing?"

Omar opened his mouth to say something, but no sound emerged. He closed it again, shaking his head slowly. For once the brilliant lawyer was lost for words. He released my hands and sank back in the seat.

"Is there any other possibility?" I continued. "Any other possible explanation? Could Mrs Strachan be right? Could they have been murdered by someone else?"

Omar shook his head, disappointed his advice was being rejected.

"Where would you start?" he said.

"The diary I guess."

"The what," he bolted upright again.

"His diary. I didn't get a chance to tell you before now."

"Do the police?"

"No. His solicitor handed it to me after the funeral."

"And …"

"No 'and'. I'm still reading it."

"I see."

"Then, there's the company, not that I'll get anywhere with them. Knock off the trustees, one by one, I suppose. All I would need was a sympathetic trustee, scared enough of being nailed for complicity to spill the beans. I would be home and dry."

"There may be no beans to spill. Anyway, they'd never talk."

"Then there are the actuaries and the scheme lawyers, of course," I continued, ignoring him.

"Forget the lawyers," Omar advised. "I know the legal adviser to the fund. It's Marcus Briggs. As nasty a piece of work as you will meet anywhere."

I raised my eyes questioningly to Omar.

"Oh yes, and he's Kelly's son-in-law."

Omar let the implication sink in as my mobile rang. We were pulling up outside my flat.

I flicked it to speak, "Julia Lighthorn."

It was Carlton Crabb. I'd never mistake his voice.

"Mr Crabb, whatever do you want at this hour?"

"I may be overstepping my brief here, Ms Lighthorn, but Mr Strachan instructed me during the last days of his life. I feel he would want you to have the fff ... following ... Have the f..f..foll ..."

He couldn't seem to get it out, and I could hear he was tired.

He tried again. "The f..f..following information."

"Which is?"

I heard him take a big breath and the rest came tumbling out. "Kelly's Brewery is re-opening for business. I have just heard. A solicitor friend of mine is handling the planning permission to restart production."

"But the company's bust."

"The old company, not the new one."

"Which will be called?"

"Kelly's Brewery."

"I don't believe this."

"T..t..t..trust me it is so."

"And the pension scheme?"

"I have no knowledge, but the normal procedure is ..."

"To liquidate."

"Quite."

"And the directors?"

"Naturally, in the circumstances, the former directors won't be on the board. But I understand it will still be a family business."

"Mother and daughter."

"Granddaughter, I think you'll f..f..find. But don't forget that the bankruptcy rules have changed."

"They can be back on the board in a little over a year."

"Quite."

"Thank you, Mr Crabb."

"It is my pleasure, Ms Lighthorn."

Omar couldn't have mistaken the fury in my eyes.

"Kelly's back in business."

I didn't need to let the implication sink in. We both knew what this meant.

"What did you expect?"

"No, don't Omar, don't say another word. Someone has to stop these crooks. They can't be allowed to keep getting away with it."

"But not you. Not now."

"Then, who else?"

Chapter Ten

10am Friday, October 12, Whitechapel

The Friday deadline came and went, relatively painlessly. I delivered my copy, and began looking for new story ideas and leads, starting with the 10 o'clock news bulletin. Another teenager had been stabbed, in Hackney this time. On the financial front, a bank and insurer had announced a merger, and a UK businessman had been jailed in the US. There was nothing for me in any of this.

But a one-paragraph story in the morning paper caught my eye. A businessman working for the actuarial consultants, Sherlock, was reported missing. Sherlock was the Glasgow firm advising Kelly's at the end.

Ludgate called.

"Good line, this stuff about Kelly's reopening."

I mentioned the missing Sherlock actuary.

"Yes, I saw that … he's done a runner."

"Maybe. Strange though, isn't it? I'm not so sure …"

"Oh …you be sure," he said. "Before we run anything."

He wasn't joking. I swallowed hard.

"What do the police say?"

"I was just about to call them."

"Good. Keep digging."

I dialled Strathclyde Police press office and spoke to a Sergeant Brown.

"This missing actuary …" I began.

"What do you call a hundred actuaries at the bottom of the ocean?"

"A good start." It was an old joke. "This missing actuary …"

"Donald Livingstone isn't missing, not officially, not yet." This time he was serious.

"He's been reported missing."

"By his wife. She says a couple of men came to the door, said they were police officers. He left with them."

"Were they officers?"

"Of course not. If I had a fiver for every middle-aged man who disappeared, on a lame excuse, after telling his wife he was going out and wouldn't be long, I'd be a very rich man."

"So the police aren't treating the report seriously?"

"I didn't say that," he protested. "But right now we've nothing to report."

The officer was right. Grown men and women walk out of their lives every day. Nine times out of ten, they simply want to disappear. Wasn't this too neat a coincidence, though, given the Kelly's connection?

I badly needed a lead on this pension story. Omar was right. The staff and pensioner trustees were saying nothing; warned off by their lawyers. My best hope was the independent trustee, the professional, appointed to run the crippled fund. So I dialled the Edinburgh number of Mr Alexander Ross for the sixth time.

"Mr Ross is away from the office." Protective secretaries were a curse in my job.

"Does he have a mobile with him?"

"Out of the question, he's at an important meeting."

Couldn't you guess.

"Will he be back later?"

"He has back-to-back meetings all week," with that, the line went dead.

I had to speak to this man. An independent trustee is appointed when schemes go down, with specific instructions to carry out a forensic investigation into what went wrong. If anything is found to be amiss, he has a legal duty to go to the courts to recover missing money. By now, he should have a good idea where at least some of the bodies, or rather bundles of cash, were buried.

As a breed though, they didn't like journalists, and this Mr Ross seemed no exception. I couldn't wait indefinitely in the hope he would call me back.

Omar was also right about wasting my time speaking to the scheme lawyers, and Sherlock was strictly 'no comment'. That left Cameron, a respected global company, and the actuaries who advised Kelly's up to three years ago. It might be willing to help, to protect its own reputation and divert blame elsewhere.

I pulled up Cameron's last valuation and report, completed six years ago in 1997, onto my screen. It was among the hundreds of documents Ken had sent me; files I hadn't opened until now. It put the investments held within the fund, ie the assets, at £3.5 billion, and the liabilities, ie the pensions due to be paid both now and in the future, at £3 billion. The margin was close, but close enough, with a cushion for comfort.

The valuation was signed by Maurice Patterson, a senior partner at Cameron.

I dialled the number.

"I'm afraid we have no listing for a Maurice Patterson."

"You must have. He's listed on the documents I have here as one of your staff." I wasn't going to be fobbed off by an officious switchboard operator.

"Hold the line."

Simon and Garfunkel's 'Bridge Over Troubled Water' clicked in. Presumably, the mood music was designed to calm clients, begging the question why so many were angry in the first place.

"Can I help you?" came a fresh voice.

"I'm trying to contact Maurice Patterson."

"I'm afraid he no longer works for us."

"Oh?"

"He retired three years ago."

"Three years ago?"

"Something like. Before my time."

"Do you know where I could reach him?"

"Even if I did, I wouldn't be able to disclose that information. It's against company policy. But I'm afraid I don't."

The line snapped shut.

So he was no longer with the company, and retired three years ago.

What should I make of that? For lack of any other inspiration, I began a Google search on Cameron and browsed its website, clicking idly through the press release archive, looking for an announcement of his retirement, or any other reference.

He was a past chairman of the professional association, had made some fairly esoteric speeches only a pension anorak could hope to understand, but that was about it.

Then, a name at the bottom of one of the releases caught my eye. 'For more information call Jamie White, senior press officer.' Jamie was an old pal, now working in Whitehall. I didn't remember him working for Cameron as a PR. I flicked through my contacts book, found his mobile number, and dialled it.

"Jules, good to hear from you, how's tricks?" His voice was warm. There was no side to Jamie.

"I came across your name on a press release. I didn't know you worked for Cameron."

"Not for long I didn't. One of those career moves where you know you've done the wrong thing the minute you step foot over the door."

"When was this? I don't remember."

"Understandable."

The penny dropped. He was talking about Philip.

"I wasn't there long, so doubt I can help, but shoot away."

"Have you any idea where a man called Maurice Patterson might live. He retired a few years ago."

"Patterson ... Patterson ... it rings a bell."

"You must have worked with him, your name's on one of his releases."

"It was such a long time ago," I could hear him wracking his brain. "Wait a minute, it's coming back. A very thin, tall, old-school type. Used words like 'pukka', 'shipshape', 'tally ho', and a favourite phrase, I recall, was 'steady old chap'.

It looked like I was about to strike gold.

"He retired a few years ago," I prompted.

"Really, he didn't seem that old."

I crossed my fingers before asking the next question.

"No idea, I guess, where he might be living today?"

"For you, d'you know, I might. It's coming back to me now. He lived in the same village as my Aunt Sally. I saw him at a village cricket match. It's called Upton Grey, Hampshire."

"I grew up not far away, in Winchester."

"So you know it. Whether he's there now or not I couldn't say."

"You wouldn't happen to have your Aunt Sally's number?"

"It's going to cost you," he muttered, as I scribbled the number down.

Chapter Eleven

10am Monday, October 15, Upton Grey, Hampshire

Marsha insisted on accompanying me to Upton Grey, staying over the night before, so we could make a reasonable start.

"Can't have you wandering the countryside alone, doll," she said, wriggling to get comfortable in the passenger seat of my Golf. "They're all mad. It's the interbreeding."

"For someone who's travelled half-way round the world, you can be unbelievably insular," I said, ramming the car into gear.

"Yeah, but I always fly out of thief-row. Never cross the M25 unless I have to," she teased, knowing Hampshire was my home.

It wasn't hard to find Jamie's Aunt Sally's house. Straight down the M3 towards Basingstoke; then follow the signs for Upton Grey. Traffic was light, so we were there in a little over an hour, and parked in the centre of the village outside St Mary's Church.

The high street was picture box pretty with thatched cottages, and large Georgian houses. Most people would die for life in such a tranquil idyll, but Marsha shuddered as we walked up the high street and opened the gate to Wisteria Cottage, where Aunt Sally lived.

A massive wisteria plant covered the wattle and daub frontage, and looked like it had been growing there for two centuries. A couple of very late lilac petals clung on, as did the faint trace of their sweet aroma.

We knocked at an iron knocker and waited.

"It's like being buried alive," Marsha whispered "All grass and rabbits."

"Hardly." All Marsha knew of nature was you were never more than 20 feet away from a rat in London, and 4,000 of the vermin were born every hour in the city.

The heavy oak door creaked slightly as it was opened by two faces, as alike each other as peas in a pod.

"I'm Sally," said a pretty, smiling woman, who could have been anything between 60 and 80 years old.

"And I'm Septimus, though everyone calls me Timmy," her companion added.

"And one of you is Julia," Sally addressed us jointly.

"I'm Julia," I put out my hand first to Sally and then to Timmy. "And this is Marsha."

"Won't you come in," Sally and Timmy said, with one voice.

We were shown into a pretty sitting room, warmed by a log fire.

"Tea?" Sally and Timmy offered again with one voice, which reminded me of the old nursery rhyme of Tweedledee and Tweedledum.

Marsha and I were not left alone on the floral settee for long. Sally reappeared a few minutes later, carrying a tray with tea-pot, china cups, saucers, and milk jug all covered with a wisteria pattern. Timmy was close behind, clutching a plate of the same design, piled high with home-made cakes.

They placed the refreshments on a table in front of the sofa and sat on two armchairs on either side, facing each other across the fire.

"D'you think we look alike?" Sally asked, as she poured the tea.

"We're twins," Timmy answered for us.

It turned out they had been widowed fast upon each other, and decided to set up home together. Now, well advanced into their seventies, they rubbed along, more content than many an old married couple. I could see where Jamie's congenial nature came from. These two happy souls seemed incapable of a cross or black moment.

When it came to Maurice Patterson, we drew blanks. Yes, they could provide an address. His home, Upton Grey House, was barely 50 yards away. More than that, they couldn't say.

"Most strange," Sally began. "Haven't seen him for years."

"Not for years," Timmy echoed.

"Once a leading light round here. Church warden …"

"Captain of the cricket team …"

"Wife, Edna, stalwart of the WI."

"Bell-ringer. St Mary's bells are famous, you know."

"Then they disappeared, just like that." Sally clicked her fingers, as if to indicate magic.

"Vanished," Timmy clicked his.

"Some illness, we all thought. If they need help, they know where we are. We all said."

"Mental illness, perhaps?" Marsha couldn't resist the opportunity to capitalise on the mental deficiency of country folk.

"More likely a stroke," Timmy suggested. "We didn't like to pry. He worked in the city."

"All that stress," Sally added.

"Dead before your time," Timmy tut-tutted

"Would you like some more tea m'dear?"

Just as Sally lifted the tea pot, the china cups began to tinkle, and I sensed a distant rumble. Next, the ground below my feet began to vibrate.

Timmy leapt to his feet. "Hold on," he shouted, as he reached to steady a standard lamp and then stretched across to catch china figures slipping from the oak fire surround. Sally threw herself over the tea tray as the whole house began to vibrate, a deafening whirring noise erupting over head.

"Don't fret. Will soon be gone. It's the Chinook helicopters from Odiham. RAF." Timmy bellowed above the noise, as he moved to steady pictures that threatened to come crashing down.

"Regular Vietnam," Sally shouted above the din. "We have complained."

The whirring subsided as quickly as it erupted. Sally straightened the tea cups and began to pour, as though nothing had happened. Timmy resumed his place opposite her.

"A nice cup of tea," she said, handing me the pretty china. "Then, perhaps you would like to see the garden before you go?"

I didn't look at Marsha; couldn't face a rolling of her eyes.

"Do you know this area?" Timmy asked, as I handed him back my empty cup.

"Indeed I do, I grew up in Winchester?"

"Marvellous. And you, Marsha, where are your family?"

"Bethnal Green."

"Marvellous," Timmy repeated, without a flicker of the eye.

I think Marsha liked that, because she followed me into the garden and joined in as I oohed and ahhhed over the winter pansies, the robin playing on the patio, and the stark leafless silver birch swaying in the breeze. They waved us off down the road, with a farewell message to 'come again any time'.

I suggested, in her own vernacular, that she 'shut it' when Marsha opened her mouth to comment on the encounter. But she couldn't resist a wry aside, as we walked towards Upton Grey House.

"Ain't it peaceful in the country."

I ignored her.

Upton Grey House was one of the most prestigious properties in this upmarket village. Not a majestic manor house, more the Bennetts than D'arcy, but a modern manor by any measure.

We crunched noisily up the gravel horse-shoe drive.

"Look," Marsha nudged me, pointing to a young boy peeing in a small lake out front. "Vulgar, ain't it?"

"It's called art." Everywhere looked deserted, just as we had been warned it would. Our feet clattered as we leapt up the stone steps onto the porch and rang the bell.

The door was opened, by a scruffy middle-aged figure.

"Mrs Patterson?" I began.

"Who wants her?"

"Not Mrs Patterson?"

"Correct. The lord spared me there. Hilda Harris."

Marsha and I exchanged glances.

"In fact, it's not Mrs Patterson we have come to see at all. Is Mr Patterson home?" I began again.

"Is he ever home?" she replied, quizzically.

Marsha sighed. "Listen, dearie. Could we stop chewing the bone, and get to the point?" She had spotted a fellow cockney abroad. "Is he home now?"

"And if he was?"

"Could we see him?" adding as afterthought, "please."

"He ain't fit for visitors, mostly," she eyed us suspiciously. I was wondering how to reassure her enough to get us past the door step, when Marsha took my breath away with a blatant lie.

"We're old friends," she said.

"Then, you'll know all about it? His sickness, like ..."

"Corse," I was beginning to think Marsha had chosen the wrong profession in social work.

"Well ... don't suppose there's any harm. He's a poor lonely soul that's for sure."

She waved us into a dingy hall. Cracked paint and a dirty, frayed carpet transformed what should have been a colour-supplement home into a sad mausoleum.

"Can't keep on top of it, any more, meself." There was something touching about Hilda Harris's embarrassed apology. "Her ladyship don't visit often. Spends her time between her daughter in Sonning and their villa in Catalonia. Won't spend the money on this."

"But she's well?" I kept up the pretence of family acquaintance, while cursing Marsha for blowing any story we might pick up by breaching the privacy, not to say entrapment, laws.

"I should say. That's why she can't stand it here. He's through in his study."

I don't know what I had expected, but it wasn't this. Study she had called it; it was the size of a large drawing room. Two walls were covered with countless newspaper cuttings flapping in a cool breeze from an open window. The stories were years out of date. The other side was plastered with equations; pages and pages of elaborate sums, the deranged work of a disturbed mind. Everything in the room was shabby and worn, and covered with thick layers of dust. The floor was carpeted in waste paper.

"Mr Patterson? You've got visitors," Hilda Harris announced.

A tall thin man, wearing a dark pin-stripe suit and red bow tie, looked up from his desk. He didn't show any signs of a stroke.

Indeed, he seemed the picture of health. He was not even very old. He broke into a warm smile when he saw us.

"Mr Patterson, we met when you were President at the professional body," I greet him, hand out-stretched. It was an easy lie. Journalists all look the same to the public.

"Splendid, splendid, jolly good show," he replied, but his gaze kept drifting from us and onto the wall dripping with equations. They looked like advanced actuarial formulae, but they meant nothing to me.

$$sjRx=\sum'' \{(vj)\ x+u+\tfrac{1}{2}\bullet\ S\ x+u\sum t(1+j)x+1+\tfrac{1}{2}$$
$$\text{Or}$$
$$P[t]= \sum (-1)r\ (t\ r+\ r)S1+rO<t<n$$
$$\text{Or}$$
$$ux=uo+x(1)\ \Delta uo+x2\Delta 2u-1+(x+1)(3)\ \Delta 3\ u-1+(x+1)\ (4)\ \Delta 4u-2+\ \dots$$

Other examples followed similar patterns, but letters were replaced by numbers. I looked at Marsha, whose deadpan stare said it all.

"I'm a journalist," I tried again. "I write about financial affairs and always admired your writings."

A daddy-longlegs flew into my face. I brushed it away, as a shiver went down my spine.

"Writings, yes, my writings," he shook my hand and stretched to greet Marsha.

"Won't you sit down," He pointed to two threat-bare chairs, before turning to his housekeeper. "That will be all Mrs Harris."

"Terrible dragon," he confided, when she left the room. "Treats me like an invalid."

"And you're not, are you?" I conspired with him.

"Goodness me, no. Just very busy."

"Busy?"

"With the problem."

"The problem?"

"The calculation, I should say."

He pointed to the wall covered in scrawled numbers and letters. A swarm of daddy-longlegs bashed against the loose papers. It was that time of year, you couldn't keep them out.

"All my life with Cameron and I never solved the problem."

"It was about Cameron I wanted to speak to you."

"Ask away, my dear. You do have a pretty face. Maybe I do remember you. I remember so little these days."

"I wanted to ask you about your dealings with Kelly's Brewery." If I had expected a reaction, I was disappointed.

"1997 will be the year to solve the problem I do believe. That gives me another 18 months."

Marsha and I exchanged glances.

"Kelly's Brewery, Mr Patterson. You advised its pension fund."

"Not me, m'dear. You are quite mistaken. It'll be the surplus you are worrying about, I suppose. That enormous cash mountain. All these arguments about who owns the surplus. Quite overlooks the fact that Britain's pensions are the envy of the world."

As he spoke, I examined the headlines on the opposite wall. None was dated later than 1995. Many covered pension scheme funding, always talking of the huge treasure chests of riches these funds had accumulated.

"You are sure you never dealt with Kelly's?" I tried one last time.

"Absolutely. Come back in eighteen months, when I've solved the problem. I might be able to help you then."

He turned back to his desk and we were dismissed. "I'll get to the bottom of it. If I multiply this by the square root of …"

A solitary daddy-longlegs rested on his hand. He didn't flinch, as I would have done.

"They always add up in the end," he muttered. "The numbers. Always add up. Never let you down."

We watched a few moments more as he scribbled and crossed-out and threw page after page onto the floor. Here was a man chased by demons.

"Envy of the world, our pensions, so proud of my life's work. So proud. Just one little problem. But I'll solve it yet."

Hilda Harris was waiting for us on the other side of the door.

"Terrible," Marsha said as we closed the door on Patterson.

Hilda Harris nodded. "He's stuck in time, pour soul. Tragedy really. Brilliant brain, got overcooked somewhere. His clock stopped ticking years ago."

"Like he's scared to face the years after ... what? 1995?" I said, mostly to myself.

"Who knows, luv? He don't that's for sure."

"Poor old sod, eh?" Marsha said, when we got back to the car. She was a sucker for anyone down on their luck.

She repeated the phrase later to Omar, when we met up for an early drink in the Axe & Cleaver.

"Poor old sod eh? One of my uncles suffered from premature Alzheimer's. Didn't know who he was most of the time, after he reached 40. Terrible to go nuts at a very young age. All that money too."

"Poor old sod nothing." I remained to be convinced.

"Are you suggesting he deserved to be struck down by psychotic illness?" Omar sounded mildly surprised.

"No, no, not exactly."

"Blimey Omar. It weren't half creepy. Nothing later than 1995. All those newspaper clippings."

"Like he's imprisoned in a lost world," Omar said thoughtfully.

"All rather convenient, don't you think?" I looked challengingly from Marsha to Omar

"You think it's an act?" Omar asked.

"No, no not exactly, but it is very convenient," I repeated.

At that moment, my mobile phone rang. It was the police. A Detective Inspector Poitu wanted to interview me at my office the following morning.

"What for?" Marsha asked, reaching for her glass.

"They said I was one of the last people to see Ken alive."

Marsha gave a ghoulish laugh. "Find the last person to see the body and you find the killer."

"It's not funny Marsha," I snapped.

"What killer?" Omar raised his voice in exasperation. "Who is saying anything about …" He stopped himself, shaking his head bewildered. "Anyway, it was ages before."

"What will you say to the old bill, doll?"

"What can I say? As far as investigations go, this one hasn't got off the ground."

Omar shook his head in disagreement. "No. There's quite a lot we do know. We know the Kelly's Brewery pension scheme collapsed owing pensions worth … " he hesitated.

"£1 billion to £2 billion, most likely," I supplied

"It's the Strachans' deaths, not the money that's needling the old bill, ain't it?" Marsha interrupted.

"I guess. Ken could never get them to buy the fraud/theft/conspiracy theory."

"Any luck with the independent trustee?" Omar asked.

"No, I keep trying. I think he's avoiding me."

"Well, try again now." Marsha picked my phone up off the table. "They should still be there."

It was not yet six so I dialled the number.

"I am so sorry. You've just missed him. He's off for a week's holiday. Shall I tell him you called, when he gets back?"

"You have to be joking." I exploded at the voice down the other end of the line. "I've been trying to get hold of him for days. Couldn't he have had the courtesy to at least …"

"I have explained to you before, Mr Ross is a very busy …"

I didn't wait to hear more, but clicked the line dead.

"He's left the country."

The other two grimaced.

"Great," said Marsha.

"Great? A vital source has left the country, the crucial lawyer is one of the family, a key actuarial adviser is missing, and the other's gone mad."

"It's not looking good, doll."

"Bit of an understatement that."

"What about the diary?" Omar changed tack.

I shook my head.

"What there's nothing in it?"

"I don't know," I shrugged.

"Are you going to tell the police about the diary?" Marsha asked.

Omar put up his hand.

"Not in my presence, please."

"Well, let's pretend you ain't here. Well dolly?"

I pulled the book out of my bag. I don't know why, but I carried it everywhere for safe-keeping.

"I don't know ... I mean, Ken seems to have gone to great lengths to leave me this diary. Why go to all that trouble unless ..."

"Withholding information from the police ..."

"Is a criminal offence, I know Marsha." I paused. "But that's rich coming from you. Omar, you should have seen her today. She broke both the privacy and entrapment laws."

"She ... don't you mean ... we. Anyway, what's entrapment laws?"

"It's when you pretend to be someone you're not, to trap them into saying things they otherwise wouldn't. You can go to jail for it."

"I really don't want to hear this." Omar put both his hands over his ears, then he removed them and stood, picking up the purple book.

"I don't think it should be on your person or premises when the police interview you. Dreadfully short of something to read right now. Do you mind?" He winked and left Marsha and me to finish our drinks.

Chapter Twelve

6.30am Tuesday, October 16, Southwark

Omar rang at 6.30 the following morning. I was awake; had been since 3.15am. I'd stopped sleeping through the night a while back.

"I'm in court all day today, but I read the diary last night. I think we need to talk." I could hear him slurping coffee at the other end.

"Did you spot anything?"

"No, you're right. Only this R business." He paused, crunching into a slice of toast. "It's the only trail you have. How are you fixed?"

I didn't need to consult a diary.

"I'm free this evening. Why don't you come here for some supper?"

"Fine, and you can tell me how you get on with her majesty's constabulary."

With that he was gone, so I got up and headed into work early, to await my interview with the detective inspector.

I had the measure of Poitu, the minute he walked through the door. There are plenty like him in the force, although they usually have names like Pitcher, Taylor or Shaw.

He had the saunter of a man who is pleased with himself. But his suit was that little bit too sharp, and his hair a trifle too sleek for me to take his aura of authority seriously. Tall and dark, I had to admit, he was not unattractive. Clearly, he saw himself as God's gift to women. Well, here was one unlikely to fall for his charms.

He had only to open his mouth, to reveal himself for the flat-footed plod he was. His questions were brief and pedestrian, as he led me through the final interview with Ken and Jim in this very office.

"Ms Light Thorn."

"Light Horn," I corrected him.

"What was the purpose of his last visit here?" His accent had that slight twang of an East London/Essex boy-made-good.

"He wanted me to open some kind of investigation into Kelly's Brewery."

"Did you?"

"No …" He didn't seem all that interested in my replies. It was a box-ticking exercise. He was going through the motions.

"You didn't think there was anything to investigate?"

"What does the SFO think?" I threw the ball back into his court, referring to the serious fraud office, known affectionately as the silly f******s.

"Well, that all seems straightforward," he said, ignoring my question. I had always found the boys in blue endearingly simple. Stick to the brief, never venture outside the authority of your rank, and don't rock the boat.

He flicked his notebook shut.

"You'll need to attend the inquest in Glasgow. Strathclyde's notified us they're calling you as a witness."

"I thought …"

"Right … Not exactly an inquest. They don't have them north of the border. Not like us. Prefer to let their dead rest in peace. Far the best way, I sometimes think."

"So …why …"

"In special circumstances, a public hearing may be held."

"And?"

"I really don't know." He stood, indicating he had nothing more to say. "My job's to inform you that you've been called. I'll notify you of final details, time, procedure, and so on, as soon as we have them. In the meantime, if you think of anything, anything at all, which could be relevant, here's my card."

"Poitu … unusual name," I said, looking down at it.

"From the French, 'Poitou'. My family came across with the Huguenots. It got anglicised over the centuries to Poitu."

"How interesting."

"It's a village in France, famous for donkeys."

Very apt I thought, as I closed the door after him. What a delightful cross-breed, the French donkey and the Essex boy.

I stopped at a delicatessen on the way home to pick up some salad to toss into supper. Omar arrived at 8pm looking tired and harassed.

"Bad day?" I asked, gently.

"Don't ask," he replied, downing, nearly in one, the glass of wine I handed him.

"What about you?" He sat on the settee and started to pick absentmindedly at the food laid out on the coffee table.

"Fairly uneventful, filed some copy for Ludgate. Don't think it'll win any awards."

Omar raised his eyebrows questioning.

"It was a load of nothing. By the way, have you seen that KNS has launched a bid for Boston National? Trust me, that man plans to take over the world."

Omar grimaced.

"I'll come back to that. First, tell me about the police. How was Poirot?"

"His name's Inspector Poitu. Nothing to tell really. Just a flat foot. He mainly came to tell me I'm called to give evidence at the inquest."

"They don't have inquests in Scotland."

"Well, the equivalent then."

"They don't have an equivalent," said the lawyer. "Unless something has gone seriously wrong and the sheriff holds a public inquiry."

"That's it." I handed him the paper Poitu had left on my desk. "You see, I've been asked to attend the Sherriff Court for a hearing in a week's time."

"Interesting."

He leant forward and picked at more lettuce with his fingers.

"The diary," he began. "Curious. This line about killing two birds … any idea what he meant?"

I shook my head.

"He was holding out on you … There're several mentions of meetings with people, whose name begins with R. We need to check them out, find out what happened in those meetings."

"What we need to know is what happened in the last one," I interrupted.

"Quite. Then there're three other meetings on April 14, May 5 and July 27. We have to find out who R could possibly have been. According to my reading of the diary, it has to be Ronnie Raeburn, David Ragland ..."

"Omar, don't you think I've been through all this already ... a hundred time ... Stephen Russell. I can recite the list in my sleep. It could be any of these or none of these."

"Don't forget Sister Robert."

"Oh perlease." He was going too far.

"Then, there's Kelly's son, Richard."

"Richard's been living on the other side of the world for the past few years."

"Interesting in itself. You have to check them all out."

"I have to check them all out?"

"It's your investigation ... .you won't get anywhere until you eliminate the Rs. This may not be the key, but it could be."

He was right of course. We ate in silence for a bit.

"You said you were coming back to Kane."

It wasn't like Omar to be shifty, but he looked down, avoiding my gaze.

"They're pressing for a court date."

"I thought you said they'd drag it out."

"I'm not God," he snapped, strain showing in his face. Boy he must have had a lousy day in court. "I make mistakes."

I said nothing. I could imagine how painful it must be to lose a case in court.

He took a deep breath.

"This business of Kane being Kelly's bankers. It worries me. Kane is not a man to keep crossing. If you persist with this pension story, you are playing a dangerous game."

"But the bankers aren't directly involved. They just cash the cheques and move the money around. You said yourself, Kane wasn't a crook."

"Not a crook, no. But they could end up carrying the can for this. Have you forgotten how you got into this mess?"

"Forgotten, how could I? It was the Mainland takeover. Kane was fighting Archie Baron at VWC to get Mainland."

"So, you haven't forgotten that Kane destroyed Baron?"

"No," I said, more gingerly now. "Pinned some association on him with that south coast bank which went bust twenty years ago … It was all lies. The bank going down had nothing to do with Baron. He was an external consultant."

"The seeds of doubt were sewn. 'Killer Kane' you called him. 'An archetype among city assassins'."

"'Kane but not able.' It was true."

"Whether it was true or not, you can't keep picking fights with him. You don't start from nowhere and end up with your name on one of the UK's biggest banks, without eating flies for breakfast … and anyone else who stands in your way."

I suddenly felt sick. "You think we'll lose in court."

"No," he shrugged with bravado, "Not at all … it's just more of their bullyboy tactics … But you have to start listening to my advice. You must stay out of trouble."

"Oh Omar," I reached for his hand.

"Don't worry," he smiled, "we'll secure an adjournment."

But his eyes were dark.

Chapter Thirteen

9.30am Wednesday, October 17, Whitechapel

The next morning I called Ronnie Raeburn's office, to be told he was leaving the country at lunchtime, had meetings all morning, but if I could get round in half-an-hour, he would squeeze me in for ten minutes.

Like most modern union bosses, his office was in town. I hailed a cab and within twenty minutes was staring up at a glass tower shooting towards the sky. How far the brothers had come in their long march.

The union was on the fourth floor. Raeburn was waiting for me in reception, with his trademark welcoming smile. I had known him for a while; liked and admired him, but could never quite bring myself to trust him. He was a model of a modern union leader; attractive, intelligent and charming, and so he looked today in his dark trousers and ice-white shirt. A Thomas Pink label peaked out behind his lemon tie.

"Julia, a pleasure as always," he held out a hand, showed me into his office, and invited me to sit on a white sofa. I sank awkwardly down among its squishy cushions. He sat upright at his desk.

Two of the walls were sheet glass, giving uninterrupted views across the city. Though the offices occupied a comparatively low floor, the outlook was impressive.

"Coffee?" he asked.

"No thanks."

"You wanted to see me about Ken Strachan?"

I nodded.

"You and everyone else, it seems." He swirled a pen between his fingers.

I raised questioning eyebrows.

"The police've been here, the regulator, you name it ..." He let the pen drop. It landed with a crack.

"The inquest's looming. They need to tie up loose ends," I suggested.

"Will you attend?" he asked.

"I've been called to give evidence. You?"

"I'm hoping to try and get there."

"I've been called, apparently, because I was one of the last to see him alive. I'm trying to establish who else may have seen him in the run up to the …"

My words faltered momentarily, then I continued. "I've some dates to run past you. Did you see him on April 14 … May 5 … July 27?"

He didn't answer but said instead, "You must stop this, Julia."

"Did you see him on those dates?"

"I saw Ken almost every week of the year. He was one of our officers." The smile had gone.

"But on those dates."

"I can't remember."

"Can't you look in your diary?"

"I don't keep my diary."

"Your secretary, then?"

He started fiddling with the cufflink at his left wrist, a chunky gold oblong.

"I haven't time for this, Julia, so I'm going to be brutal. You have to stop this. Keep this up and no one will thank you."

"Just walk away?"

"Oh grow up. I hate to shatter your illusions, but Ken was not the angel you always took him for."

"Really?"

"Yes, really." He picked the pen up again and started tapping it rhythmically on the desk. "Do you remember the walkout over the Hannigan sacking?"

"The catholic kid? About eight years ago?"

"Ken took a back-hander from Kelly to get the men to return to work. Hannigan was the victim of a nasty piece of sectarian bigotry. Foreman, leading member of Glasgow's Orange lodge, took a dislike to the kid."

"Hannigan was reinstated, I remember."

"Officially. Strachan agreed a deal to get him shipped back to Ireland, the men back to work, and a big new extension for his wife."

I felt like I had been kicked in the stomach "I don't believe it."

"Oh, you believe it alright." He stood now. "I must go, plane to catch. Take my advice, let sleeping dogs lie."

As we shook hands, his cufflink caught my eye again. A tiny gold crate. The symbol of the Brewery Owners' Association. A gift, no doubt.

Traffic was building up, so I took the tube back to the office, turning his words over in my mind. Could it be true? Corruption in unions was widespread a decade ago, which was why new brooms like Raeburn were brought in to clean out the dirty corners. But Ken, of all people?

Back in the office, I called Richard Crippledown's press team. A spokesman was clear, the junior industry minister had never met Mr Strachan. He relied on the local MP, David Ragland, to liaise with the union men on the ground. So that ruled Crippledown out.

Next, I called Ragland's office, and asked for an interview.

"We'll get back," the voice at the other end of the line promised.

While I waited, I dialled Stephen Russell, the head teacher at Clydebank School, where Ken helped out with the football.

"I still can't believe it," Russell said. "I keep trying to understand."

"Me, too."

"It defies understanding, I'm afraid. We just have to …"

"Move on," how many times had I heard those words.

"And remember the good times, and his achievements." This headmaster had missed his vocation. He should have been a priest.

"Are you going to the inquest, Julia?"

"Yes."

"Me, too. Maybe it will shed some light."

"Let's hope. But 'til then I'm trying to trace his movements before he died."

"If I can help …"

"There're a couple of dates I'm interested in. Did you see Ken on April 14, May 5 or July …"

I didn't get to finish.

"My dear, I saw Ken all the time. He was a regular visitor to the school. He helped out with football. In the holidays, he would offer to do odd jobs round the premises. He took an interest in some of my difficult pupils."

"I see."

"Ken and I were old friends, at school together. Sometimes, I would tell him about a particularly troublesome youth. Confide in him. Some of my kids' lives aren't exactly a bed of roses. No male role model at home. Threatened, sometimes abused by mum's boyfriends. Not much by way of love. Ken would find time for this lad or that one. Let them know they weren't alone in the world."

I got the picture.

"He was often at the school. I couldn't give specific dates."

"In the last few days before he died? Could he 'ave been with you or your pupils?"

"Oh yes, most certainly."

This conversation left me almost as confused as the last, but further speculation was interrupted by the ringing telephone. It was Ragland's office.

"Mr Ragland is inviting you to take tea with him this afternoon in the members' room," a voice at the other end informed me. "He must be back in the House by 4pm for the debate on the health service. Can you make three?"

I agreed.

"Good, he'll meet you in the foyer." The phone clicked dead.

The House of Commons always put me in mind of Wordsworth's freak show at Bartholomew Fair. A Parliament of Monsters, it was indeed. If only he had lived to see today's political freak show, I thought as I walked down central corridor, past statues and paintings of our great leaders. What writing it might have spurred. Still, Rory

Bremner did his best.

Through no fault of his own, David Ragland had been born with an unusually small head. An affliction which cost him dear. It was not unknown for some of his crueller opponents on the opposition benches to shout 'pinhead', when heckling his speeches. Even from a distance, there was something odd about the way he moved, the way he held himself.

We greeted each other with a cool handshake, and he led the way to the members' room, holding the door for me to enter its museum-cum-library atmosphere. An undercurrent of conversation simmered as members entertained their guests. We sat at a table by a window. Boats glided past on the Thames.

"You're troubled by this Strachan business, Ms Lighthorn," he began, decently enough.

"Shocked is more the word."

Across the room, I saw a woman wipe a tear from her eye with a lace handkerchief. I hadn't seen a lace handkerchief since I was a child. Carlton Crabb and his huge cotton handkerchief flashed into my mind, and the bird and the hat.

Presumably, she was a constituent, pleading with her MP about some problem in her life.

"We are all shocked." He was quick to reply, ordering tea for two. He insisted on paying. "I can't be bought, you see," he smiled, at his little joke.

"I'm trying to find out who Ken saw in the last few days before ..."

"To what purpose?"

"In case he said anything, or indicated anything."

"The police are examining these matters."

"Did you see him the week before he died?"

"I met Ken Strachan on a regular basis. When I was in the constituency, he would drop into the office quite frequently."

"You were friends?" The woman with the handkerchief was snivelling quietly, and the middle-aged man sitting opposite looked distinctly uncomfortable. I wondered what she was appealing about.

A personal tragedy? Could she be lobbying on behalf of others? Maybe it was simply a planning matter. People could behave so strangely, when their bricks and mortar were threatened.

"That would probably be overstating our relationship," he replied, as the tea arrived. We sipped in silence for a moment.

"Do you remember seeing him on April 14, or May 5 or …"

"I would never speak ill of the dead, but I have already explained that Ken Strachan could be quite a nuisance at my constituency office and here too."

"In the few days before he died?"

"Monday is my day in the constituency. It's possible. I honestly don't remember."

"Your diary?"

"It wouldn't be logged, but before you turn this man into a hero."

"I have no intention …"

"There were always suspicions." He paused. "This is very difficult."

"Go on."

"He spent a great deal of time at Clydebank School and the asylum seekers centre … There were doubts about his motives."

"As in?"

"Must I spell it out for you? There were stories."

"Stories of what?"

"You force me to be plain. Why does a middle-aged man hang round centres full of displaced, vulnerable children and teenagers?"

"On what evidence?"

"There is evidence, I believe."

"The police?"

"Their investigations have closed." He hesitated before adding, "for the time being."

"Will they stay closed?"

"That rather depends."

"Depends on what?"

"On whether we all agree to let sleeping dogs lie."

'Sleeping dogs lie' - Raeburn's words exactly. The threat was clear. My meeting was over. The woman with the lace handkerchief continued to weep.

Chapter Fourteen

4pm Wednesday, October 17, Whitechapel

Ludgate called shortly after I got back to the office.

"Can you make dinner tomorrow evening? I have some things I want to discuss."

There was something about his tone that made me uneasy.

"Sure."

"I'll head over your way. How about the Oxo Tower?"

"Fine."

"I'll see you there, about eight."

Omar stopped off on his way home from court. He seemed more cheerful. I suspected his case was turning.

"How did you get on?" he asked.

"Not brill." I recounted the day's interviews.

"Well, you can count Crippledown out."

"I guess."

"What do you think about these allegations?" I asked Omar after repeating Raeburn's and Ragland's smears.

Marsha joined us, sitting in an armchair she had rescued from a skip on the Old Kent Road. My desk, which, like me, had seen better days, had been salvaged from another in Northumberland wharf.

"What's this, doll?" Marsha asked.

"Raeburn, the union guy, warned me off. Said Ken had taken backhanders. Do you remember the case of Hannigan?"

"The young catholic who was sacked?"

I nodded. "Said Ken cut a deal to ship him back to Ireland for the price of a new extension."

"D'you believe it?" I didn't know how to answer her.

"That's not all Marsha," Omar nodded to me to continue.

"Ragland hinted at worse."

"Like?"

"I don't know exactly. Underage sex, grooming minors … I don't know."

"They both have motives for discrediting Strachan," Omar said.

"Ragland's a piece of piss," Marsha put it more colourfully.

"What do you think, Jules?" Omar asked. That was the problem. I didn't know anymore.

"Three months ago, I would have laughed my head off. But now, after everything …" I trailed off.

"We never really get inside someone else's head," Marsha's voice was kindly.

I nodded again. "The possibilities, as far as I can see, are either someone broke into the house and killed them all."

"But why?"

"I don't know, Omar, maybe a burglary."

"Nothing was taken."

"Maybe he was disturbed?"

"He'd have to be bloody disturbed to wipe out a whole family for the sake of a bit of petty thieving," Marsha interjected. "That sort don't carry shot guns. It's not the way it works, doll."

"Well, then, maybe Ken was on to something. Maybe he got some conclusive proof of something, something to do with the pension scheme, maybe this meeting with R …"

"So the actuaries gunned down his entire family," Omar's voice dripped with sarcasm. "I don't think so."

"Which only leaves … I mean, if he was the good man that Stephen Russell believes, how could he shoot his family? How could he have done such a thing?" My voice caught on the words. "I just can't understand it …"

Omar and Marsha both watched me intently, waiting for me to go on.

"If he wasn't a good man, if he was something other than we thought …"

"Steady, doll," Marsha stood and placed a soothing hand at the base of my neck.

"But if he wasn't a good man, if I misjudged him for years, if he was bad, that means anything is possible."

"Not at all," Omar's voice was quiet and calm. "Nothing here is clear."

"A bad man wouldn't care about murdering his family," I said.

"Ain't so, gal. You know what they say about thick as thieves. Family's all some crooks have to hold on to."

"Jules, you may have to accept ..." Omar stopped, as if trying to choose his words with extreme delicacy.

"Julia," he began again. "Sometimes we have to accept that any one of us, no matter how good, kind and courageous ..." He hesitated. "All of us ... every one of us ... at a certain time in our lives, in certain circumstances, any one of us might ..." His voice petered out.

"You believe he did it, don't you?"

Omar didn't answer, although in a way he did.

Chapter Fifteen

8pm Thursday, October 18, the Oxo Tower

"Ask for evidence," Ludgate said, when I ran through the interviews with him the following evening. "Until either of them produces something, keep it in the back of your mind. It's not strictly relevant to your primary investigation."

"The pension collapse?"

"And the company. If they took money out of the pension, what did they take out of the company before it went down?"

"The creditors?"

"Exactly."

We had a window table, looking over the Thames, with a view of the North Bank stretching from Westminster down to Canary Wharf. The lights of London were brash against the dark.

"Look Julia, there's no easy way for me to say this." Ludgate's face was sombre. "You are not making the progress on this story we need."

"It's difficult."

"Too difficult for you?"

I didn't respond.

"Getting anywhere with that missing Sherlock man?"

"No, nothing yet." I had called Strathclyde police ahead of this meeting, as I had all my contacts, desperate for a new lead. There was nothing.

"Police aren't even treating it as a missing person. Not seriously."

"Was there nothing from the meeting with Patterson?"

I shook my head.

"We can't afford to let this stall, Julia. My instincts tell me there's something going on here. Have you been through the company accounts?"

I had to admit I hadn't. The pension scheme accounts had been my main focus.

"I've been going through them. Pure fiction. Who makes 80 per cent on cans of lager?"

"I'll check them out."

"Do that. I know the Kellys of old, remember."

I nodded, taking a sip of wine.

"The inquest's next Wednesday, there may well …"

He cut me dead. "The time for the 'may wells' are over. This story needs a crack operator. I've given you the best chance I can. Either you come up with the goods and soon. Or we put someone else on the story."

That last sip of wine regurgitated back into my mouth.

The days before the inquest dragged. On Monday, I called Sister Robert's asylum centre to make an appointment to see her after the inquest. I might as well check her out while in town. I spent the rest of the day going through the company's profit and loss accounts for the past five years. Ludgate was right. Sales volumes were falling year on year, yet revenue was rising. I spotted several well-known tricks used to smooth out the numbers, such as sale-and-leaseback of buildings; disposal of assets at inflated prices to family members; scantily-accounted-for special cash inflows.

As a private company, these accounts would escape the scrutiny which listed plcs had to withstand from investment analysts. The more you looked into them, the more they fell apart.

I sensed I was wasting my time here in London. There was only so much you could achieve on the phone and by going through old documents. I would have to pull off a minor scoop on Wednesday, at the inquest, or I was in deep trouble.

Marsha knew I was feeling down. On Monday evening, she invited me to join her at the project's soup kitchen for the down and outs at Waterloo, although why she thought mingling among London's rejects would lift my spirits I wasn't sure.

"It'll be fun."

"If you say so," I replied, reaching for my coat. It was the best invitation I had. The only one.

The kitchen was a lock-up under one of the old arches close to Southwark Cathedral. I'd always meant to get involved. It was on my doorstep. Marsha was a regular volunteer, which made me feel bad. She crossed the river to help people living, as she put it, on my manor.

Marsha was obviously a favourite with the regulars. She had that touch of magic that marks people out from the crowd. For sure, someone needed to be cheerful to lift the gloom of those who idled in. It would have taken a heart of stone not to ache for the plight of, particularly the young, who were sleeping in the streets. Bedraggled, dirty and without hope, many struggled with their English. Illegal immigrants, young girls and boys, discovered the hard way that the promise of London could be brutal and empty.

"Like your new coat, Susie, very stylish," Marsha flattered one client, as she filled up a soup bowl and handed it across. "Harrods or Harvey Nicks?"

"Got it off a tip down the Elephant, nice though," Susie smiled, looking pleased.

"Still at the Bermondsey hostel, Dougie?" she asked another.

"Na, that bitch of a social worker got me kicked out."

"Bad luck. Tell you what, what do you call 100 social workers at the bottom of the sea?"

"A good start," a chorus replied. This 'bottom of the sea joke' seemed universally adaptable.

It was a bitter sweet scene despite the laughter. Drugs, prostitution, mental illness, abuse, family breakdown; the underbelly of one of the richest cities in the world.

"It breaks your heart," I said to Marsha, as we walked away.

"No, doll. There's a lot of help out there," she replied. "A lot of people doing good work. They ain't abandoned."

Chapter Sixteen

10am Wednesday, October 24, Glasgow

It was the strangest inquest I had ever attended, probably because it wasn't one. I did my homework before heading for the airport. Omar was right. Scotland has no tradition of public inquests after a suspicious death. The Procurator Fiscal hears evidence in private and decides whether murder investigations should be initiated. On rare occasions, evidence could be heard by the Sheriff in public, at what the Scots call a Fatal Accident Inquiry. Someone had lobbied hard for this inquiry, and my money was on Mrs Strachan.

The court was packed, I guessed with friends, neighbours and other associates of this much-loved family, all searching for an answer to the question that kept them, like me, awake at night. What made him do it?

I recognised a few faces in the crowd; Stephen Russell, the Clydebank Head, a priest, who spoke at the funeral, other funeral followers. No sign of Raeburn. There was one I couldn't miss. She sat up front with Jim Sugden, her funeral coat and hat as pristine as the day of the burial.

The Sheriff's court in the heart of Glasgow's Merchant City was lavish; domed ceilings, marbled columns, gold-crusted statues of ancient Gods, stained-glass windows, and heavy wooden panelling.

I found an empty seat near the front, and as I took up my position, I spotted someone waving to me from the side benches. It was Inspector Poitu. What was be doing here?

The clerk hammered on the table, announcing the Sheriff was on his way.

"Court rise for Sheriff Johnston!"

A bespectacled Sheriff Johnston, bewigged and begowned, took his seat on the bench and proceedings began. First to give evidence was PC Barry Fraser. He reported attending the Bearsden address, accompanied by armed officers, after an emergency call reporting shots just after 3 o'clock on October 3.

"And you entered the house?" the Sheriff asked. The proceedings weren't adversarial, like a normal court. The Sheriff took the role of inquisitor.

"Not immediately, no," came the hesitant reply. Fraser clutched his note book tightly. He looked nervous.

"You waited?" the Sheriff asked again.

"Until it was safe."

"Safe?" The Sheriff took off his thick-rimmed glasses and polished them on his black gown. He wasn't looking at the witness, but he was listening to him.

"Until we were sure there was no gunman left alive," Fraser explained.

"And how long was that?"

He must have known the answer, but Fraser flicked the pages of his notebook backwards and forwards, before replying. "Something like eight hours."

A gasp echoed round the court room. Fraser blushed. The Sheriff replaced his glasses on his nose and glared at the constable.

"You waited eight hours … until nearly midnight?"

"It wasn't midnight,"

"After 11pm?"

"Yes," he replied, although too quietly to be strictly audible.

"Why so long?"

"Policy," Fraser replied, pronouncing it the Scottish way, like 'pawlissy'.

"When you entered, what did you find?"

"Nothing in the hall. A body in the lounge, lying on the carpet with a wound to the back of her head."

"Mrs Strachan?"

"So she was later identified."

"Was she breathing?"

"She didn't appear to be."

"What did you do next, constable?"

"The patio doors were open. We went into the garden. There were two more bodies. An adolescent male and female."

"Also wounded?"

"Aye, they had bullet wounds. In the back for the boy, but lower down at the top of the leg for the girl."

"Did you search the house further?"

"Indeed. In the study we found a man, slumped across a desk. There was a shotgun by his side."

The court rumbled as those present took in these remarks. The clerk silenced them with his hammer.

"Mr Strachan?"

"He was later identified as such."

"Did you find anything else?"

"There was a note on the desk."

"Did you draw any conclusions about what had taken place?"

"It looked like the man had crept up on his wife and shot her in the back of the head. She wouldn't have known anything about it."

"And the adolescents?"

"Must've been alerted by the noise from the lounge and were trying to escape over the back garden."

"He shot them in flight?"

"It would seem."

The court gasped as one, and some of those present vented their disgust with murmurs of 'monster', 'bastard', 'murderer'.

My eyes were drawn as if by a magnet to Mrs Strachan. Her stiff back did not move.

"And then?"

"We concluded that he had returned to the study and shot himself."

"None of them was breathing?"

"We thought not at the time."

"But subsequently?"

"The paramedics discovered a faint pulse in the adolescent female. She was taken to hospital."

"The daughter, Emma?"

"Yes."

"Still breathing?"

"I couldn't say …"

"But a faint pulse."

"Yes."

This was the first time it was revealed anyone had been found alive. The clerk hammered to silence the court.

"She was alive?" the Sheriff continued.

"Yes. But we didn't know. Not at the time …"

"And died later, in the hospital?"

"Yes …"

Another gasp from those present. My gaze drifted to the motionless figure of old woman Strachan. I caught Poitu out of the corner of my eye. He smiled inanely, and I wondered, again, what on earth was he doing there?

"Were any other lines of inquiry pursued? Was anyone seen running from the scene?"

"No other suspects were sought. All the evidence pointed to …" He didn't finish.

"That will be all constable." The policeman was dismissed.

The next to give evidence was Professor Fergus MacIntosh, a professor of pathology at Glasgow University. Dressed in a light tweed suit, he was tall and thin, with a wispy beard and failing hair. He looked more like Old Father Time than Dr Death.

He replied to the Sheriff's questions softly and with maximum courtesy. He would not be startling the court room with tales of blood and gore. Mrs Jane Strachan had probably been killed instantly by a massive shotgun wound to the head. Similarly Robbie would have died within seconds of being hit.

Then he came to Emma.

"The wound was not fatal," he tried to break the news as gently as he could. "There were signs on the ground that she attempted to drag her body, perhaps to get help."

"The wound was serious?"

74

"It was too serious to permit her to travel far. But it was not a fatal wound. She died subsequently through loss of blood."

"If the police had entered sooner, is it your opinion she might have lived?"

"I am certain she would be alive today."

The clerk lifted his hammer to quiet the storm he expected these words to produce, but an eerie silence descended.

"That will be all. Thank you Professor MacIntosh. Can I next call Dr Hullah, the Strachan's GP."

Dr Hullah reported that the Strachans were a healthy normal family, with no obvious medical problems.

"I knew the family well, GP for some 20 years. Mr Strachan had developed late onset diabetes about two years ago, so I saw him for regular monitoring. I saw him a fortnight before the incident."

"Was he depressed in any way? Did he give you any cause to suspect he might be suicidal?"

"None. He was fighting mad about this problem with the works pensions. But completely himself. Vintage Ken Strachan I would say."

Dr Hullah gave some further details about recent consultations by other members of the family, but they were routine matters, grist to the mill of a typical surgery.

Jim Sugden was called next. He ran through some of the details of the problems with the pension fund, and Ken's outrage when the scale of the black hole came to light.

"He were that mad," Sugden told the court. "He swore they wouldn't get away with it."

"Away with what?" the Sheriff asked.

"With the theft. That's what Ken always said it were."

"Is it possible, Mr Strachan became morbid about the whole business? Did it prey on his mind?"

"He were worried, but not morbid. No, not Ken."

"In your experience, is it possible that problems of this nature can affect the mind? Worry the nerves?"

My heart went out to Jim, as I waited for him to answer. His thumbs twitched erratically along the edge of the witness box.

"Aye, it can. It can affect a man's nerves. This business has ruined the health of several of our members."

The Sheriff coughed, and signalled for the usher to attend the clerk, who gave him a piece of paper to take to the witness.

"Can you say if this is Mr Strachan's handwriting?"

Jim screwed his eyes up.

"Mr Sugden?" the Sheriff prompted.

Jim took his reading glasses out of his top pocket, but he didn't put them on, as though afraid. His hands trembled, as he studied the scrap of paper.

"Aye, I'd say so. But I couldn't be sure."

"Thank you, Mr Sugden." The Sheriff's tone softened. "Could I please ask you to read the note to the court."

Jim opened his lips, but nothing came out.

"Speak up, Mr Sugden."

Jim took a deep breath. "It says, 'I'm sorry.'"

"Thank you, Mr Sugden, that will be all." The Sheriff signalled he could step down.

"Please call Ms Julia Lighthorn to the stand," the usher's voice echoed round the court. My turn had come. I made my way to the stand.

"Ms Lighthorn, you were visited by Mr Strachan in the week before he died?"

"Yes, with Mr Sugden."

"Did he seem distressed?"

"He was absolutely incandescent with rage."

"About the pensions?"

"Yes."

"Was there anything about his behaviour … did suicide ever occur to you?"

Ah how to answer that one. Suicide had loomed large in my mind, but not for Ken.

76

"No. absolutely not, not with regards to Ken."

"How did you find him?"

"He was angry, as we have heard. He felt betrayed and very much alone."

"Distressed?"

"No, not distressed." Then an image of Ken thumping my desk came to mind. "Yes, I suppose he was distressed."

"Angry enough to harm himself or his family?"

"I shouldn't have thought so. Ken was a wily operator. He loved a good fight."

"You are absolutely confident, he could never have been violent?"

I went to answer 'absolutely,' but the word died in my throat. I found myself thinking of my wedding day. My handsome husband, my beautiful dress, the music, the cake, Mum and Dad, Peter, a huge crowd of friends.

"Ms Lighthorn, can you please answer the question." The Sheriff called me back.

"I'm sorry ..." I was flustered.

"Are you confident Mr Strachan was incapable of violence?"

Why couldn't I answer?

"Ms Lighthorn, can I ask you for the last time. In your opinion was Ken Strachan capable of murdering his family."

"I'm sorry, I don't know."

The court grumbled as I left the witness box, and Mr Alexander Ross was called to the stand. So here, at last, was the elusive Mr Ross, the independent trustee, who had been avoiding my calls for weeks.

He was not what I had expected. Blond grey hair crowned a youthful face, softened by blue eyes. Here was a man people would warm to and trust.

"Mr Ross, you are investigating the collapse of the Kelly's Brewery pension fund, I understand," the Sheriff asked.

"Yes, so I knew Ken Strachan well." Ross spoke briskly and openly.

"He was convinced money had been stolen from the fund?"

"Stolen is an emotive word."

"Were there grounds for his suspicions?"

"We are currently investigating certain financial transactions. That is all I can say at this stage."

"Did you see him regularly?"

"Very regularly."

"Did you see him in the week before he died?"

"I saw him the day before he died."

"Was he depressed?"

"Not about the pension fund. If anything, he was rather more optimistic than I had seen him for ages. He seemed convinced he was on the verge of some breakthrough."

"Was he?"

"Not that I'm aware. Oh yes, and he said someone had come on board what he always called 'our great campaign for justice', someone who would ensure they won the day."

"Did he say whom?"

"I believe it was a journalist." His tone became unmistakeably drier. I felt my face blush. "I believe it may have been Ms Lighthorn, who you have just heard from."

"Would you say he was capable of shooting his family?"

"I am an actuary, not a psychiatrist."

"As a human being then, would anything about his behaviour indicate he may have been on the brink of something drastic."

"Absolutely not. I find it unbelievable, and will until the day I die."

A wave of approval thundered through the benches as Ross left the stand. I felt ashamed, I had not been able to give such unequivocal assurance. The clerk hammered his desk, and the noise subsided.

A deadly hush descended when the usher called Mrs Margaret Strachan to the stand. With poker-straight back, the old woman rose.

"Mrs Strachan," the Sheriff's voice noticeably softened. "Did you see your son in the days prior to this terrible event?"

"Aye. I saw Kenny every day of his life."

"Did you see him the day he died?"

"Aye. He came round for a cup of tea on his way out for the day, like he always did."

"Did he say anything which seemed unusual?"

"Nay, he did not."

"Did he seem in any way ..."

"Mr Sheriff. My son never murdered anybody."

"Was he being threatened by anyone? Was there anyone else who could have done such a thing?"

"Somebody murdered my family. It's for the polis to investigate."

The Sheriff thanked Mrs Strachan and the frail figure hobbled on her stick back to her seat. She was the final witness, but the hearing was not adjourned as I had expected.

Instead, the Sheriff looked down at his bench and shuffled papers around for a bit, before taking off his glasses and staring into the distance. For a few moments, we all stared with him into the comfortable suburb of Bearsden, at teatime on October 3.

Then, he cleared his throat, and the clerk began hammering on his table, indicating an announcement was imminent.

The Sheriff began, "I am concerned at the police handling of this case. It is possible that a teenage girl died because of the delay in entering the house. I am commissioning a full investigation into Strathclyde police procedures, to be led by Scotland Yard's DI Poitu, who is in court today.

"I will not, however, be requiring further investigations into the deaths of the Strachan family. I am satisfied that Ken Strachan shot his family, while the balance of his mind was disturbed, and then turned the gun on himself."

A piercing cry erupted from the front bench, where Mrs Strachan was sitting. The frail figure leapt to her feet and screamed, "It was murder I tell, you. Murder. My son loved his wee wife and weans. Is there no justice in this country?"

But the Sheriff was too quick for her. He jumped to his feet and disappeared from the court. Mrs Strachan crumpled, sobbing, onto her chair, a tiny, broken, pathetic figure.

Part of me wanted to go to her, but I didn't know what to say, so I left the court quickly. I wanted to catch a word with the elusive Mr Ross. I reached the foyer in time to catch a glimpse of Carlton Crabb disappearing down the broad, winding staircase.

I waited for Ross to emerge.

"Mr Ross, you are a very difficult man to get hold of. I'm Julia Lighthorn," I stretched out a hand, with what I hoped was an engaging smile.

"I know who you are, Ms Lighthorn," he turned strikingly blue eyes towards me.

"I'm investigating the Kelly's pension fund collapse."

"How nice for you," his tone dripped irony.

"Ken asked me to …"

"Ken Strachan had a great deal of faith in you."

I tried one more time. "Can I make an appointment to see you before I go back?"

"I am a very busy man Ms Lighthorn …"

He was cut dead by screams from inside the court. "Get a doctor, get a doctor," people were shouting.

Ross pushed his way, against the flow of the crowd, back into the court room. I followed close behind. Professor MacIntosh and Dr Hullah were laying Mrs Strachan out on the floor. She was as limp as a rag doll. In turns, they pumped her chest and tried to breathe life into her.

I looked at Ross in horror.

"Congratulations, Ms Lighthorn." The blue eyes darkened. "You came for a story and it looks like you are about to get one."

With that, he pushed through the crowd to Mrs Strachan's body. He spoke to Professor MacIntosh and then to the police who were standing around the patient. It could not have been more apparent, while I was an outsider, he was a trusted member of this community.

I watched for maybe twenty minutes, as they tried to resuscitate the old lady. Someone called an ambulance, and paramedics arrived with more equipment. But it was hopeless.

I left the court room as they were placing her body on a stretcher ready for removal. Poitu was waiting for me at the bottom of the winding stair case.

"You look as if you could do with a cup of tea," he said, leading the way through huge wooden doors.

Chapter Seventeen

12.45pm Wednesday, October 24, Glasgow

I followed Poitu across the road.

"Hard to believe this used to be a prison," he said, as we entered a restaurant. "Makes the Scrubs look a bit basic."

His constant chirpiness was maddening. We found a table in a corner, but I didn't sit.

"Hungry?" he asked. My stomach heaved at the thought of food.

"I have to call the office," I needed to let them know Mrs Strachan was dead. I left him scanning the menu, returning to the lobby and dialling Ludgate direct. He picked up after one ring.

"Julia. Shoot."

"Big story. Old Ma Strachan collapsed at the inquest. She's dead."

"So, the old dame croaked, eh?"

"Heart attack, stroke or something."

"Broken-heart and stress … Anyone else there?"

"There'll be some local press, but that's all. No one from London."

"Good, how soon can you file?"

"There're some loose ends I want to tie up first. I'll be across before six."

"Anything else out of the inquest?"

"Loads."

"Good girl, keep at it."

The line clicked dead. I rejoined Poitu. His food arrived. Full works; steak, fried egg, tomatoes, sausage, mushrooms, griddle cakes, black pudding, baked beans and chips. Not a green vegetable in sight.

He had ordered me coffee. The strong black liquid hit my nervous system like a shot of Valium.

"So, what are you really doing here?" I asked him.

"You heard didn't you?" Steak and tomato juices ran down his chin. "I'm the lucky bugger who gets to investigate Strathclyde."

"That won't win you any friends. They screwed up, didn't they?"

"Oh yes," his face darkened. "They screwed up big time. That little girl might well be alive if ..." he stopped, as if forgetting himself, and quickly resumed his customary broad grin.

"Of course, this is idle chatter." He was cutting into his steak again. "I have no idea what the investigation will show."

"Quite. But that hearing was pretty damning."

"Damning. It was a shambles. What did you think about the forensics?"

"I don't remember ..." now he mentioned it, what had they said about the scene of the crime, DNA and so forth?

"They weren't mentioned. The Scottish legal system is a disgrace. Deaths are buried behind closed doors. There's no routine system of public inquests. Even when one is conducted, like today, it's sheer theatre. And they're talking about introducing this system down south."

"But we did learn ..."

"I learnt nothing they didn't want us to learn, which we didn't know already," he interrupted. "As for getting poor Jim Sugden to read that note. Why didn't the copper read it?"

"Maybe the Sheriff thought ..."

"Maybe they thought it would be more damning from the mouth of a friend. Pure theatre," he repeated.

"I see." I was beginning to suspect there might be more to this Essex donkey than I'd given credit for.

He finished his food, pushed the plate aside and wiped his mouth with a serviette.

"I've got an offer to put to you."

I said nothing.

"You're right," he continued. "It's gonna be lonely for me working here. The tartan mafia will do everything they can to block my inquiries."

"My heart is bleeding."

"Let's pool our resources."

"What d'you mean?"

"We both have a lot of unanswered questions."

"We're not necessarily asking the …"

"Same questions. Yes, I know. You're close to this story. You understand things I'll struggle with. I can do stuff you can't."

Police and press often traded information.

"What's your brief?" I asked.

"I find out why the Scots mucked up."

"Not who murdered Ken and his family?"

"Murdered? There's no evidence they were murdered." There was a look in his eyes, I couldn't quite put my finger on. It was gone in a flash.

"You said yourself that the inquest …"

"Was a joke, doesn't mean it reached the wrong conclusion."

"Mrs Strachan was convinced someone had murdered them all."

"She was biased, God rest her soul."

He had a point.

"The money?" I said.

"Don't care, not my business. Who cares about pensions … just a load of dead money."

"Dead money, huh," that was one way of describing it.

"I'll never solve your mysteries for you. But, work with me and I'll put what I can your way, if you …"

"Put anything I pick up your way."

"Goddit. We're neither of us popular up here. Let's be friends. We could make a good team."

"Team?" I laughed.

"You know, like Holmes and Watson, Morse and Lewis, Barnaby and Troy …"

"Laurel and Hardy?" I was in no position to turn down his offer, but I still didn't trust him.

"OK," he said, as if reading my thoughts. "Let me show you my good faith. Ask me for a favour."

I told him about Raeburn's allegations regarding possible corruption in the Hannigan case.

"And there's something else."

I repeated Ragland's insinuations; neither seemed to come as news to him.

"He implied there were police files," I added.

"I'll look into them both. If there are files, I'll find them and see what I can share with you."

"Do you think it could be true?"

"That he was a paedophile?" I flinched at the word. "He was your friend."

"I guess …"

"People let you down, that's life." He tipped his cup right up to drain the dregs.

"So you think …"

"I don't think anything. This is just the start," he said, placing it back in the saucer.

"Where will you work?"

"They're giving me an office here. But I'll be heading back south in a day or two … You?"

"I'm off to the asylum centre, then I've copy to file. I'd also give anything to see the independent trustee before I go home."

"Alexander Ross?"

I nodded.

"Good man. Best I've met up here, so far."

"Doesn't like journalists. Won't take my calls."

"I'll give you his mobile. Don't say it came from me."

Poitu was rising in my estimation.

"You may need to try a few times. Don't leave a message. I find he doesn't call you back."

"It's reassuring to know mine aren't the only calls he ignores," I smiled.

"He's a busy man, runs the company."

I nodded.

"He's a widower, with four kids. They run him ragged. What with this case, the firm and the kids, I'm not surprised his secretary guards him like a hawk."

I digested this information, as I punched the number into my mobile, before pulling on my jacket to leave.

"Three tenners should do it," he said, pointing to the table. The cheek, but I took the notes out of my purse and threw them down.

"One more thing," I remembered. "That missing actuary. Any news?"

"You know as much as I do. But hey, grown-ups walk out on their lives all the time. Often the best thing. Better than …" He stopped himself suddenly, and looked up at me sheepishly.

"Than blasting their family away," I finished for him.

"Ciao, Hornlight," he waved.

I left the restaurant, wondering, for all the 'big pals' act, just how much Poitu knew, and what information he was keeping from me.

I walked back to George Square in search of a cab, and found myself passing Carlton Crabb's office. On an impulse, I inquired at reception whether he was in. I was told to go through.

Crabb was sitting behind his gold-embossed desk, the grandfather clock ticking away in the corner.

"Ms Lighthorn," he stood to greet me. "What terrible news from the inquest. I had already left."

"I thought I saw you there." We both sat.

"Did you see poor Mrs Strachan?"

"I'm afraid I did."

"Terrible, terrible. I understand she didn't suffer."

I raised my eyebrows. The poor woman had suffered a great deal.

"At the end I mean."

I changed the subject. "Mr Crabb, as a Scottish lawyer, what did you make of the inquest?"

"Ah. Not our finest moment, I think we can say."

"Were you convinced by it?"

"That rather depends what you want cc..ccc..convincing of?" His 'Cs' were still proving troublesome.

"Indeed."

"My interest is largely in the will," he explained. "It's proving difficult, more difficult now that Mrs Strachan is gone, of course. I've her will too, to sort out, now."

"Who are the beneficiaries?"

"As I remember, Mr Strachan and his family are his mother's beneficiaries. Now they're pre-deceased, I would expect a fight over both estates. Mrs Jane Strachan's family in Inverness has a claim, there's a nephew in Milton Keynes, and some distant cousins in Canada."

"Is there much at stake?"

"Not so much. No. Mr Strachan had remortgaged his house after losing his job. There's not much equity left there. He did have substantial life insurance, though."

"Will these pay?"

"The inquest verdict is ccc..cc..crucial. Not on a suicide. But they were joint life policies. They pay out on the first death. The inquest ruled that Mrs Jane Strachan died first. So they should pay out."

"Do they pay out on murder?" He didn't reply. I looked at my watch. I'd stayed longer than I intended. "I'll have to go or I'll be late. Thank you for seeing me."

"Always a pleasure Ms Lighthorn. So sorry your trip has been a sad one again. At least, Mrs Strachan is at peace now." He held the door open for me.

"Another funeral of course," he said.

"How's the hat?" I thought of him walking away from me in the battered, stained topper. "Did it clean up?"

"Unfortunately, not. C..c..completely ruined. I've had to buy a replacement."

"Oh dear,"

"In fact, it is what you might call deceased."

Good grief, I thought, as I walked back down the stairs. Carlton Crabb had just cracked a joke.

Chapter Eighteen

3pm Wednesday, October 24, Stella Maris

It was raining now, that blinding west coast rain that descends in a moment and silences the seabirds. I hailed a cab and asked the driver to take me to the Star of the Sea community centre. According to my map, it was on the banks of the Clyde, a mile or two beyond an area called Black Top.

The road out of the city was drab, pitted with ugly housing schemes. Further along, we passed vast mountains of rubbish. I'd heard gags about Glasgow being the best place to dump garbage. But it was no joke. Taking in other people's rubbish was one industry at which the city excelled. Industrial stacks of debris were piled high, one after another.

The rain had eased to a spit by the time we pulled into the gates of the Stella Maris Catholic Church and community complex. The modern church looked like a UFO, squat like a flying saucer, with a huge triangular spire towering from its middle. By its side was a tidy building, surrounded by neatly trimmed lawns. People cared about this place. A statue of Stella Maris, the star of the sea, stood alone on the front lawn. The former shipbuilding community could be a superstitious lot.

I paid the cabbie and made my way to reception. Another effigy of the Star of the Sea stood in a corner on a wooden shelf.

"Can you tell Sister Robert I am here," I asked the receptionist.
But she didn't have to. I heard a door slam along the corridor, and saw a diminutive figure coming towards me.

What she lacked in height she made up for in presence. When she reached me, I realised there was nothing small about her.

"My dear child, what dreadful news. Poor Mrs Strachan," she took both my hands in hers. "Were you there?"

I nodded. "She didn't suffer." I found myself repeating Crabb's words.

"Dear Ken," her eyes softened. "He's a great loss to us. And now this."

"It's about Ken I wanted to see you."

"I know. I'm glad you've come. But first can I show you something of our little centre. He was very proud of it. We all are."

And she was off, kitten heels clicking.

"Without his efforts, we would never have opened our doors," she continued down the corridor. "He helped fundraise to build this place. Lobbied the bishops to get them to release the land. He wasn't even a catholic. Charmed the locals into not objecting, badgered the authorities until they funded us."

She was right to be proud, the centre was an achievement. Marsha would have loved it. She led me through a lecture room, computer room, language lab, home cinema, a small recording studio, and a huge gym. Along the way, I heard more different languages than you would in Heathrow's Terminal Three.

Sister Robert spoke to several individuals on the tour. She knew most of them by name, mainly men. I guessed their womenfolk were either still back in their home country, or secured behind closed doors in one of the housing schemes.

Next, she pounded through double swing doors into the canteen, leaving me to follow. It was busy, and the bubble of conversation, again all in different languages, sounded like the Tower of Babel.

What had brought them here, I wondered, with their many cultures and languages? What awful pasts were they escaping, this kaleidoscope of nationalities, that they preferred life marooned in a Glasgow ghetto, to all they had left behind?

"You must be ready for a cup of tea yourself," Sister Robert interrupted my thoughts, swinging out through the double doors, and leading the way back up the corridor to her office.

It was a simple room, with white walls and red carpet, but quite spacious. At one end, was a small desk with PC. The other looked like a sitting area, with sofa, armchair and plasma television. A door opened into a kitchen alcove. A wooden crucifix hung above it.

"Sit down and make yourself comfortable," she said pointing to the settee. "I won't be long." She disappeared for a few minutes into the kitchen, returning with two mugs of tea, and sitting near me on the armchair.

"The asylum seekers …" I began. "Are they all legal?"

"We don't ask."

"So some could be illegal immigrants?"

"It doesn't matter to us. We are here to help whoever we can. They are all God's children."

"In what way exactly … help I mean."

"We try to help them find work, if possible. We have contacts. Usually, though, they need to boost their language first, find somewhere decent to live. We make sure they are claiming all the benefits due to them. Get the children into school."

"And the whole family to communion," I mumbled cynically.

"You have a sharp tongue, Ms Lighthorn. You should watch it, it'll get you into trouble."

I blushed. She had got me in one. "You are so right, Sister. Me and my tongue. I apologise."

"Ken always spoke highly of you."

"Yes, that's what brought me here. I'm trying to trace his movements in the weeks before he … Did he visit the centre?"

"Yes, most definitely. But as for dates … it's hard to be precise. We are a drop-in centre. People come and go. We keep no record of their movements. I'm sure you understand …"

I understood alright. Records would scare the living daylights out of illegals.

"Helped with language, mainly." She paused, running a ring round the top of her mug with an index finger, as if choosing her next words carefully.

"He'd taken to spending a great deal of time with a girl we all called Roxy … that's what we all called her anyway. She came from the Ukraine."

I nodded for her to continue.

"A sad case. I found her in the church a few months ago, sobbing her heart out. Her mother had died, when she was young. Her father was a chemist. He'd been promised a job in a lab here in Glasgow, so they made the journey."

"Legally?"

Sister Robert wouldn't be drawn. The implication was clear that they had entered the UK illegally.

"She and her sister Marietta were put to work in a sewing factory somewhere in the city. Her father worked in a chemical lab. These factories are death traps. There was a fire late one night. He was killed. She didn't know the full story. They just told her he was dead. Not long after that, her sister disappeared. When I found her, the child had reached the end of a long, agonised road. She was alone and desperate."

"Why weren't the police informed?"

"Julia, may I call you Julia? You have to understand, these people are invisibles. If someone doesn't exist, there is nothing to investigate when they die or vanish."

"It doesn't seem possible in the 21st century," I shook my head. "What did you do?"

"We did the best we could for the child. Gave her love, and a home of sorts, when she wasn't at the sewing factory. She was devoted to Our Lady. Would pray to the Star of the Sea for hours."

"And Ken befriended her you say." I thought of the diary entry, *'Hoping to see R tomorrow. Then the game will be up.'*

Could this Roxy be R? Had he somehow got involved in all this?

"Sister, do you know if there's any possibility he saw her the Monday before he died?"

"Most definitely. He did see her. I saw them here together."

"That's fantastic. Can I see the girl? Where is she now?"

"That's the problem Julia, I have no idea. She disappeared the night Ken died. We haven't seen her since."

I felt sick.

"Where was she working? Where was she living?"

"I explained. We don't keep records. We don't ask any questions. We just give our love."

"Did you call the police?" I knew the question was pointless.

"To say what? Someone who doesn't exist has disappeared. This centre would empty overnight, if we called in the authorities every time someone stopped coming."

I nodded, and took a deep breath.

"Sister Robert, do you believe Ken Strachan killed his family?"

"God is our judge. I leave such matters to him."

"What can we do to find the girl?"

"I've been praying for her every night."

"With all due respect …"

"I know, but what else can I do. My hands are tied. But you Julia, you could look for her. Find her for me please. She was such a sweet child. I'm worried something's happened to her."

"Will you help me?"

"I'll do what I can. I'll ask the regulars to put the word out." Her voice dropped. "Did you notice, it is mainly men in the centre?"

"I had."

"The girls stop coming once they hit a certain age."

"What age is that?"

"She is only 13."

Chapter Nineteen

5pm Wednesday, October 24, Glasgow

I made it back to the hotel in time to meet the 6pm deadline. My report of the inquest shamelessly milked the drama of Mrs Margaret Strachan's collapse for all it was worth. She deserved a good send off.

Andrew fired back an email saying he was delighted with the material, and confirming it looked like we would break the story. But his hero-gram failed to dispel the gloom left by Stella Maris.

I felt deeply uncomfortable after the interview with Sister Robert. The girl Roxy complicated everything. If she were the R, what was Strachan up to? I thought of Ragland's words, "Why does a middle-aged man hang round centres full of displaced, vulnerable children and teenagers?" And Raeburn's, "No one will thank you."

Then I remembered Andrew saying, "Let them present the evidence. Otherwise keep going."

What if I did keep going? What if I did what Sister Robert asked and found the child? What can of worms might I be opening?

I called Ross's mobile. He didn't reply. I clicked the line dead without leaving a message. I tried Poitu. He didn't pick up either.

Finally, I called Omar.

"How'd the inquest go?"

"Terrible. His mother dropped dead at the end."

"It happens in court hearings. What was the verdict?"

"Strachan killed his family then killed himself. There was an eight hour delay going into the house, apparently. The Sheriff has ordered a Met officer to launch an inquiry into Strathclyde's conduct that night."

"Interesting, who?"

"It is interesting actually. They've appointed the inspector who came to see me. He was at the hearing."

"Ah, Hercule. Did you speak to him?"

"Yes, he was pretty scathing about the inquest, and the lack of forensic evidence."

"I see."

"And I dropped in on Carlton Crabb. He agreed. They both seem to think it was all a bit of a charade."

"Was Crabb at the inquest?"

"He's trying to sort out the will. There could be a big insurance payout."

"The Strachan's weren't murdered over an insurance payout."

"No." I agreed. "But there is another development."

He cut me dead. "Julia, there's a cab at the door. I'm late for a dinner. Let's catch up properly when you get back."

"Sure," and he was gone.

I flicked on the television, for lack of anything better to do, and caught the old Raymond Chandler movie, 'The Big Sleep'. What I could do with the insight of Philip Marlow.

I called Ross twice more during the commercial breaks. No answer. I was beginning to give up on seeing him before I flew home, when my mobile rang around nine, as the film was coming to a climax.

"Have you been trying to contact me?"

"Mr Ross?" I tried to sound as courteous as possible. "It's Julia Lighthorn. I wondered if you could spare me a few moments, before I catch my flight home tomorrow."

"I've meetings most of the day."

"Please. I'd only take a few minutes of your time."

He sighed.

"Can you be here at 10am? I may have a few minutes free then."

"At your office in Melville Street?"

"Right."

"I'll be there."

We clicked off, simultaneously.

I woke just before six and stretched a sleepy hand to the television controller to switch on the news. Within seconds, I was sitting bolt upright and wide-awake. A body had been fished out of the Clyde late the previous evening. I got straight on to the police press office.

"No, we have no idea who the deceased might be." The duty officer sounded as though he had been fielding calls since the small hours.

"Will you be calling Mrs Livingstone …"

"Not yet. The body is badly decomposed … nearly a fortnight in the water … identification is going to be …"

"I see."

"Don't jump to conclusions," he warned. "This could be anyone. Drunks fall into the river all the time. And then …"

"Plenty more get pushed," I finished for him.

Time was running on, so I dressed quickly and headed for Queen Street Station, where I grabbed a bacon roll, and made the 8.45am to Edinburgh. The train rattled through the bleak landscape of Falkirk, on to prettier Linlithgow, then crept slowly under the shadow of the castle, into Waverley Station.

It was cold, infinitely colder than Glasgow, but I was glad of the icy east wind to sharpen my wits, as I walked to his office. I was greeted in reception by Mrs Morag McKenzie, and recognised her voice immediately. She was far more personable than her telephone manner, and her face was kindly. This was disconcerting.

She had disappointing news, though.

"I'm afraid Mr Ross has been delayed. He will be with you as soon as he can. I'll show you into his office."

I followed her into a room. It was a modern office, but not a large one, not for the boss.

"Can I get you a coffee?"

I smiled, appreciatively.

The room had a comfortable feel to it. A strengthening autumn sun flooded every corner with an ocean of light. The desk was awash with paper, and I had to smoother an urge to start sifting through the documents strewn across it. So I walked over to the window and gazed out. A steady stream of human traffic rumbled by; businessmen in dark suits, late for work; business women, too, dressed like them in sober colours and cuts. This was Edinburgh's Square Mile; the heart of the financial district. Elegant Georgian town houses were given over to investment banks, fund managers, insurance companies, actuaries, advisers and their staff. Discreet, stoic and refined, it couldn't be more different from the brash whirlwind of the city of London.

Mrs McKenzie re-entered carrying a tray, drawing my attention back to the inside of the room.

"He shouldn't be much longer. Meeting overran. Make yourself at home."

She put the tray down on his desk, and left me. I moved towards it to pour a cup for myself, but, as I reached for the coffee pot, my eyes rested on a family photograph, pinned to the side of his computer screen. Four children, two boys, two girls, with their father. I was not good with children's ages any more, but they looked about six to fourteen, the youngest, not much more than a baby.

No mother, of course. In fact, no picture of her anywhere, as if he had airbrushed her out of their lives. I guess it hurt too much. Something hurt inside me too, as I gazed at the picture of the happy little group and thought of an appointment I had to keep the next day, a journey I had been blocking out. I had intended to go alone, but Marsha insisted on keeping me company. I didn't want to think about tomorrow right now. Not yet.

So instead, I did what I had promised myself I would not. I put a hand on one of the buff files on the desk, the first to catch my eye. I stroked its smooth cover. It had a label, 'Kelly's Brewery'. I opened it. The first few pages were formal letters of appointment. Then, I came to some handwritten notes. The writing was difficult to decipher. I concentrated harder, but it meant nothing, just columns of crazy figures and equations. I had seen that writing before. Could it be, I wondered, as the door opened and Ross walked in.

"Those are private documents," he said. I blushed scarlet.

"I … I … was just pouring the coffee." It was a pathetic excuse.

"I think you'll find the coffee pot is that thing with the handle," he pointed to the tray. Moving to the desk, he picked up the pot and poured two cups, while closing the file with his free hand.

I took my place in the chair opposite him.

"You're taller than I remembered," I attempted to break the ice.

"Well, you've not grown-up any," he screwed his eyes up and stared at me. I flinched. "Shall we get down to business?" he continued. "My time is …"

"I know … precious."

I chose my words carefully. I wanted him to respect me, like me even. I thought of Ken Strachan and the interview that day in my office. Now the boot was on the other foot. I needed help.

"I'm investigating the missing pension money."

"On what authority?"

"Authority?"

"Are you with the police? Has a court appointed you? Is an interested party paying you?"

"I'm a journalist. The public has a right to the truth. The victims have a right to the truth."

"Ah, the truth. We all know how truth is your industry's particular stock in trade."

It was a cheap jibe, so I ignored it.

"Ken Strachan asked me to investigate. He was an old …" somehow the word 'friend' wouldn't come out.

Ross cut me short. "I'm not interested in your scandal. All I want is to sort out this mess and get as much money for the members as I can. That's my only concern."

"The murders …"

"In the past year, I have had the misfortune of watching seventeen people die without any compensation for the loss of their life's work and savings. I saw an old woman drop dead yesterday."

"It was tragic."

"And that's what you're after, isn't it, Ms Lighthorn? Fodder for your newspaper? Scandals that sell copies?"

"No," I protested, knowing there was at least a grain of truth somewhere in those words.

"I have a difficult job, which needs sensitive handling. I have a legal duty to do the best I can for those who've lost out, but I mustn't raise expectations unrealistically."

His face darkened.

"I don't want any more dead bodies on my hands."

"Of course, I understand." I spoke softly. This was going as badly as it could, and I didn't know how to turn it around.

So I softened my voice, and tried a different tack. "Did you hear they pulled a body out of the Clyde last night?"

"No ... yes ... of course, I've heard. I've been with the police since dawn."

Well that might explain a lot.

"Could it be the missing actuary who worked for Sherlock?"

"Maybe it is," he threw at me. "Maybe this guy stole all the money for Kelly, so had to be silenced. What a story that would make for your readers!"

"It's the truth my readers want."

"Well, if it's truth you're after, it probably has nothing to do with anything. Some drunk lost his footing."

"Is that what you think?"

"Actually, I don't care. It doesn't help me recover the cash."

"Will you get it back?"

His voice softened and he loosened his tie, as if relaxing.

"Not all of it, no."

"How much is missing?"

"Even that's not clear yet. We're gathering the data. It depends on how much the Government will pick up. It has some liabilities, the records are a mess ..." He touched the buff files in front of him irritably. "The cost of annuities are rising all the time."

"Then there are your fees, of course. They'll have to come out before anyone else gets a penny."

He didn't move a muscle. I thought of Sister Robert, and quickly apologised, before he threw me out.

"I'm sorry, that was unfair."

He let it go.

"Mr Ross, the only valuation I've seen was done about six years ago. The fund was in surplus then. I've not seen the one Sherlock did three years later."

"No, they don't broadcast the numbers. According to Sherlock it was still roughly breaking even ... assets and liabilities roughly matching at around £3 billion."

"Can you trust these numbers?"

"Sherlock's, what do you think?" He shook his head. "My first priority was to carry out a valuation. I haven't filed the formal report yet. But I can only find £1 billion in the kitty."

I sucked in a breath sharply. "More than £2 billion short."

"Off the record, but probably half of that is markets."

"But the other half ... d'you know what happened to that, where it went?"

"It's not that simple."

"But you're on the trail?"

"Investigating a number of avenues, yes."

He opened a file on his desk, as if about to share something with me, then thought better of it and closed it again.

"What do you know about Kellys?" he asked.

"Not a huge amount ... old family firm ... got left behind in the brave new world of the 21st century. Not the first, won't be the last."

"That's about it," he said. "In their heyday, they were one of the most powerful families in Scotland. The brewery dates back to the early 1800s. It was Jack Kelly's great, great, great, grandfather who first began brewing the stuff. The conditions of working class life gave them a terrible thirst."

"An escape."

"The Kellys have always been teetotallers, did you know that? So many of the drinks families were. High church, too. Beer and whisky made their fortunes, but they had the sense never to touch a drop."

"Kind of endearing, huh?"

"They got a good living out of it for a couple of generations, bought a nice house in town, an estate on the west coast, property on the islands and a place in society. But it was Mary Kelly's husband, Robert …"

"Jack's father?"

"Uh..huh. He was the one with the big plans. Took the business global."

"Global?"

"Prohibition was his fortune. Supposed to have supplied half of Boston with booze at one stage. Made some very important political contacts."

"Bootlegging, I see. And when prohibition ended?"

"Kelly was well placed to put his business on a legitimate footing. He expanded into whisky, soft drinks, you name it. He even had a share in a small oil rig at one point."

"That's why the scheme was so big?"

"The American's love all things Scottish, particularly Scotch whisky," he nodded. "Then, there was the Japanese market."

"And the depression and the war."

"Exactly. Our fellow man was never without a reason to want a drink."

"So what went wrong?"

"Look round you, any night you go out. What are we drinking these days? White wine, and the odd bottle of red. By the ocean. You can't grow grapes in Scotland."

"The rest of the group?"

"Long gone. They sold it off, bit by bit, to keep the brewery going. But they always hung on to the pension funds."

"Ready for raiding?"

He opened the file in front of him, again.

"Here's a story. Ask the Pensions Regulator about the monthly transfers of £15 million out of the fund, which started five years ago."

This was jaw-dropping stuff, but I kept a stiff lower lip.

"Five years ago, Cameron was acting. What do they say?"

"Not much."

"Was it legal?"

"That depends where the money went?"

"If the company pocketed it, you mean?"

"It's a bit more complicated than that. Employers could help themselves to surpluses, if the funds had more money than they needed."

"Which it was at the time of the Cameron valuation."

"Exactly. But valuations are an art, not a science."

"They can be manipulated."

"To an extent."

"But Cameron is a very respectable firm, famous for being conservative."

"They stopped acting pretty quickly afterwards."

"By actuarial standards," I couldn't resist. He smiled.

"Indeed. And the guy in charge of the account retired suddenly. Lives in Hampshire now. I'm going down to see him next week. He must know something."

"You'll be wasting your time, I'm afraid. I've already done that one." I gave him quick rundown of our visit.

"Oh no ..." He looked downcast.

"So the valuations are key?" I continued.

"Key to keeping the directors, trustees and their advisers out of jail, yes."

"If the valuations were misleading, either Cameron's or Sherlock's, then we could prove fraud."

"We'd be in with a chance ..."

"And you could sue their insurers?"

"And everyone else in sight, in theory. But proving wilful fraud is nigh on impossible. Very few claims have been successful."

"The trustees ... it's their job to make sure this sort of thing can't happen."

"A toothless bunch, but anyway, if the advisers say it's OK, there's nothing they can do."

He was right, of course.

"Back to these transfers; you know, as well as I do, that the regulator won't say a word."

"Find a way to get the story out. But leave me out of it."

I nodded, wondering how on earth I could pull that one off. Hell, I could trust this man. If it came to it, I would take one God-almighty-seat-of-the-pants flyer.

He looked at his watch. My eyes flicked to the clock on the wall. It was 11.04am. I had overstayed my welcome. It was time to go. I needed to get moving myself, if I was to make my flight home.

"Thanks, for everything," I stood, gingerly holding out my hand to say goodbye. He took it, and was still holding it, when I ran one more line by him.

"Have you heard anything about a missing child? Someone Strachan had befriended?"

He stared hard into my face, then dropped both my hand and his gaze.

"My job is to find the money," he said.

How had I known this would not be news to him?

Chapter Twenty

12.45pm Thursday, October 25, Edinburgh Airport

I made the flight by the skin of my teeth and had roughed out a story by the time it landed. Determined to get it away in the next morning's edition, I took a cab direct from City Airport to the office. My first call was the pension police, or chief regulator. My regular contact Toby Cartwright picked up the phone.

"Julia," he said. "To what do we owe this honour. Clean out of whipping dogs are we?"

Watchdogs liked to bar their teeth to ward off trouble.

"Toby, what can you tell me about a series of £15 million monthly withdrawals from the Kelly's pension fund, going back five years?"

"There is an investigation taking place into the whole Kelly's affair, as you know perfectly well. We will have nothing to say until it's completed."

"So you're denying you're investigating these transactions?" I was determined to trap him.

"I'm doing no such thing. I'm neither denying nor confirming."

"So you're not denying you're looking into the Kelly's collapse?"

"Heavens help me. The fund has imploded and people have lost their pensions. You know there's an investigation under way."

"But these transfers?"

"I'm saying nothing." He paused. I waited … and waited … and waited. Sometimes, saying nothing could be the most productive modus operandi.

The strategy worked.

"The missing money went somewhere didn't it, pet?" he said, if only to get me off the phone. Toby could be slightly camp at times, not to mention endearingly indiscreet.

I put the phone down. I had all I needed. He had given me a green light to proceed, an off-the-record nod confirming I was working along the right lines.

I called Ludgate directly.

"Bloody hell, good work," he said. Then he began pushing me. "Where did the money go?"

"We don't know."

"Get back to your source."

"He doesn't know."

"Who ordered the transfer?"

"We don't know."

"Are we sure about this?"

"My source is impeccable."

"What does the regulator say?"

"No comment."

"For crying out loud, Julia!" His patience was running thin.

"Look let me write it. Then, see what you think. See if it's strong enough to run."

"OK."

I put down the phone and began to type:

> *'Watchdogs have launched an urgent investigation into £15 million monthly withdrawals from the disgraced brewery pension fund, which began five years ago.*
>
> *The suspicious withdrawals came to light as part of an investigation into the collapse of what was once one of Britain's greatest drinks giants.'*

I included all the caveats, such as the pension's regulator refusing to comment, and a similar one from the independent trustee. Before filing, I put in a call to the liquidator and to the new company of Kelly's Brewery. Both refused to take my call, simply saying 'no comment'.

Andrew called a few moments after I had filed. My heart sank at his words.

"It's a bit thin, now I look at it. I'll see what the lawyers say."

Within an hour Matthew Sharp was on the phone, firing questions, putting me through the wringer. I thanked God, though, he was on duty. Matthew was crushingly tough, but unlike many lawyers, he seemed to understand his job was to help us get stories into the newspaper, not spike them.

"We are just bandying around unfounded allegations," he stated the obvious.

"No, we're not. This has come from a senior source."

"Name it."

"I can't."

"We have to get someone to confirm something."

"No one will."

"Then we can't run it without being sued."

"Truth is a defence."

"Only if it is true."

"It is."

"That money was transferred or that it was suspicious?"

"I don't know, both I guess."

"You need another source."

He put the phone down. I looked at my watch. Time was running out. It was 8pm. Where would I find another source at this time of night? I reached across my desk, and, as I did, I sent a mug of coffee flying. I tried to catch it mid air, but made it worse, knocking it sideways. It came crashing down on the desk, where the mug neatly cracked in three. A sticky brown liquid spilled everywhere.

"Damn," I felt something trickling down my inside leg, seeping right through my underwear. I stood up, shaking my skirt with one hand, stretching to grab the fragments of the wretched mug, to throw in the bin, with the other. As I stretched, I had a flashback of Jamie's Aunt Sally bending to save the tea pot and cups, when helicopters turned her village into 'Nam.

"Guess she gets more practice," I thought, as I shook coffee grains off some soaked papers. As I stood there shaking, a light switched on in my brain.

"That's it."

I dialled Jamie's number.

"Jamie."

"Julia. Hear you had a great time with the old folks? Did you get what you wanted?"

"Yes, no, not exactly. Look, I'm desperate. I wouldn't ask you."

"Go on," his tone was dry.

"When you were at Cameron, when you were working for Maurice Paterson …"

"Yeeees."

"Look. It's to do with the Kelly's Brewery pension fund."

"Obviously."

"I've discovered that big monthly withdrawals were made, that may partly account for the missing money, going back to Cameron's time."

"Impossible," he answered sharply. "They're too straight."

"I'm not saying they did anything wrong. Not exactly."

"Which means, not yet you aren't. Where do I come in?"

"Did you ever see anything, or hear anything …"

Jamie was as honest as the day was long. If money had been misappropriated, he would not hesitate to shop the culprits.

"How much time do you have?"

I laughed down the line, indicating none.

"I have some old files. Never looked at most of it. Give me half an hour?" Sensible operators took discreet copies of everything they came across. It paid to be cautious.

He put the phone down. Precisely 30 minutes later he rang again. The friendliness in his voice had gone, replaced by a new grimness.

"There's a letter here to Kelly's bankers authorising monthly transactions to an account number. The sum specified is £15 million. Is that enough?"

"Will you fax it to me, I have to see it."

"You keep me out of it?"

"Trust me."

"OK."

I rang Ludgate to tell him a fax would soon be with him. He said nothing. The fax departed.

Then Matthew called.

"This is all very well, but all it proves is that Cameron ordered a few transfers. We still don't know there is anything suspicious. The transfers may have been made prior to a big investment, or to buy a raft of annuities."

"That's not what my contact thinks."

"Cameron will take us to the cleaners over this."

"Then leave them out of it. The story stands, without any reference to them. This was just meant to be more reassurance for you."

He went quiet.

"I'll talk to Andrew. Where are you by the way?"

"I'm in the office. I'll be going home shortly. Call me there if you need me."

He called me almost every hour until 2am, each time pulling the story to shreds in a different way. At 2am, the final deadline passed. I was no nearer to knowing whether it would be used or spiked.

I dreamt fitfully; of Mrs Strachan at the inquest, of Poitu's offer to work together, of Sister Robert and a girl called Roxy, and of Alexander Ross's expression, when he learned Maurice Patterson had lost his mind. "Oh no," he said over and over again in the dream.

I woke to the sound of the newspapers hitting the mat. I picked up my copy of Square Mile with trembling hands. It was all there in 72 point:

'Watchdogs probe suspicious Kelly transfers.'

Chapter Twenty-one

10am Friday, October 26, Southwark

By the time Marsha arrived at my flat, I had checked out the competition on the internet. Two of the most prominent titles had followed us up, pretty much verbatim, without being able to verify a word.

Ordinarily this would have been a source of satisfaction, but not today. The phone had begun ringing at regular intervals. I let it switch onto answer machine. Their questions could wait. There was something more important to do. It was October 26. Three years to the day that Philip had died.

Marsha parked her one luxury, a 20-year-old MG, on double yellow lines outside my flat, and honked the horn until I joined her. She was dressed more soberly than usual, in a dark skirt, which must have taken ten times more material than her usual tight above-the-knee numbers.

I wore my yellow silk suit. Yellow had been his favourite colour. The Southwark street was quiet. Many residents had joined the cattle trek to the city hours ago. Others, who worked from home, writers, graphic designers, advertising copywriters, were already glued to their computers. A postman went from house to house making his delivery. There was a woman, in a grey trench coat, I didn't recognise.

Marsha stopped at a flower shop, picked out two dozen white roses and waited patiently, while I stood looking at the display. Flowers are what we take when we visit the graves of loved ones, but they seemed to have nothing to do with me. There was nothing in the shop I wanted.

Marsha picked up another dozen yellow roses this time, and paid for them at the counter. "These will do for both of us," she said.

We got back in the car and drove to the cemetery where Philip was buried. It had not changed since our last visit, a year ago. It was deserted, the lives commemorated here forgotten by the outside world. Tall thin trees lurched in an east wind.

Marsha opened her bag, took out a damp cloth and cleaning materials, and set to work on the head stone. She rubbed and wiped and polished for a good ten minutes, while I stood watching. Next, she tipped out the dead flower-pots, cleaned those too, and filled them with fresh water from a tap along the way. Finally, she cut the roses, arranged them in the pots, and placed them neatly around the stone.

Then, she stepped back and we gazed at the grave in silence.

'Philip Anthony Lighthorn' I read, although I'm not sure anyone else would have heard. 'We will never forget you.'

That was all it said. And then the tears came, like they did every October 26. I tried to stop them, I really tried. But part of me knew, I would never be strong enough to control this grief. I cried for the happy summers I would never see, the young man who had been taken from me and the grandchildren I would never cradle.

I cried for Ken Strachan, and his family. And I thought of Alexander Ross. He must have stood at such a gravestone, grieving for his lost wife, and wondering how he could cope with the years ahead. And I thought of Sister Robert and the lost girl. A wave of despair engulfed me.

"Come away now," Marsha said, wrapping her arm around my shoulder. We walked slowly back to the car. A light had come on in the little church. Another funeral. Another bereavement. More tears.

As Marsha revved the engine, I saw a shadow of a figure emerge from the chapel. It vanished the instant after it caught my eye. I could have sworn it was the woman in the grey trench coat I'd seen hanging about my road. But no, it couldn't be. My nerves were strained.

"Did you see someone, over there?" I pointed to the chapel porch as we drove passed.

Marsha gave me a strange look.

"I need a drink," she said, moving her hand from the gear stick and placing it over mine. If there were any ghosts lurking in the shadows, they would have to cross her first.

She pulled into a pub. We were the first visitors of the day. Its brown wooden chairs and iron tables were reassuringly old-fashioned. A fire glowed in the grate. I sat staring into the flames, while Marsha went to the bar. A big swig of whisky hit the right spot.

"Three years … it seems like …" I stopped. What did it seem like? Like a life-time. Like no time.

Marsha said nothing, just listened.

"All this business with Strachan. It brought it all back."

"I was afraid for you, Jules, so was Omar."

"I still can't believe Ken harmed his family. Men don't become violent over night. There are signs. I know the signs."

Her mouth was a flat line. I knew she wanted me to stop.

"My God, I should know the signs. I was married to one."

"You survived," she put a hand over mine.

"I never saw it in Strachan, the need to control."

"We never really know other people."

"And people change," I added.

Our drinks were empty, so Marsha went to the bar again, leaving me thinking of my wedding day and all that had followed. The second whisky burned that satisfying combination of pleasure and pain.

"You mustn't blame yourself," she said.

What else could I do but blame myself, for my rotten marriage, for Philip, for Strachan, for throwing away my career.

"It was the job," I tried to excuse it all.

She nodded.

"Do you still think about …"

"Every day. Not a day passes, not a minute …"

"Yes."

"I did love him, Marsha."

"I know you did."

"In many ways, he was wonderful. Truly, you didn't know him then. He was witty and funny, but he could be passionate and driven.

It was love at first sight. And it was perfect, those early years. Me, working for the Examiner. Him on the foreign desk at the Globe. Out every night, parties, receptions, concerts …"

"Then he went to the Middle East."

Marsha had heard this story before. A million times.

"Embedded with a platoon." The whisky had loosened my tongue. "He was shocked by the brutality and casual violence. But it changed him."

"It does change people," Marsha understood. "They become brutalised. Violence can be addictive, like heroin. They crave the next fix."

I nodded. "I wouldn't hear from him for months. Then he'd turn up, demanding and possessive. The slightest thing would spark a rage of jealousy. He started using me as a punch bag."

"They were all casualties."

"I know. I forgave him a long time ago."

"But it still hurts?"

I nodded.

"You have to let go, Julia." She hardly ever called me Julia. "You have to … you have to learn to trust again, to trust another man."

"No. I tried that once and it's not for me."

"Give yourself another chance."

"I'll never marry again. Never."

"Lor' I said nothing about marry. Just let go. Try letting someone into your life."

"You don't, and what about Omar?" She could hardly deny her own celibacy. But Marsha had her family. It comprised every waif and stray, down and out in London.

Her reply, though, struck me as odd.

"Omar will marry, and he's very fond of you."

"Not in that way. He's waiting for his parents to arrange a marriage. He's told me a hundred times."

"That's not what he's waiting for." She looked at me pointedly, then picked up her purse to leave.

I wondered how Marsha, normally so astute, could have misread my friendship with Omar so badly.

A smell of pizza greeted us as we walked up the stairs to the office, and we could hear Mina shouting at Omar about the stench.

"Good on yer mate," Marsha greeted him, biting into a warm slice. "We're hank marvin, ain't, we gal."

Mina hugged me close for a moment, although I wasn't entirely sure whether this was in solidarity at my grief or in disgust at the greasy cheese smell. Then, she left us. Omar looked across nervously.

"All went well?"

"It was fine," Marsha answered for us both,

"Some good stuff in today's edition, Jules," he continued.

"Thanks."

"So a productive trip up north?"

I sat at my desk. Marsha pulled up a chair, and I finally got round to telling them about Sister Robert, the story of the lost girl, and the body in the Clyde.

"So Poitu held out on you?" he said.

"Looks that way, he must know more than he's letting on."

"But Ross seems to have come through?"

"Yes and no. He's using me."

"Don't knock it. At least we're getting somewhere with the money."

"Yes. According to Ross the fund's £2 billion short."

"And nearly £1 billion was withdrawn in these £15 million slugs." Omar reached for another slice.

"That we know of … There could be others. The markets will account for some of the loss."

"Could these withdrawals have been made legitimately?"

"Some of them, possibly, in Cameron days, maybe. Ross implied to prove fraud you'd need to prove the valuations were fraudulent."

"Ah fraud …"

"I know, hellish difficult to prove."

"Get back to Hercule." He couldn't resist a joke at Poitu's expense.

"You need to chase him on that Hannigan case and find out if he has files on the paedophilia accusation and the child's disappearance."

"What about the body?" Marsha interrupted. "He must know something, even if the local bill are saying nothing."

"You must keep pushing Poirot."

"His name is Poitu."

Mina was right, the pizza smell was disgusting. I got up to open a window.

"What about the girl?" Marsha asked. "Can we try and find her?"

"How? It'd be like looking for a needle in a hay stack."

I stared out at the by-passers in the street below.

"That poor girl … if she's alive," Marsha said.

"Isn't all this just the way capitalism is supposed to work?" I was angry, the day was taking its toll. "The girl, the Strachans, the pension fund. Don't we just have to get used to it?"

"Don't think we can blame capitalism here, my dear friend." Omar had sucked in a love of enterprise with his mother's milk. "You can't blame the market place for the failings of individuals."

"The market, the market, that's all we bloody hear. What about its victims, Omar?" Marsha spat.

"The great free-market economists accepted there would be victims, but as Adam Smith said, their numbers would be 'psychologically small'."

"Psychologically small, eh, Omar?" I retorted. "Tell that to Sugden and Strachan …"

I gazed out the window, as Omar and Marsha continued arguing the theory of economic ethics. My eyes rested on a stall below, selling eastern trinkets. How glamorous it looked and how I wished I were the other side of the world. Then I saw her again … the woman in the grey trench coat. A third sighting couldn't be a coincidence. Who was she, and what did she want?

Chapter Twenty-two

3pm Friday, October 26, Whitechapel

"What is it doll?" Marsha had seen me pull back from the window.

"Nothing, nothing," I mumbled, not ready to share my suspicions. Journalists often found themselves more spied upon than spying, particularly when they break a big story. Interested parties can be desperate to trace your sources. I knew of several organisations which kept detailed files on me, and my phone had been tapped on three occasions in the past. But I'd never been followed before.

"I must go," Omar stood. "Before I do, I've bad news. I'm so sorry, Julia, to bring it today of all days."

"You couldn't get an adjournment?"

"No. There will be a preliminary hearing in a month."

"Dear God."

"Don't panic, it'll be fine. It's all just part of the game."

"What if …?"

"No ifs … just put the date in your diary. November 13." With these words, he left.

"I must get moving too," Marsha said, leaving me alone.

I switched on Sky News to catch the latest headlines; two more suicide bombs in the Middle East, a stabbing in Manchester, a racist attack in Govan, oil price up, market down, another pension fund closed. No news though on any identification of the mystery Clyde corpse or the disappearing actuary.

There was an item about Victor Kane. He'd pulled off the bid for the Boston Bank, but 10,000 jobs worldwide would have to go. I froze as his face appeared on the screen, and I could feel my pulse racing. Yet there was nothing physically scary about this man. He looked like any other banker, which reminded me he was Kelly's Banker, or rather his director David Black was.

The news moved quickly on to other matters, so I clicked it off and tapped into my emails, downloading 64. One, a herogramme from

Ludgate, ended with his instruction, now we were way ahead of the race, to make sure we stayed there. Easier said than done. There were 15 calls on the answer machine, one from Alexander Ross, asking me to call him. And another from Poitu.

"It's time to make a list," I muttered, pushing the keyboard away and pulling an A4 lined pad in front of me.

I sucked the pen for a moment and then wrote a big '1' at the top of the list, with 'Black' beside it.

What I would give to talk to him, but the libel case ruled out making any approach to him. I could imagine what Omar would say if I even thought about trying. I wrote 'no' beside his name.

'2. Briggs'; the fund's legal adviser, but he was Kelly's son-in-law. Another 'No'.

'3. Jack Kelly.' It was time I confronted Mr Kelly. I put a tick beside him.

'4. Poitu.' He got a long line of exclamation marks.

The phone rang. It was Ross. "I'm flying down tomorrow. I'm going to see Patterson. D'you want to come?"

My stomach caught at the sound of his voice. What was he up to now?

"Ahmmm … it's a Saturday … I'm not sure whether …"

"Fine, it was just a thought."

"No, no, wait …" I said, hesitatingly. "Yes, I can probably do that."

"Good. Meet me at Heathrow in your car … I take it you have a car … and you can drive me down."

"So you were just after a free ride?"

"Something like that. I'm landing at 10am, Terminal 1."

"Ok. I'll be there."

How strange, I thought, replacing the receiver. He never mentioned the article. If he hadn't liked it, I was pretty sure he wouldn't have held back from telling me.

Next I dialled Poitu, to be told he was away for the weekend. Would I like to make an appointment to see him at the station on Monday?

"No, tell him I want to see him in my office." I knew he would come.

"I'll make sure he gets the message," said the voice at the other end. I was pretty sure he'd get the message.

I picked up my pen and added 'Sister Robert' to the list. It was time I called her. I got through quickly. No, there was no news about the girl, and yes, she had put the word around.

"My numbers are falling, though," she confided. "People are getting nervous."

"Nervous, of what?"

"Just nervous."

I cut the phone off at the base, but continued to hold the receiver. I desperately needed an interview with Jack Kelly. Taking a deep breath, I dialled the head office of Kelly's Brewery and requested the interview. I was put through to his secretary.

"Mr Kelly doesn't give interviews," came the reply.

"Will you ask him please if he will see me?"

"I will ask him, but I shouldn't hold out much hope."

"Ask him and please call me back. My number is ..." I reeled off my mobile. This was one call, I wanted to make sure I took, whatever the hour of day or night.

I decided to call it an early night, but before I left I put in one more call, to Jamie's Aunt Sally.

"My, my, did you hear that, Timmy?" which he couldn't have done, not being on the phone. "Julia's coming to Upton Grey tomorrow to see us. And she's bringing her young man."

"Not my young man. A colleague. We'll pop in for a quick cup of tea." It made sense to catch up with the local gossip.

"We are popular all of a sudden. Well, not so much us, as Grey House. Visitors almost every day."

"Really?"

"Oh my, yes. Goodness knows what the Pattersons make of it all. By the way ..."

I waited patiently.

"Mrs Pike in the post office told me, and she got it off Hilda Harris."

"And?"

"The Pattersons are getting divorced. How strange at their time of life? Anyway, we can chatter more about all that when I see you tomorrow. And you're bringing your young man," she repeated.

"A colleague," I stressed again, before putting down the phone. So, the Pattersons were getting divorced.

How interesting. And what sudden development could have brought that on?

Chapter Twenty-three

11am Saturday, October 27, M3 near the Windsor turnoff

"A divorce?" Ross digested this snippet, as we headed down the M3 towards Upton Grey.

"According to local gossip."

"She's taken advice. Someone has warned her to get as much safely ring-fenced for herself while she can."

"She's afraid he's going to be sued?"

"It's a sensible precaution in the circumstances."

Ross flicked his mobile phone to pick up a text message as he spoke.

"What would it take for a case to be successful, against Cameron, say?" I asked.

"Proving the valuations were fraudulent would be a good place to start." With that, he began a detailed explanation of the laws governing pension valuations.

I listened as carefully as I could, while mainly keeping my eyes glued to the road. I watched him too, stealing across occasional glances. I had to admit I found him fascinating. He must have been gorgeous when he was younger, or maybe, he was one of those annoying men who became strikingly attractive with age, just as we women were falling apart at the seams.

"You see, valuations operate within a range and within that range they are legit. But, assets and liabilities can be assessed in different ways," he explained.

"So different actuaries can come to different conclusions, and that's fine?"

"Exactly," he continued. "Take a loaf of bread. You might look at it and think you'll get ten sandwiches out of it. But I might expect to get fourteen or fifteen. We might both be right."

"Depending on how thickly we cut the bread."

"Then, there are the liabilities."

"The pensions?"

"These have to be valued, and it is an even more uncertain calculation. You have to decide how long people will live and a whole range of other stuff. The pension age and discount rate can have a huge impact."

"The discount rate?"

"It's the rate at which future liabilities are discounted. It's difficult to explain, but it's like an interest rate."

All the time he spoke, I was studying him, with one eye on the road. It was hard to put a finger on his particular charm. His eyes were like two blue shiny magnets, which drew you in. His grey-blond hair added a touch of glamour. His mouth was warm and honest, and his bone structure intelligent. They all fitted together perfectly to make the kind of face you wanted to know better.

"And the pension age?"

"You reduce the pensions bill every time you push up the pension age."

"I see. So what you're saying is, the withdrawals may have been legitimate, if the valuations were within the acceptable range."

"Most actuaries value somewhere close to the middle of the range. Patterson's last valuation was way out there on the edge."

"Could he have taken a backhander …? Damn," I hit the brakes, as a juggernaut swung into the fast lane, before swerving back into its own lane again.

"I don't think so," Ross spoke slowly, like he couldn't be sure. "He did retire soon after."

His mobile rang and he spent the rest of the journey with it glued to his ear. As we pulled into Upton Grey village, I heard him wishing someone good luck. His voice had lost its usual edge and seemed softer.

"Laura, my daughter," he said, by way of explanation. "It's her piano exam this afternoon. They're all with my mother. Ah … we've arrived."

When we reached Upton Grey House, I pulled into the sweeping drive and watched him soak up its magnificence. Hilda Harris opened the door. She greeted Ross courteously, but ignored me, as if we had never met.

The entrance hall was unchanged since my last visit, but if Ross noticed the shabby neglect, he didn't show it.

"I'd better warn you. He's having one of his blue days," she said, leading the way through.

Patterson was sitting at the same desk in the same room, curtains flapping in the breeze of the open windows, as they had been the day Marsha and I visited. He wore the same pin-striped suit and red bow tie. The room, though, had moved on. Even more cuttings were plastered along the walls. And more equations than ever were scribbled on every surface.

If the spectacle surprised Ross, he showed no sign, but greeted Patterson courteously, one actuary to another. He had brought with him a huge pile of documents.

"Thank you for seeing me at such short notice," he said, offering Patterson his hand. "I believe you've already met Ms Lighthorn?"

"I'm sorry, I don't remember. I used to remember everything. I was so sharp, but now, there's nothing in my mind at all. I seem to lose everything. Quite frightening."

"It's nothing to be afraid of Mr Patterson. I have a few valuations I wanted to discuss with you. They relate to Kelly's Brewery. D'you remember advising them?"

"Kelly's Brewery, Kelly's Brewery. It's all anyone asks about."

"Others have been here asking?" Ross's voice was gentle, as if coaxing a child.

"Never leave me in peace. I have my work to get on with. I'm getting so close." He was trembling and seemed more agitated than when I had seen him last.

"Can I see your workings?" Ross tried to calm him. Patterson pushed some papers his way and invited him to sit, as if glad of a kindred spirit.

"I can see your fascination," Ross murmured. "It is beautiful. What

120

a brilliant piece of work."

"Thank you, I'm so glad you understand."

They bent their heads over the papers for about five minutes mumbling in a language, which meant nothing to me. I stared at the cuttings. Still nothing later than 1995. The glory days of the pensions industry, with no hint at the chaos to come.

Ross slipped one of his reports onto the desk.

"Mr Patterson," he began. "Do you remember which discount rate you used to reach this valuation?" He flicked the page over deftly. "And on what grounds did you authorise this withdrawal?"

"The discount rate is there. It is always included. I can't remember anything about any withdrawals."

"And this. Do you know anything about this authorisation?"

"I'm sorry, I can't remember, I can't remember, I remember nothing." His agitation was rising.

Then he started to sob, "Sorry, sorry, sorry, I can't remember … sorry, sorry … I'm so sorry."

He sat on his chair, rocking backwards and forwards, gently sobbing.

"Sorry … sorry … sorry …"

I watched Ross gaze round the room, and saw a look I didn't recognise as he took in its whole absurdity. In an instant, it was gone.

"Please don't trouble yourself, Mr Patterson. We'll leave you now. Thank you again for your time."

And we walked out, leaving the deranged figure rocking backwards and forwards on the chair.

"A wasted journey," Ross said, as we pulled out of the drive.

"What did you expect?"

"Oh, I don't know. Those equations are gibberish, by the way."

"Completely meaningless?"

"Not completely, I suppose. He's reworking the same sums over and over again, using different assumptions each time, trying to get them to add up."

"And they don't any more? And he can't face it?"

"Something like that."

"D'you think he's really ill?"

"I don't know. I'm not a doctor. It seems genuine enough."

"We're neither of us psychiatrists."

"No, but I am an actuary. And this is a very smart house, even for a senior partner."

Ross was no fool. When I stopped outside Wisteria Cottage, the door opened immediately and Sally and Timmy came out to greet us. I was sure I saw a wry look of amusement flicker momentarily in Ross's eyes.

Before we could get inside, a distant rumble quickly swelled into the deafening whirr of overhead helicopters. Timmy ran to the front door and steadied various pots of winter pansies.

"We complain all the time," Sally shouted.

"Get's us nowhere," Timmy agreed.

"Deaf to democracy."

"Death to democracy?" Ross repeated.

"No deaf, my dear, deaf. The people are powerless. Come in, come in."

I led the way through to the sitting room.

"This is Alexander Ross," I introduced him.

"Call me Sandy," he said, shaking hands with them both.

"Sandy, how delightful, short for Alexander of course."

A tea tray full of fancies was already laid, and Timmy brought boiling water for the pot. I watched Ross inspect the wisteria on the cup and saucer and cake plate. When he looked up, our eyes met, but he didn't smirk, although I suspected that he wanted to.

"Was your meeting with Mr Patterson successful?" Sally addressed the question to me.

"It's a long way to come for a wasted journey," Timmy added.

I looked at Ross. He didn't respond.

"You say Patterson's had a number of visitors recently?" I asked.

"Seems to have become something of a celebrity," Sally answered. "I've been stopped twice in the high street and asked to give directions to Grey House."

"And don't forget Mrs Pike," Timmy reminded her.

"Yes, Mrs Pike said she's had about three gentlemen in the post office asking for Grey House."

"And then there's Marjory."

"Oh yes. Marjory. She's one of our church cleaning volunteers. She's a Tuesday. So it must have been last Tuesday. She was on her hands and knees behind the altar … there'd been an accident with some wine, she was trying to get it out … when someone appeared from nowhere. Gave her quite a fright. Anyway, this gentleman wanted to know where he could find the Pattersons."

"What was he like?" Ross asked.

"Marjory said he was wearing a suit, but didn't look quite City."

"Marjory's such a snob," Timmy couldn't resist.

"Don't be unkind Timmy," his sister chided him, gently. "Then there was that chap you saw. You said he looked weird."

"Distinctly weird. He had a ponytail. A dark ponytail."

"And a tattoo, you said."

"That's right Sally, a tattoo on his forearm. He stopped me, to ask directions, and he was leaning his arm on the open car window.

"A tattoo?" Ross seemed interested.

"It was a boat … And there was writing, a name perhaps. It looked like the Sea Witch."

Ross's jaw dropped slightly, but, if he was going to say something, he was interrupted by his mobile vibrating.

"Ah," he said reading a message. "It's from my daughter. She's just out of her piano exam," he explained to our hosts. "It went well."

"Marvellous," Timmy congratulated him. "Do you have other children?"

"I have two daughters and two sons."

"How wonderful," Sally clapped, "but a handful. Does your wife work?"

I cringed, but was stunned by his next words. "I'm divorced. The children said they wanted to stay with me."

Poitu told me he'd been widowed.

"Which reminds me," he said, as if to change the subject as quickly as he could. "I believe the Pattersons are getting divorced."

"So we're hearing," Timmy replied.

"Well, if you hear anything more, let us know," I said.

"And maybe keep a tab on who's coming and going," Ross added.

"Like private detectives?" Sally suggested.

"Eyes and ears," Timmy said, touching first his ears and then his eyes.

After a few more polite exchanges we left.

I waited until we were pulling out of the village to speak.

"I didn't realise you were divorced."

"Yes," his voice was deadpan. "My wife left me three years ago."

I moved up a gear thinking what I wouldn't say and do to Poitu when we next met, for supplying me with yet another piece of dud information.

That pleasure came sooner than I expected ...

Chapter Twenty-four

Midnight Sunday, October 28, Southwark

It was midnight, when the buzzer went. I was in bed, but not asleep, listening to the midnight news. I ignored it. It went again and then a third time, loud and intrusive, so I hauled myself to the front door.

"Who is it?"

"It's me," I recognised the voice immediately.

"Poitu. What on earth are you doing here at this hour?"

"I got a message, saying you wanted to see me urgently."

"Tomorrow. Tomorrow would have done. I thought you were away."

"I was. But I flew back specially when I heard you wanted me."

His speech was slurred. He was drunk.

"What do you want?"

"What do I want? Where shall I begin? A rich widow to die and leave me all her money. A vineyard in France. A passionate lover. But the question is, what do you want?"

My heart sank. A drunken cop on my doorstep on a Sunday night was all I needed.

"You'd better come in, before you wake the neighbourhood." I released the lock and opened my door for him to enter.

"You're drunk." I greeted him.

"You are right, Lightweight. But tomorrow I will be sober. Whereas tomorrow you will still be …"

"Just don't!" I cut him dead. "What do you want, apart from some strong coffee?"

"It's what you want isn't it? I thought you wanted to talk."

"Sit down," I pushed him towards the settee and went into the kitchen, hoping he would be asleep by the time I returned. No such luck. He was staggering around the room, inspecting my DVD collection, having already put a CD of Tina Turner's 'Steamy Windows' on to play.

"This is madness," I handed him a cup.

He slumped on the settee and slurped a few sips.

"What's so urgent?" he asked.

"Look, it's late."

"I'm busy tomorrow. I'm in court. If you want to talk urgently, it's now."

Where to begin. The child, my suspicion that I was being followed, the misinformation about Ross's marriage, the old Hannigan chestnut, the police report into paedophilia accusations, the forensic report, the body in the Clyde …

Instead I began, "Have you seen Jack Kelly yet?"

"No, nor will I. All I'm interested in is Strathclyde police. I've told you a dozen times, I'm not interested in your dead money."

I stared at him.

"You don't believe me, do you?" He rubbed it in.

"I thought we had a deal."

"We do have a deal."

"Then, why didn't you tell me about the missing child?"

"What missing child?"

"You know perfectly well which child?"

He scratched his head, as if thinking for a moment.

"Do you mean your Mr Strachan's very special friend?"

I started counting slowly to stop me hitting him.

"Do I have to tell you about every investigation taking place in Britain?"

"Yes, if it has anything to do with this case. That was the deal."

"And what would you've said, if I'd told you your precious Mr Strachan was screwing a child?"

I let it go. He was drunk. "Did you find the report? The one I asked for?"

"All good things come to those who wait." He tried to tap the side of his nose three times, missing with each attempt.

"What about the forensic report of the Strachan deaths."

"Now that is interesting, seems to have vanished, just like your little girlie."

I was digesting this information, when he lurched nearer to me, an annoying smile spread across his stupid face.

"I think you fancy me … go on, say it, those three liddel words."

"Jesus, it's half-past midnight, and I'm having to listen to this."

"Go on … just those three little words."

"OK then. Here's three little words for you. I'm being followed."

"Strictly speaking that's four," he fell back on the cushions again.

"So?"

"So what?

"So, don't you want to know by whom?"

"Do you want to tell me?"

"I don't know."

"Well, there we are then. It's probably all in your imagination. Have you thought about seeing a shrink?"

"Is it your lot?"

He laughed, like he was enjoying himself.

"You flatter yourself, you really do."

"What about Alexander Ross?"

"Ahh,"

"And that sob story about his wife."

"Right … well … yeah … I guess, Thornhorn, I'll have to cough to that one."

"Why did you lie to me?"

"It was for your own good. Call me a softie, but I'm just an old romantic at heart. I wanted you to like him. You two were never gonna hit it off … both totally …" He seemed to be searching for a word and then grimaced, like he had found it, but then thought better than to utter.

"We needed him, or your investigation, and possibly mine, was going nowhere. I wanted to oil things along …"

"You're deranged."

"Quite possibly. They tell me I am crazy between the sheets."

This was too much. I got to my feet, and pointed to the door.

"Get out. Get out of my flat."

He got the message, stood, albeit unsteadily, and walked towards the door. I watched as he closed it behind him, but before I could sigh with relief, the door opened again and his stupid, grinning face thrust back in the room.

"Did anyone ever tell you, you're beautiful when you're angry?"

This was more than I could take. I picked up the nearest thing to hand, which was his half-emptied coffee cup, and threw it at him. He ducked. I missed.

"Temper ... temper," he tutted. I reached for something else to throw, but this time the door slammed shut.

I was standing, shaking with fury, when my mobile phone rang. I picked it up ready to give Poitu another piece of my mind. But it wasn't Poitu. It was a man with a foreign accent.

"You looking for Ukrainian girl, Roxy."

I said nothing.

"I help, for money."

I'd never paid for a story and had no intention of beginning now.

"Also, I has picture. You pay me money, I give to you. I call again."

"Who are you? Where did you get my number?" but the phone clicked dead.

Chapter Twenty-five

7.30am Monday, October 29, Southwark

I woke with a blazing headache. It was one of those stifling winter days, when the sun streams blindingly through the window, even though the temperature outside is freezing. I couldn't face rushing in first thing, but spent the morning going over the previous night's interview with Poitu. This whole investigation was in danger of disintegrating into farce.

The call troubled me, though. If Sister Robert had put the word around, it might have been a hoax or someone after easy money. But it could have been genuine, which at least meant the child was alive. I'd have to wait until they called again.

Foolishly, I didn't bother to check my emails before leaving for the office, so more surprises were waiting for me there. Ragland's office said he wanted to see me at lunchtime. It was too late. I had missed that appointment. Damn, my leisurely morning, and damn Poitu.

But there was some good news; an email from Kelly's Brewery inviting me to interview Jack Kelly on Wednesday. Excellent. I dialled his secretary and fixed a time after lunch.

I called Ragland's office. No, it would not be possible to reschedule this afternoon. No, his private secretary did not know what the right honourable member had wished to discuss with me. He had been called to his constituency on urgent business. No, we do not know his next availability.

Ludgate called. He was delighted to hear I would be seeing Kelly before the week was out, but wanted to know where I was getting with the body they had fished out of the Clyde.

"Not very far."

"Have you tried Sherlock?"

"Can't seem to get through."

"If they've stopped answering the phones, get on to the FSA."

"Will do."

"And Strathclyde?"

"They're not saying any more than you'll see on the wires." One thing Poitu and I had in common was a deep-rooted distrust of that force.

"Keep trying. In fact, go up to Glasgow tonight and door-step the family."

I hung up determined to ignore that last instruction. There would be plenty of time to see the family, in the unlikely event they wanted to see me. I didn't have to rush up tonight.

But I did spend a couple of hours dialling every number I could find for Sherlock. The best I got was an automatic recording asking me to leave a message. Most of the numbers simply rang out.

So I called the Financial Services Authority and told them I couldn't get through.

"There have been developments," my press contact informed me. "At this precise moment we can't comment. We'll be making a statement in due course."

Interesting.

I was booking my flights for Thursday, when Marsha poked her head round the door.

"You look all in," she said.

"No, no, I'm OK. It's just …"

"Getting nowhere fast," she nodded understandingly. "Why don't we get out of here? It's a lovely evening. Let's go for a drink by the river?"

We caught the bus to St Katherine's Dock, and sat outside the Dickens Inn. It was a beautiful evening. The air was chill, but the sun was strong, as it had been that morning; winter strong, not strong like in summer, but strong enough to sit outside.

Yachts bobbed about in front of us on their moorings, their riggings tinkling, as if calling to adventure. This place never failed to bewitch me, and with good reason. My ancestors were born and bred in St Katherine's Dock in the 19th century, when it was home to poor dockers' families. This was my heritage.

Marsha and I sat in comfortable silence, watching the boats and sipping our drinks. We were neither of us in a hurry. A group of students arrived. Some of them wore the sweat shirts and T-shirts of University College London. We watched, as they clowned around on the Quay, not a care in the world. One of them, a young buck, decided he wanted a swim and began peeling off his clothes.

"He's nuts, it'll be freezin'," Marsha whispered. "Should we say something?"

"Leave them, they'll be fine. A cold dip won't hurt him."

A loud splash was followed by another, and another, as his pals followed him into the water. They climbed out up the wooden ladder fixed into the harbour wall, and no sooner than were they on dry land than they ran again leaping straight back into the marina.

Over and over again, they jumped off the wharf edge. Screams of excitement, bravado, and blind terror filled the air. Each time, they took a longer run at the water, so they could jump even higher, until they had fallen back to our table to launch their take-offs.

"You must be mad," Marsha said to one of the females, whose soaking clothes clung to her. She trembled with cold. "You'll catch pneumonia."

She laughed at us.

"It's fabulous. The water's lovely and warm. You should give it a go," and she was off, running at top speed, before vaulting high into the air, shrieking, all the while, with joy and fear. She hit the water with an almighty explosion.

I don't know what crazy demon took possession of me, but I stood, took off my jacket, pulled Marsha's off, and grabbed her by the hand.

"Come on," I said, "Come on."

Not stopping to think, we ran, a dark unsteady "Yeeeeeeooooooo" sounding from somewhere deep inside. And together, hand in hand, we jumped off the quay. The student was right. The eternity between leaving the harbour and hitting the water was like heaven. But she was wrong about the water. It was ice. I went down, down, down, before natural buoyancy brought me back up to the surface.

I couldn't see Marsha, and called her frantically. Seconds later, she too emerged, emitting a string of profanities.

"Get me out of here before I die," she screamed.

We swam towards the steps and climbed out. The crowd of youngsters cheered and clapped us, as we emerged. One came towards us with towels, which allowed us to dry a bit.

"We'd better get home sharpish, before we catch our death," Marsha said, heading back to the table to pick up our bags and jackets. I checked Strachan's diary was safe. It was. We flagged three taxis, before one would agree to take us to Marsha's flat in Bethnal Green. We soon warmed up on the journey back. Marsha went into the bathroom first, after handing me towels and a dressing gown, and setting the tumble drier going for my underwear.

Ten minutes later, she vacated the bathroom for me, with the words, "I'll sort out something for you to wear, doll."

I tried not to worry what that would be, as I closed the door behind her. I couldn't see myself in one of her little leather numbers.

The bath was heavenly, and, as I lay there soaking up its warmth, I felt happier and freer than for ages. Jumping off that quay had been a moment of sheer madness, but madness can be so liberating.

Marsha was soon knocking at the bathroom door.

"Blue jeans or black cords?"

"I'll take the cords." The door squeezed opened a crack, and a hand appeared, placing cords, polo and my dry undies on a stool.

"There you go," she said, her hand disappearing again.

As I reached for the towel, I heard her phone ring.

"Right ... right ... right," I heard Marsha's voice. "Thanks. You're a diamond."

I emerged from the bathroom, as she dialled another number. The phone was answered at the other end.

"It's Marsha Rosenblum. I've had a tip off. Children being held in St John's flats ... that's right... fourth floor ... number 48."

She paused.

"Right now. Sure."

She replaced the receiver.

"One of my contacts at the Met. They're going straight in. Want me to be there. For the kids. I've got to go."

"Can I come with you?"

She looked at me without saying anything, and left the flat. I grabbed one of her coats, locked the door, and jumped down her steps two at a time. We were running together again, but this time, I didn't have a clue where we were going, or why. Nothing could have prepared me for what was in store.

Chapter Twenty-six

10.30pm Monday, October 29, Bethnal Green

Marsha led the way past boarded up shops, and down a twisted alley. I was struggling to keep up with her, my pulse racing. Music throbbed, in the distance at first, and then grew louder. The alley opened out into a street party in a dingy square. It was like stepping out downtown on a sub-Saharan Saturday night.

Rap music boomed from three houses. Two open-topped cars, packed with black and white youths, revved their engines then braked, then revved again, as they attempted to navigate a race between the crowds of people just hanging around. Music blared from their cars too, and each time they revved, they screamed out gang chants like war cries. One of the drivers had a gun, and fired shots intermittently into the sky. It didn't take much imagination to see that the girls were hookers and the men pimps and clients.

"Just look down," Marsha said, as she took my hand firmly and led the way across the square to another alley opposite. She knew this place, and knew exactly where we were going. We crossed unchallenged, apart from a few catcalls in our direction. But relief at escaping the square was short-lived. We had reached Blow Job Alley. I had heard of it, but as an urban myth, an allegory of our time.

"Look the other way," Marsha whispered as we passed through the shadows. But I couldn't. And it wasn't a myth. This was for real.

The bottom of the alley opened onto lock-ups in front of a run-down 1970s council block.

The police had beaten us there. Half-a-dozen police cars and two vans were parked outside. A team of police had begun to lay a cordon. Marsha flashed a pass, and we made it through in time, before the area was sealed.

Police sieges were nothing new to me. As a young reporter I had covered the police beat for one of my employers and spent many a cold night outside hostage situations, a few of which had ended in bloodshed.

The stairs stank of urine. We raced up them, to the fourth floor, and ran along a balcony in time to see police batter down the front door.

We were not allowed to follow, but had to wait and guess what was going on inside, amid the noise of screams, bangs and general pandemonium that had broken out. Discoloured paint was peeling off the front window. It was hung with a twisted, filthy net.

"Out," one of the coppers shouted.

Three hooded figures were led away, hands cuffed behind their backs. They struggled and kicked against their escort. But they knew the game was up. We waited patiently outside. A WPC joined us. Then another woman. Marsha seemed to know them both. Social Services, I guessed.

After a bit, one of the officers came out and told the three women they could enter, but to be prepared. His face was grim.

The passage was dirty, lined with cracked and grime-engrained lino. Another officer barred the door to the first room we came to, but through the opening, I could see about a dozen sheepish looking men, being questioned by other uniforms. They would have some explaining to do to their wives, girlfriends and bosses, when the story made the local rag.

Nothing could have prepared me for the rooms, which followed. Children. I'm not good with ages any more, but they were maybe eight to 14. All girls. Painfully thin. In the dingy light, their skin looked pale as death and their eyes were frightened.

I watched Marsha, the WPC, and the other woman, work the room. Each sat beside one child on stained mattresses. Not too close. They talked in a low voice. I walked back to the passage and on to another room, filled with more children, and another filled with more still.

I wanted to reach out to the poor mites. But I wasn't trained. I went back to Marsha to seek instructions. She was inspecting weal marks on one child's back.

"Ambulances on the way," a PC stuck his head round the door, flinching at what he saw. The NHS would patch up their violated bodies. Who would repair their minds?

I went back into the other room and sat beside one of the children. I tried speaking to her, but she didn't understand. She had Slavic features, but I couldn't say where she came from. Another looked African. Each had hair pulled back tight into a ponytail. Their lips were plastered a grotesque red. They wore halter-neck tops, and skirts the size of handkerchiefs. I noticed blood oozing down the inside of one of the girls' legs.

Marsha joined me now, and as I smiled at her in mutual sadness, I heard a new voice in the background. A voice I knew.

The next minute Poitu appeared in the door way.

"What the hell ..." he looked shocked to see me and turned back to the officers in the passage.

"What cretin let the press in," his voice filled with anger.

A young PC rushed forward, making excuses, clearly cowed by the superior officer.

"She came with ..." he pointed at Marsha.

"Get her out, and get her out now," he yelled.

Two officers grabbed me by the arms and frog-marched me out of the flat.

Chapter Twenty-seven

1.30am Tuesday, October 30, Southwark

A police car took me home. When I closed the door, I realised I was shaking. I got into a bath and scrubbed and scrubbed, trying to rub away those young faces. But they haunted me throughout the night.

"The girls stop coming once they hit a certain age." Sister Robert's words came back to me.

Was this the fate of the missing child, Roxy, always supposing she was still alive? Was this what Sister Robert was hinting at?

At 4.30am, I switched on the bedside light and took Strachan's diary out of my bag. The entry of September 28, the last time I had seen him, had always bothered me:

'Couldn't tell her the half, of course. In good time. Then we'll crack both birds with one stone.'

What half, what birds, what did it mean? I switched off the light and slipped into a shallow, fitful sleep. I dreamed of that flat again; of Mrs Strachan at the funeral; the look of disbelief on Alexander Ross's face as he surveyed the scene at Patterson's.

I rang Ludgate from the office and mentioned the previous night's incident, but it wasn't a story to interest the readers of the Square Mile. Anyway, charges had already been laid, which outlawed further coverage as sub judice.

I slept better the following night and was more refreshed when I headed off to the airport next morning. My nerves, though, were on edge at the thought of the coming meeting. This was my big chance and I couldn't afford to screw it up. I had spent the previous day planning the interview. What did I want from him? Confirmation of the withdrawals, and some idea where the money went, would be a good start. Who was I kidding? Kelly was a class act. Only rookie hacks were arrogant enough to think you could catch such people out with killer questions. What did I expect him to say? 'Yes, I stole the money. Yes, I killed Ken Strachan and his family.'

I tried to read my notes during the flight, and rehearse the questions again, but I was distracted by a little girl sitting beside me. She must have been about nine or ten and seemed to need to chat incessantly. I welcomed the diversion. She had been staying with her Daddy, who lived in London and was flying back up to her Mummy. She clutched a simple rag doll, called Amy. By the time the flight landed, I knew everything there was to know about her brother and sister, aunts, uncles, both sets of grandparents, and pretty much every girl in her class.

I offered to take her to find her mummy, but airline security was tight, and the stewardess said 'no'. So I said goodbye aboard the plane and headed for a taxi, instructing it to take me to Kelly's offices. The brewery had depots scattered around the UK, but its head office was sited some 100 yards from the main operation, roughly half an hour's drive from central Glasgow.

As the taxi pulled up at the main gate, we were overtaken by a white, windowless van, which was waved straight through security. While we waited for a green light to proceed, I watched the van pull up across the forecourt and disgorge maybe 20 worn-looking faces. It didn't take Sherlock Holmes to work out that these were foreign hands, working for rock bottom rates.

We drove on to the main building, and the driver paused outside to let me out. They were unlike any offices I had ever seen before, let alone on a Glasgow factory site. Built in solid concrete, they were a cement-maker's fantasy of arches, columns and vaulted windows; an exercise in ego. Why did this not surprise me? The smell of the brewery hit full force, as I climbed out of the taxi and paid the driver; a sickly putrid smell.

The entrance hall was like a cathedral, white marble everywhere. The receptionist offered to take my red coat and overnight bag, but I said I would keep them with me.

"I'll let them know you're here," she pointed to a seated area.

I didn't sit, but studied the many pictures, certificates, and trophies decorating the walls. I didn't bother to count how many times Kelly had won Brewer of the Year, other than noting the last time was a few months before the company went bust.

Some of the pictures dated back to early last century; charming sepia shots of horses and carts pulling barrels of beer.

There were several family groupings. One, particularly, caught my eye. Positioned prominently, as if in pride of place, was a shot of Joseph Kennedy, father of Jack Kennedy, the US president, who was assassinated. Founder of one of America's most famous dynasties, Joseph was a prohibition bootlegger; a taint of corruption never far from his name.

"This picture?" I asked the receptionist.

"The Kennedys, with Mr Jack's mother and father, Mary and Robert."

"Fascinating."

"Yes, they're rather special." Her phone rang. She picked it up.

Photographs of Jack Kelly dominated the collection. There were various gatherings of staff, awards ceremonies, retirement do's. And my, my, look who was guest speaker at this one? None other than David Ragland. Ronnie Raeburn was centre stage in another photograph with a group of brewery workers. All very cosy.

A buzzer sounded. "They're ready for you." The receptionist beckoned me to follow her. A lump hardened in my throat, as I climbed the stairs; my heart thumping.

"Stay calm," I whispered to myself.

Jack Kelly stood to greet me. He was everything I expected … big built, larger than life. He was handsome, too. If my newspaper story had wounded him, he didn't show it. His iron grey hair looked the sort that wouldn't budge in a gale. His smile was fixed and wide, but it didn't fool me. This man would eat me for breakfast given half the chance.

"It's little red riding hood, on an errand of mercy," he said.

"I'm glad you like my coat," I quipped, refusing to be patronised.

"Colour of highland tartan, isn't it? Battle tartan, they call it."

"Colour of blood, don't you mean …" he sniped back. "We don't take sides, never have. Politics and business," he shook his head, "Bitter cocktail. Sit down." He pointed to the chair opposite his desk.

I sat, taking in the room. It was masculine, Teutonic and above all black. Whereas the entrance had been startlingly white, this room, though well enough lit, was suffocatingly dark. Black units and cupboards lined the walls. They were shiny. Surely they couldn't be marble too. He sat at a black desk almost the size of a billiard table, raised on a platform, like an altar.

"You wanted to see me?" he began again.

"I have some questions about your company and the pension fund."

"Ah, your little …" he hesitated, choosing the next word carefully, "obsession."

"It's not an obsession, Mr Kelly. A number of people have legitimate questions."

"Red, I'm a brewer and distiller, not a pension's expert. I make beer and whisky. I used to be good at it. I know nothing about pensions. I leave that to my advisers."

"And they say?"

"They tell me your recent article was well-informed, if mistaken."

"Mistaken?"

"My lawyers are considering what action we'll be taking next."

His words didn't frighten me. He was in no position to begin a libel action. Kane could afford to sue, Kelly couldn't. There was a knock on the door. A dark-skinned woman arrived with a tray of tea and biscuits.

"Shall I be grand-mamma," he asked, as she closed the door behind her. "Or does Riding Hood want to pour?"

He was deliberately taunting me, but I refused to be baited, so he began pouring. I resumed my questioning.

"Remind me, Kelly's went into liquidation about six months ago."

"March fourth," he volunteered.

"What happened?"

140

"This Government is what happened. You know what happened. Our costs rose with every bit of new legislation. We couldn't go on."

"And sales were falling."

"Sales were OK," he contradicted me.

"The pension fund?"

"It was crippling us."

"Did you authorise those withdrawals?"

"What if I did? It was my money."

"Hardly fair. It was your employees' pensions."

He smiled that flashing smile, with teeth lined up like white nail files.

"I told you, I left all that to my advisers. When they said I could take money out, I took money out."

"So you did make those withdrawals?"

"I'm not saying that, I'm not saying any withdrawals were ever made. If you think they were, publish the evidence. You haven't published any so far. All I'm saying is, if any money came out, I was legitimately entitled to take it. It was my money."

"How can it have been? Your workforce had been paying into a pension, in some cases for forty years. They lost all their savings. What happened to that money?"

"I don't know anything about that."

"You're a trustee, you're responsible."

"I'm a brewer. That's what I do. When it comes to pensions I follow advice. What's the point of paying for it otherwise? You don't keep a dog and bark yourself."

"Don't you feel any responsibility?"

"Do I look like a charity?" he grinned, that sinister grin again. "My priority was saving the brewery."

"Enough to raid the pension scheme."

"Any money that came out, came out legally. It was all signed off by our legal and actuarial advisers."

"I think that may be a moot point."

"Do I look like an idiot? Why would I take money that didn't belong to me, when it would be clearly documented, and could put me in jail?"

I could have replied, 'by paying crooked advisers'.

"These people have rights, there are laws." I said instead

"Get real Red. Grow up. The rights are all mine. I pay the bills."

I changed tack. He was never going to admit pocketing those withdrawals. "How well did you know Ken Strachan?"

"Strachan was a pain of a man."

"What did you make of his death?"

"He always struck me as a few pints short of a barrel … Don't get me wrong it was a tragedy … tragedy for the family."

The phone rang. I sensed the interview was over.

"I have to go," he said, when he replaced the receiver. "Look Red, let's be friends. I'm hosting a dinner tonight at Loch Lomond. Few local dignitaries and businessmen. Join us. I'd be honoured. It'll help you find out a bit more about our business and the people we deal with."

"I've nothing to wear," I was suspicious of his olive branch.

"Come as you are," his ran his eye over me. "You look …" he hesitated, "… ravishing."

"Oh don't you worry. I can ravish alright," I responded dryly. I decided to accept his invitation, though. It was too tempting an opportunity to pass up.

"Good. Where are you staying?"

"The Clanachan."

"We'll send a car at 7pm."

I nodded again.

"And Red …" he called after me, as I opened the door. "Remember your fairy stories. Wolves do bite."

Chapter Twenty-eight

3.30pm Wednesday, October 31, Glasgow

The receptionist had arranged a car for me, and I didn't argue. The driver spoke English, but with a strong accent. He said he was from Romania and his name was Piotr. "It's the same as Peter." He had been in Scotland for 18 months, liked the work, the weather, the food and the whisky. Yes, he missed his native Bucharest. He would go back one day, maybe.

As we approached George Square, gaudy Christmas decorations sparkled in the darkness. Barely November, and already the countdown to the holiday had begun.

"Good to see you again," the receptionist at the Clanachan greeted me. "Not another funeral, I hope?"

"No, thank heavens. Not yet anyway."

She smiled. "We're pretty full. Does it matter, bath or shower?"

I shook my head and reached for my credit cards. The lift was broken as usual, so I walked the three flights. A familiar musty smell hit me as I entered the room; that faintly fusty odour, which seeps out of old curtains and carpets. But it was spotlessly clean, cheap, and central. What it lacked in luxury, the staff made up for in warmth.

I hung up my coat, switched on the kettle and dialled Poitu's number. We hadn't spoken since he had me kicked out of the Bethnal Green flat. I needed him to get me in to see Mrs Livingstone.

"It's Foghorn," he greeted me. He was still mad. "Contaminated any good scenes of crime today?"

"The other night … I only wanted to help."

"How? What could you do to help?"

He was right. There had been nothing for me to do that night.

"I'm in Glasgow."

"Thank heaven for small mercies. Remind me to cancel my next flight up."

"Don't be so mean. What about our deal?"

143

"It's pretty much one-way from where I'm sitting."

"I want to talk to Livingstone's wife."

"You, and a million other hacks."

"She's not talking?"

"What do you think?"

"Can you fix it for me?"

"And what do I get in return?"

"Don't be so annoying. Can you fix it?"

"I could fix it, probably."

"Then will you?"

There was silence at the other end of the line. I knew he was playing with me, teasing.

"Please."

"That's better. We'll teach you some manners, yet."

"Is there any news on the body?"

"There may be soon, actually," he said seriously. "I think they're getting close to an identification."

"So Mrs Livingstone? Can you fix it?"

"I don't know if I can be …" His other phone went. He answered it, leaving me waiting.

"Look, I'll see what I can do," he said, when he finally came back.

I made some coffee, drank it quickly, and then went out to shop. A House of Fraser department store was a few doors up. I picked out a classic black velvet skirt and ivory white blouse. If I was dining out with local dignitaries and bigwigs, I would at least look the part. I wasn't long back at the hotel when my mobile rang. It was Poitu.

"She'll see you at 10am tomorrow morning, Mrs Livingstone. Got the address?"

"It's Cardonald, isn't it?"

"Just off Paisley Road West."

"Her name?"

"Heather."

"You're an angel," I could have bitten my tongue out, as soon as the words left my lips.

"I knew you'd see it one day."

I ignored him.

"Guess where I'm going tonight?"

"As long as I won't be there, I don't care."

"I saw Jack Kelly this afternoon. He's invited me to dinner tonight."

"Very cosy."

"It's a function he's hosting."

"Ah … well, let me know how you get on."

"I will … About the other night." I was curious to know whether any charges had been brought.

"Stick to playing with numbers, Lightweight. It's not a nice world outside."

He could be so patronising.

A car arrived at 7pm to take me to Lomond Castle. Once the lights of Glasgow receded, the night was pitch-black. I could see nothing from the car, so I dozed lightly in the back. I opened my eyes again, as rows of blazing torches, burning magnificently, came into view. The taxi joined a procession of limousines gliding down the flaming drive, towards a spectacular towered and turreted castle. The driver let me out at the main entrance.

To my surprise, someone was waiting to greet me.

"Julia," he put out a friendly hand. "I'm Tom Kelly. The one that doesn't gobble up little girls in red," he smiled warmly. "My father told me about your meeting. Don't pay too much attention, his bark's worse than his bite."

I doubted that. Tom, though, seemed different. He was as unorthodox as his father was conventional. He wore a dark dinner suit with trousers, unlike the rest of the guests who sported kilts of various tartan. His thick, jet-black hair was pulled back into a ponytail. He had his father's wide mouth, but his lips were red and generous. Perhaps this was Jack Kelly as a younger man.

"A quick drink at the bar, then I'll take you in to dinner," he said.

The bar was a kaleidoscope of faces. Tom never left my side, but introduced me to a couple of guests. Everyone was connected with the drinks industry.

"Wonderful to see Kelly's back in business," one bucolic-looking veteran said, shaking Tom's hand warmly.

"Can't keep a good man down," Tom quipped.

"I knew it wouldn't be long before the barrels began rolling again."

My teeth bit on my glass so hard, I thought it might shatter. Another overweight, ruddy-faced, body joined us. Tom introduced us.

"This is Julia Lighthorn. She's a journalist. She's convinced my father is Al Capone. Julia, Jonathan Hume, from Hume Whisky and Richard Munro from Munro Brewery." He pointed to the two men.

"Is she the one persecuting your poor father?" Hume was a blatant media-hater.

"I've been asking legitimate questions about what happened to the pension fund, that's all."

"I blame the media," Munro joined in. "It's all their fault."

"I've told my advisers," Hume continued. "If I'm forced to pay any more into the pension fund, I will shut the company down. Go to hell with their jobs. I've had enough of this."

"If only I had a pound, for every time I'm told it's all the media's fault," I muttered to Tom, as the master of ceremonies called us in to dinner.

The banqueting hall, packed with tables, was also lit with blazing torches. Tom seemed to know where we were sitting, and led the way through the crowd.

There was a long top table for the guests of honour. We joined a round table close by. My heart sank when Hume and Munro joined us at our table.

The banging of a gavel announced the proceedings were about to begin, and we stood to welcome the top table, which was piped in to 'Scotland the Brave'. I nearly fell back in my seat, when Jack Kelly took his place at the centre, with none other than David Ragland at his side.

No expense was spared on the meal or its setting. We began with

146

Scottish poached salmon, and moved onto venison. The wine was a good quality Bordeaux, but only a token amount was drunk before the men moved back to their beloved whisky.

"How well does your father know David Ragland?" I asked Tom.

"He's our local member of parliament … an important contact."

"And where do you fit in?"

"Fit in?"

"In the business."

"Oh, here and there, you know."

"Go on …"

"It's dad's business."

"But will be yours one day?"

"I have my own business interests."

"How fascinating. Tell me about them."

So he did. He had not initially wanted anything at all to do with the brewery, and went to Glasgow Art School. Afterwards, he put money into various business enterprises, which he hoped would produce a sufficient income to maintain his independence from the family and allow him to pursue his interest in art.

"So art's your great love?" I asked.

"Art and sailing. I've a boat on the coast. And my nightclub, of course."

"Nightclub?"

"I've several clubs actually. But the big one, on Sauchiehall Street, is my baby … the flagship. More of an entertainment centre. We stage all kinds of acts and events."

"Like an arena?"

"I guess."

"And is it successful?"

"It ticks over. You must come one evening."

"Yes, I'd like that." I was surprised to find I meant it. After dinner there were some short speeches, all in fulsome praise of the achievements of the Kelly family. This was followed by some Scottish music, a final reading of some Robbie Burns and then it was time to go.

Tom accompanied me once more to the sumptuous drive at the front of the castle, where cars were waiting. I was about to get into one, when I heard David Ragland's voice. I stepped back to let another guest leave before me.

"Mr Ragland," I approached him as he came out. "It's Julia Lighthorn. You were trying to get hold of me."

"Ms Lighthorn. What a surprise, and, may I say, a pleasure to see you."

"Your office called to say you wanted to see me …"

"Did they really? Now there's a mystery … I've no idea what they had in mind … No … complete mystery," and with those words he stepped into the next available car.

Chapter Twenty-nine

10am Thursday, November 1, Cardonald

The press pack was already in position outside the Livingstone home in Cardonald, when I pushed my way towards the front gate. Two policemen stood as sentries, but they let me pass when I mentioned my name. A police woman opened the front door, and waved me through to the lounge. Again she seemed to be expecting me.

It was the sort of room I found hard to breathe in. Net curtains hung at a bow window; carpet orange nylon; furniture teak.

The woman sitting on the sofa was unusually thin for Glasgow, where fashion was to the large. She looked drained.

"Mrs Livingstone." I walked towards her, with hand outstretched. "I'm Julia Lighthorn. Thank you for giving me a few moments at this difficult time." She looked up at me without responding. She seemed disconnected from the scene around her. I let my hand fall and sat in an armchair by her side.

"I'll make a brew," the WPC said, disappearing into the kitchen.

"Mrs Livingstone, I know this is a very difficult time for you," I repeated. "But publicity may help to get to the bottom of what has happened. We all want to help you find out what happened to your husband."

She looked at me again, but said nothing. It was as if she were somewhere else entirely. All this was going on around her, but she had no part in it.

"Tell me about your husband," I tried again, gently. "When did you meet?" It always paid to start a good distance from the current traumatic event, at a happier time.

She began to open up, gradually. "We were both working in an office in George St. We were married within a year. That was 25 years ago."

"Your husband wasn't working for Sherlock then?"

"No, he only joined them three years ago. I told him he was making a mistake. Been with his old firm more than two decades. But he said we needed more money. They offered him a small fortune to move."

"Was he happy?"

"He never discussed work."

"Was he happy at home?"

"He was never here. Work, work, work. That was all he did. Except when we were on holidays. Then he'd go back to being the old Donald, his old self."

"What happened the night he disappeared?"

"Two men came to the door. He said they were policemen and he had to go with them."

"And he went,"

"Of course, it seemed strange." She shook her head, as if in disbelief. "We thought it some mistake. We're respectable law-abiding people. But Donald said he'd go down to the station with them and sort it out. He said he wouldn't be long."

"And that was the last time you saw him?"

She nodded.

"What do Sherlock's say?"

"At first they were very good. Said they would do everything to help me and the police."

"And then?"

"It's all gone very quiet. Can't find anyone to speak to. Like they've all gone into hiding."

"And you've got no idea what all this could be about?"

"None at all. I knew it was strange, that they couldn't be policemen. One of them had a gold earring."

"A gold earring?"

"Yes. It was round with a cross hanging below. I thought at the time, policemen don't wear earrings."

The WPC came in with tea on a tray. I stayed a while longer. We talked about the children.

"Thank you for coming," Mrs Livingstone said, as I rose to leave.

Her frail courtesy took the wind out of my lungs. My heart went out to the poor woman. She was decent and kind. But I sensed, before the day was out, her peace would be shattered forever.

Chapter Thirty

1pm Thursday, November 1, Glasgow

I filed the interview from the airport, and headed home. The phone rang at 9pm. It was Poitu.

"Strathclyde believe the body is Livingstone. DNA results have come in. Positive ID tomorrow."

"What took them so long?" I said, but he was gone.

I didn't waste time trying to get confirmation. He was a prime police source. That was good enough. I called Ludgate, and agreed to file a news story within the next 20 minutes.

As I logged on to my computer, an email came in from the FSA. Sherlock had gone into wind-up. The company was liquidating.

I called Ludgate back. "Wrap it all up," he said.

So I did, and the paper splashed with the story of the identification of actuary Donald Livingstone, as the body pulled out of the Clyde, and the collapse of his company, Sherlock. Inside, we had the first exclusive interview with the widow.

Strathclyde police called before I was out of bed. "Who gave you a positive identification?" an angry copper snarled down the line. I implied it had been a lucky guess. He was far from satisfied, but the division confirmed the story with a general release an hour later.

A congratulatory email was in my inbox when I arrived at the office. Ludgate sounded like the cat that got the cream. We had annihilated the opposition.

He called later that morning. "I've got a tedious banking dinner at the Mansion House, tonight, 7.30pm, black tie. Someone here's dropped out. Would you like to come with me?"

"Sure." It was never smart to say "No" to the boss.

"You'll need an invite. I'll see you outside."

The next email to land was from Alexander Ross informing me he would be in London on Monday, and suggesting we meet up:

"… *always supposing the flight is on time. I've got meetings all*

morning and am seeing someone for lunch. Shall I see you afterwards
in our offices? You know where they are? About 3pm. Go to reception
and ask for me."

I was dying to talk to him about the latest Livingstone and Sherlock developments and replied by return, saying I'd be there, and asking him if he'd seen that morning's Square Mile.

He replied noncommittally, saying he was looking forward to seeing me again. I was sure he had read my copy.

Andrew was waiting for me outside the Mansion House, looking glamorous in his penguin suit. I wore one too, of sorts. I'd never had the figure for slinky, off the shoulder evening dresses, and felt more comfortable beside the men in a white tuxedo, embossed red waistcoat and black silk three-quarter-length trousers. He waved our invites at me, but held on to them.

We had a quick drink at the bar before heading into dinner. Just enough time to swap greetings with the bankers we knew by sight. Andrew knew more than me, but I had plenty of contacts too. The bar was so squashed and noisy, it was impossible to do more than say hello.

It was soon time, anyway, to head towards the dining room. Andrew checked the seating plan for the table. We were 34. He showed both tickets at the door.

We made our way through the crowded, buzzing banqueting hall, stopping briefly, again, to say hello to acquaintances. We were both chatting to one such, when I spotted table 34. My heart stopped dead. Besides a metal spike displaying the number, was another with the name of the table host. 'KNS' was printed in big red letters.

I grabbed Ludgate on the arm, but he continued chatting to his contact. When he finished, he turned to me and raised his eyebrows.

"It's Kane's table, we're sitting on Kane's table."

"I know, don't worry, he won't be there."

"I can't. The case …"

"You have to break the ice sometime, Julia. You can't run away forever. We all get complaints and legal problems. Don't take it so personally. It's part of the job."

"I'm not running away, it's just …"

"Look … they're a big bank. Like it or not, we have to work with them."

"I can't. It's so embarrassing."

"Yes, you can." He got behind me and gave me a hard shove in the direction of the table.

"My lawyer will have a fit."

"Whenever did you worry about giving a lawyer a heart attack?" he whispered in my ear, as we arrived at the table.

The host, John Westwood, from the investment side of the bank, greeted Ludgate warmly, if formally, and extended similar courtesy to me. He introduced us to the rest of the table. I had Guy Peters from foreign exchange on one side, and William Crowther, from credit insurance, on the other. Westwood worked his way around the table with introductions, until he reached David Black. My heart skipped a beat. So this was David Black, Jack Kelly's banker?

Things got worse. When the top table arrived, Victor Kane was third to walk in and take his seat. Victor Kane, the man who had cost my job. I shot a look to Ludgate, who smiled back. He had set me up.

The meal passed uneventfully, although the food could have been better. A watery tomato soup was followed by leathery chicken. I kept the conversation going as best I could with the two men on either side, who were courteous and attentive. When I could, I stole a glance at Black.

He had the kind of face, in other circumstances, I would have warmed to. Dark-haired, even features, he seemed to smile a great deal. For a banker, he had a lot of charm.

I also spent time studying Kane. I found myself comparing him with Kelly. Physically, Jack Kelly was a giant of a man. Though Kane was tall, he didn't have his bulk. In real life, he also wore round spectacles, he must discard for television. These made him look strangely vulnerable. But then, so did half the German high command in the last war, I couldn't help reminding myself.

After pudding, before coffee and speeches, guests were invited to take a break and leave the table, so some began milling round, while others went out for a smoke. I took the chance to escape to the ladies.

When I returned, I found Andrew engrossed in conversation with another man. Both their backs were to me, so I slipped unobtrusively back into my seat. There was a cigarette burning red in the hand of the man Ludgate was talking to. Smoking was strictly prohibited in the banqueting hall.

"Julia, you're back," I heard Andrew's voice. "Can I introduce you to Victor Kane?"

I couldn't move. It was if I was paralysed. "Victor, this is Julia Lighthorn," I heard his voice again and couldn't believe Andrew was doing this to me.

"Good to meet you, Ms Lighthorn." I struggled to my feet as Kane turned towards me. He spoke softly, with little trace of a Scottish accent. I wondered if he was as embarrassed as I was.

"Julia is our new pensions guru, she's concentrating on the Kelly's case for us," Andrew wasn't giving up.

"Ah, the Kelly case. Bad business."

"You're Kelly's bankers, aren't you?" I found my voice at last.

"I can't discuss individual clients, as you know." He had brown eyes, but the whites were fading with age.

"Wasn't there anything you could have done to save the business or the pension fund?"

"Ms Lighthorn, I'm not my brother's keeper. I'm a banker. I pay my clients' cheques. I don't run their businesses."

At that point, the master of ceremonies called the guests back to their seats. The speeches were about to begin. The first speech was tedious, so I decided to call it a night. The exchange with Kane had shaken me. I made my excuses to our host, Westwood, then said farewell to Andrew, who was getting stuck into the port.

David Black also rose, I thought to visit the boys' room, but he followed me out to the entrance lobby.

"Ms Lighthorn, I didn't get a chance to introduce myself. I'm David Black. I was Kelly's banker."

"Was?"

"The relationship's been terminated, although that's strictly off the record. I'm aware of your interest and I wanted to give you my card."

He handed me his details. I turned the card over in my fingers.

"It's difficult. There's not much I can say to you. Client confidentiality and all that. But, if at some stage, you need someone to …" he paused, "to bounce ideas off, call me."

"We know money went out. What we don't know is where it went … and whose pocket it ultimately ended up in."

"I can't give you that information," he said. "It's strictly confidential. But we both have an interest in …" he trailed off, reluctant to be specific about precisely what Kane's interest was.

"Thank you, it's very generous of you. I'll be in touch," I said, slipping the card into my tuxedo pocket.

"Good," and with that he turned and went back to the dinner, leaving me to wonder why a valuable new source of information had just opened up for me.

Chapter Thirty-one

10.45pm Friday, November 2, London

In the taxi home, I called Omar, despite the late hour, and was relieved when he picked up. He was dining with some lawyer friends in the West End, and left the table to find a quiet spot. I told him about the dinner, the exchange with Kane, and Black's offer at the end.

"So, you spent the evening schmoozing with KNS? D'you think that wise?"

"Not schmoozing. I couldn't help it. Ludgate didn't give me any choice."

He was quiet again for a few seconds.

"It may not be such a bad thing ... Ludgate knows his business."

"This offer from Black?"

"I shouldn't get too excited. Banks may bend every rule in the book, except the holy of holies."

"Client confidentiality?"

"They would be finished if they were found to breach that, and to a journalist, too. No, more likely he wants to pick your brains, see what you know. You've been ahead of the pack on this story all along."

It was meant as a compliment, but his words left me slightly deflated.

I spent Saturday morning cleaning the flat, followed by a visit to the dry cleaners. My cleaning bill was astronomic, but there was no way round it. All the time, I thought about Sherlock and the liquidation. There was nothing to stop the directors winding up a company voluntarily, if there was enough money to meet all their obligations. From the looks of it, there must have been.

Naturally, that wouldn't have been the case if a claim had been lodged in respect of Kelly's Brewery. But no claim had been lodged.

Still, I decided to spend Monday tracking down someone to speak to, either at the company or its liquidators. I crossed the river on foot and caught a tube down to the office. Then, as I approached our door, beside the entrance to the Bangladeshi supermarket, I saw her again; the woman in the trench coat. I hadn't seen her for a few days now, but she was there, as if waiting for me; browsing a few stalls down. This couldn't be a coincidence.

I thought of approaching her, challenging her, but what if I was wrong?

"Ignore her," a little voice said. So I leapt up the stairs to the office, and began the day's work. Not that I got very far. It was as if all the executive and non-executive officers of Sherlock had etherised, and the liquidators were saying nothing.

I consoled myself with the thought that I would see Ross again, soon, in just a few hours. He might have picked up some industry gossip about Sherlock. His office was near the Tower, so I decided to leave early, and enjoy a sandwich and walk through the castle gardens. The tube flashed through dark tunnels at unusually high speed. Dazzling winter sunshine burst on me when I emerged from Tower Hill station. The air was crisp, the sky a brilliant blue and the river glistened silver.

There was a spring in my step, as I marched along the embankment. The tower, the river, and the gardens never failed to lift my spirits. A group of school children were feeding a colony of pigeons. Beefeaters chatted to strollers meandering by. It took me back to my own childhood and walking through these same gardens with Mum, Dad and Peter. What a happy time that had been. I did miss them, especially Dad. But, after all that had happened, I was better off with them living on the other side of the world. They would have suffocated me with their love and kindness.

A tug boat glided past, sending waves rippling to the shore. I looked at my watch. Still a little time. The river was as busy as ever. Big boats, small boats, boats of all shapes and colours, crested the waves faster than looked possible. Vessels of various dimensions transported goods, commuters, party-goers and trippers along its channels. If there was some kind of highway code, I couldn't fathom it, but crashes were rare, so there must be some rules of engagement.

Three entertainment boats sailed by. A firework was dispatched from one. Of course, it was November the 5th. Disco music boomed out from it, while scantily-clad young women jived on deck, oblivious to the season or the time of day.

The next had a small chamber orchestra playing on deck, while diners in black ties sat at formal tables.

The third looked like a business lunch boat. Passengers were moving away from their tables, as it prepared to dock at the jetty of a hotel, up-river.

And then I saw them. Alexander Ross stood on deck, with a woman, their heads bent together in conversation. I recognised her immediately. She was wearing the same grey trench coat. So this was his 'lunch'.

The vessel lurched and he placed an arm round her to steady her, as they disembarked. I stepped behind a pillar, not wanting to be seen. The pigeons took to the air in fright at my abrupt movement, but the frantic flapping of their wings hardly registered. My thoughts were locked on the scene I had witnessed. What the hell was going on here? Don't tell me, he'd been the one tailing me.

I looked at my watch, 2.45pm. I waited another five minutes, then headed for his office and arrived at the dot of three, determined to get answers. I was shown quickly to his office.

"Julia," he smiled warmly, an unmistakeable post-lunch glow about him. "How's the big investigation going?"

"I thought you're the one who's supposed to be carrying out an investigation."

"I do my best … So you found us, OK?"

I nodded. "How was lunch?"

A spark lit his eyes.

"It was fine."

I was sure he was trying to stifle a smirk.

"I saw you getting off the boat. That woman you were with … know her well?"

He opened his mouth, as if to say something, but closed it again. He sat, waiting for me to go on.

"I've seen her several times recently," I continued. "She's been hanging round outside my office, and flat. In fact, would you think I was crazy, if I said, I think she's been following me?"

"Ah …"

"Know who she is?"

"Well …"

"Do you?"

"She's a private detective."

I felt like I'd been punched in the stomach.

"You hired her to follow me?"

"Don't be ridiculous."

"Then what was the lunch all about? I don't believe you …"

"Please yourself …"

"If not you, then who?"

"How should I know? She contacted me."

"To question you, about me?"

"And other things."

"What other things?"

He raised his eyes to heaven.

"What makes you think you're the only one interested in what's been going on?"

"What d' you mean?"

"Work it out for yourself." His next words, he pronounced one at a time, like I was an imbecile. "Who has most to lose?"

"The other trustees?"

"Who's got money a court could come after?"

"The advisers?"

"Who's got the big money?"

He had lost me.

"What exactly is your agenda?" My blood was rising. "Who are you working for?"

His eyes hardened. The glow had gone. My time was up.

"I don't see any point in continuing this conversation. I've a plane to catch in an hour. I've got …"

"Don't tell me … a parents' evening."

He jumped to his feet. I had gone too far.

"I think it's time you left."

His dismissal annoyed me, so I went for the jugular, regretting my next words almost before they were out.

"No wonder your wife left you," I spat at him.

"How dare you. How dare you." He was furious. "Your husband died, so you think that gives you the liberty …"

"My husband didn't die …"

"Philip died. You visited his grave."

"Of course, you know everything about me, thanks to your private dick."

His face was white with rage. "How can I get it through your thick skull …"

"And to think I nearly trusted you."

"Trust? You don't know the meaning of the word. Your right hand wouldn't trust your own left hand."

I shook my head. When I spoke again my voice was calm and steady.

"Philip wasn't my husband," I said. "He was my son."

With those words, I walked out of the room and slammed the door.

Chapter Thirty-two

4pm Monday, November 5, Whitechapel

I was still fuming when I got back to the office, although a big part of me was more hurt than angry. He had no right to snoop into my private affairs.

"That phone's not stopped ringing for the last 'alf-hour," Mina greeted me. "Drivin' me crazy."

"Try answering it for a change, you lazy …"

"Julia …" Marsha shouted from her room, stopping me saying something I would regret.

It rang again, the minute I sat at my desk.

"Yes," I snapped down the line.

It was Ross.

"Look. We could both have handled that better."

I said nothing.

"Can I apologise. I'll cancel the flight. Do you want to …"

"Don't bother," I slammed the phone down. What a nerve. After all he had said and done.

It rang again almost immediately.

"What now," I shouted into the receiver.

"I have a call for you, madam." It was the refined voice of a Scot. I waited, the line clicked again and, this time, a gentle female voice spoke.

"I am Mrs Kelly. Mary Kelly. I believe you know my son, Jack."

I was stunned.

"Ms Lighthorn," she continued. "I'd like us to meet, when you're next in Scotland. Do you know when you will be coming north again?"

"My next trip isn't planned," I replied.

"I see. Perhaps you could let us know when you're next in town. I'm sure a meeting will be useful for us both."

"Of course," I said.

"Good. I'll put my secretary, Angus, back on the line."

I scribbled down her number, although this was one invitation I would be in no hurry to accept. I could imagine the white-washed version of events, I would be force-fed. These old dames excelled in blanking out reality where their precious family was concerned.

I hadn't long hung up when the phone rang again. It was Poitu.

"What do you want?"

"I'm in the Blind Beggar, waiting for someone to buy me a pint."

"What do you do with your police salary?" I snarled.

"Oh well, I'll keep my bit of news to myself then."

"Get the order in, I'll be down in five."

Poitu was standing at the bar, sipping his pint. I ordered a half, and paid for them both. We moved to a table and sat down.

"So what's new?" I began.

"Hello, inspector, how are you, what have you been getting up to today?" he said, sarcastically.

"Yeah, well, all of that too."

"My, my, someone has upset you."

"The only person who upsets me, is you," I glanced irritably away from him and round the bar, where notorious East End gangster Ronnie Kray had shot dead his gangland rival.

"And I thought I was your angel."

"Angel of darkness." The murder, for which the Krays were finally jailed, took place in full view of countless witnesses.

"That's hurtful."

"The problem with criminals," I said, going off on a tangent, "is they get arrogant and start to believe they're untouchable."

"Same could be said of journalists," he replied.

"Not to mention the police …"

"Change the record, Hornworm. Do you want my news or not?"

I nodded.

"First, tell me, how you got on with Mrs Livingstone."

"Buy the newspaper."

"Can't afford it … OK, OK," he held up both hands as to surrender.

"I was only joking. What has got into you today?" He took a sip of his beer. "I've read your pieces. Learn anything else?"

"Not anything you don't know."

"No. I guess not. But your favourite inspector does have some news for you."

"As in?"

"Remember the Hannigan case?"

How could I forget? "The one Raeburn suggested Strachan had taken a back-hander over?"

He nodded. "We sent someone to make inquiries. There may have been something in those stories."

My stomach churned.

"Hannigan was paid to go home," he continued.

"Did it have anything to do with Strachan?"

"He arranged the deal."

This sounded bad.

"What deal?"

"The kid got £10,000 to go home. It kept the bigots at the works happy and production flowing."

"I see. How was he? Angry?"

"Not about going home. It was what he wanted. He'd had his fill of bonny Scotland. Things worked out OK for him. Strachan found him a job, a good job. The payoff allowed him to buy a house. He loves the guy, eternally grateful."

"Did he think Strachan took a bung?"

"Extremely unlikely, he thought. Couldn't see it at all."

"Any report on the other accusation." I couldn't bring myself to say paedophilia.

"I'm still looking."

I told him about the call from Mary Kelly.

"Interesting, Hawthorn. Will you be going?"

"I've no plans right now."

I wanted to tell him about Ross and the private eye, but something held me back.

Instead, I said, "I don't trust Ross."

"You don't trust anyone." He was right enough there.

"You don't think he could be in league with …"

"Kelly? No chance."

"What about the actuaries or the bankers?"

"He'll be working with anyone he can to sort this mess out."

His words had the ring of truth.

"Sherlock?"

"Only if he can find them, when no one else can."

He was quiet for a moment, thinking.

"There's something else you should know," he began slowly. "The word on the street is that someone is offering a big reward for information." His eyes went to a line of men standing at the bar. He had informants all over London.

"About what?"

"The offer's vague. But there's a big reward out for information about Strachan's death and anything connected with it."

"The pension, the missing girl …"

"I guess."

"How much?"

"Hold onto your tonsils, Lightweight … it's for half-a-million."

"Christ, that should flush something out."

"You'd think so, always supposing there's something to flush out."

Poitu dipped his middle finger into his glass.

"What d'you think, Poitu? You never said? What do you really think happened that night?"

"It's not what I think, it's what I know."

"As in?"

"There was no suicide note." His glass hummed, as he ran his finger round the rim.

"There was a note," I said. "That young police officer said there was at the inquest."

"He said what he was told to say." He took a swig of his beer, then stared at the glass, as if concentrating hard.

"Sugden confirmed it. He said it was Ken's writing," the words tasted bitter in my mouth.

"He confirmed nothing," The glass chimed as he stroked the rim again, lower this time, a sustained ringing. He continued, "I told you that inquest was pure theatre. Did you see his hand shaking? And the way he squinted at that note? And the light over the witness box? He's short-sighted. Didn't even put his reading glasses on."

He took a final swig, emptying his glass, before handing it to me. "Your turn I think."

I rose and went to the bar.

"So they brainwashed Jim, convinced him Ken had left a note," I said, when I sat again with our drinks.

"Trust me, there was no note." Poitu sipped his pint.

"How can you be so sure?" I asked.

"If there'd been one, I'd have seen it." He had a strange look in his eyes. And suddenly the fog cleared.

"You were there, weren't you?" I said, as the penny finally dropped. "At the scene of the murder?"

He nodded slowly. "They knew there'd be an outcry over the delay going in. So they called for a tame copper to give them a clean bill of health. Thought someone from the Met would have bigger fish to fry, than worrying about a domestic."

"Poitu, I'm sorry. I never knew. It must have been awful."

"Awful … I'm a police inspector."

"Even so … tell me about it." I desperately wanted to hear, in his own words, what he'd seen that night.

But he wasn't playing ball.

"You've heard it all already at the inquest, except for the note."

"You say you don't believe there was one. Why?"

"Nothing had been removed from the house when I entered it, except for Emma, the daughter, who was being brought out on a stretcher when I arrived. There was no note on his desk."

"What if someone had moved it before you got there?"

"Well, if they did, it has vanished now, just like the forensics?"

"Gone from the file?"

He nodded. I could hate Poitu for always being two steps ahead of me.

"You think it was a forgery?"

"Maybe yes, maybe no. It could have been Strachan's writing, they may have found a note he started to write about something entirely different."

"Is that likely?"

"No, not really."

"What do you think happened then?" I continued.

"I don't know. He could have killed them and shot himself. Anything else doesn't make sense. Why would an outsider wipe out a whole family? It doesn't add up."

He was right.

"Did you realise the wife and kids had been away for a few days at her sister at Inverness?" I asked.

"Yes, she told us. How did you know?"

I pretended I couldn't remember. I'd never told him about the diary.

"What if they weren't meant to be there?" I added. "What if they came home early?"

"It's a possibility, I suppose. She didn't say."

"Did you ask?"

"I'm not sure we did. I'll call her tomorrow." He looked at his watch. "It's gone six, I'd better be going."

"Me too."

I headed to the tube, while Poitu walked back down the Whitechapel Road. I watched him stroll along the stalls. What a day. First the business with Ross, and then the disclosure Poitu had been at the scene of the murder. I was beginning to suspect I might have read him all wrong from the start.

I stood watching him still, when my mobile rang.

It was Ross. "Look, I want to apologise. We need to talk …"

"I thought you had a parent's evening …"

"I'm still down here. I thought …" Suddenly, I felt sorry for him.

167

"I see …" the heat had gone out of my anger.

"Look, the meeting with that detective. There was nothing sinister about it. I don't know why you reacted …"

"You think I over-reacted?"

"I'm not saying that," he was struggling to be diplomatic.

"It doesn't matter now." The fight had left me.

"Let me buy you supper."

"I thought you'd already eaten?"

"I can cope with lunch and dinner."

I wasn't sure I could. "I was looking forward to a quiet night," I said. He chuckled at the other end of the line.

"It's firework night. You can't possibly have a quiet night. There's a display starting on the Thames in half-an-hour. It might be fun."

In the end, I agreed to meet him by Cleopatra's Needle. Fun was something I could do with, it had been in short supply. If nothing else, I could clear up, once and for all, what he was doing with that private detective, who had been following me for days.

Chapter Thirty-three

6.45pm Monday, November 5, Thames Embankment

Ross was waiting for me by the Needle, as we agreed, and my heart melted the moment I saw him. It was already dark, there was no moon, but the river was lit on both banks, and across its bridges. It didn't need fireworks to look magical.

He had secured a spot down by the waterfront, and waved for me to join him. I felt a warm rush, when he placed an arm around me to ease me into the gap.

The fireworks began almost immediately, to William Walton's 'Battle in the Air' music. The first salvo unleashed a colony of silver spiders, swarming across a black sky from the south bank, to edgy violins. We watched in silence as they got nearer, beautiful, but creepy. They finally exploded above our heads in a cascade of diamonds to "oohs" and "ahs" from the crowd.

Blue fountains, like torchlights scouring the river, were lit next, to a quieter section of the music, finally making speech possible.

"Enjoying it?" Ross asked. I detected a trace of nervousness behind his warm smile.

"It's great, particularly the music," I smiled back.

"Spitfire music, hmm," he grinned, "very apt."

The fireworks and music were getting louder, so he drew close and whispered in my ear.

"Look I'm sorry about earlier. I can see how upset you were. This woman rang me and asked to meet. I knew absolutely nothing about any surveillance."

A battery of rockets whooshed into the sky, like a doodlebug attack, lighting the darkness red, gold, blue, and yellow, with ear-splitting blasts. A dog started to bark furiously. Another volley of explosions followed immediately, and another. The crowd was screaming with delight and terror. Ross moved towards me again, and this time shouted in my ear, in order to be heard above the crowd.

169

"You don't think you could be mistaken do you? It seems a bit ..."

His next words were drowned out by a massive detonation of firecrackers, sizzling and blistering, like popcorn in boiling oil. I was beginning to feel I had seen and heard enough.

"This is hopeless I said," pointing back to the road. "Let's walk, we can enjoy the fireworks, without being deafened."

He smiled, and we moved away from the river frontage, passing some children with fists full of sparklers, who were painting weird, glittery patterns around the Needle.

"Did she ask about me?" I asked, as the bangs faded.

"A bit."

"What did you say?"

"Not much," he could be infuriatingly discreet.

"Did she say who'd instructed her?"

"No, she wouldn't," he shook his head.

"But you have an idea?"

"I could guess."

"It must be Kelly or Cameron," I suggested, but his face was a mask. Whatever he thought, he was giving nothing away.

"If you think you're being followed you should tell the inspector," he changed the subject.

"I have. He told me to see a shrink." Ross swallowed a laugh, before trying, with only limited success, to straighten his face.

"So I've no intention of mentioning it to him ever again," I continued, ignoring his enjoyment of the joke at my expense. "Someone is anxious for information, though." I reported Poitu's news that someone was offering half-a-million for a lead.

"Phew," he whistled. "That's a great deal of money."

I also told him about Poitu being present at the crime scene, but this didn't seem to come as news.

We were crossing Waterloo Bridge when Elgar's 'Pomp and Circumstance' began to boom from of the loudspeakers. The river lit up, as a million candles gushed colour into the darkness. A group of tourists moved from one side of the bridge to the other, leaving a gap by the wall. We filled their empty space, and watched the spectacular finale from on high. When the music reached 'Land of Hope and Glory', the crowds were singing with all their might, but you couldn't hear them for the batter of blasts, as a barrage of rockets again lit the sky, showering rubies, emeralds and diamonds down onto the silver-glistening water below.

And then it was over, and people started to drift away. We continued to cross the bridge in the direction of my home.

"Let's get something to eat," he said, when we reached the bank. "There are some good restaurants further along."

We continued walking. I told him about my meeting with Jack Kelly, the dinner at Loch Lomond, and seeing Ragland. He didn't seem to think it was suspicious.

"Prestigious meeting of the drinks' clan," he said. "Ragland's the local MP. He relies on their patronage."

"I spent most of the evening with Tom Kelly," I said. "I was rather taken by him."

"Uh … huh," Ross said, guardedly.

"Not at all like his father," I continued, looking for a response from him.

"Uh … huh" he said, again.

"He seemed fun, like a breath of fresh air."

"Is that what you thought, Julia?"

"Do you know him?"

"A bit."

"What do you think?"

"I think only a fool would take Tom Kelly at face value."

No love lost there then.

"He says he owns a night club." I continued. "Is it respectable?"

"I don't go to nightclubs, another question for your inspector."

We had passed several restaurants by this point, but neither of us suggested going inside. They looked full, anyway, with long queues forming outside. I was enjoying the walk, the fresh air, and, if I was honest, the opportunity to be alone. Not that we were alone. The

South Bank was buzzing with entertainers.

"What do you make of this Sherlock business?" I asked, as he stopped to give a few pounds to a beggar, who had approached us.

"Story is they've all left the country," he said, as we walked on.

"How can they get away with that?"

"It's Glasgow," he shrugged. "How was the wife, by the way?"

"Distraught."

"Does she have any ideas …"

"No. As far as she's concerned, her husband was a respectable professional. They are living a quiet, ordinary life, and then one day he disappears. A fortnight later he's fished out the Clyde."

Ross sighed a deep sigh. "Do you want to stop here?" he pointed to a spaghetti house, which looked a bit quieter.

"No, let's keep walking for a bit." The air was cool, but not cold, the river shrouded in the coloured mist, which fireworks leave in their wake.

"It's all so depressing," I said.

He nodded slowly, before adding, "Shall we change the subject?"

"Good idea. Why don't you tell me about yourself," I said, looking at him tentatively, nervous he might resent this new line of questioning. He began to open up, slowly at first. He talked of the time he spent training with a big firm, and then ran through the other companies he worked for, before becoming an independent trustee.

"I was bored. This work is more challenging. I like sorting out muddles," He had started to relax.

"Not a million miles from journalism," I suggested.

"I sincerely hope so," he said, raising his eyebrows with a smile.

He asked about my career. I told him about how it had all seemed pretty easy, like I had my own lucky star, until I stupidly threw it all away.

"Kane but not able," he smirked.

I blushed. "How did you know?"

"We actuaries have our contacts too."

We laughed, our eyes meeting. He looked away first. We were

approaching Southwark Cathedral now. My flat was on the other side.

"When are you going back?" I asked.

"I'll have to get off first thing in the morning ... the children."

I nodded understandingly

"How long is it?"

"Three years ..."

"It must be hard."

"I'm told it gets easier." His jaw set hard for a moment. "We had always been the perfect family. I had no idea she was unhappy."

"She probably wasn't," I attempted to reassure him. "People rewrite history to suit themselves. Had you been together a long time?"

"It seemed like forever. We met at school. We were kids together, grew up together. Then one day she announced she was moving out, leaving me for one of our oldest friends."

"Ouch, that must have hurt."

"She said we had drifted apart and I'd been too busy to notice."

"The children?"

"They chose to stay with me. I wouldn't have stopped them, if they had wanted ..." he paused. "The other couple had children too. It was all such a muddle. It seemed best for mine to stay with me, at least until things settled down."

I could see the attraction of sorting out number muddles, when real life was such a tangled mess.

"You had a son?" His own frankness had earned him the right to ask.

"Philip, yes," I spoke hesitantly.

"And?" he pressed me further.

"Oh, you might as well know, my marriage was a disaster, an aberration. Not at first ..."

"You don't have to tell me," he interrupted.

"No, it's OK. Marsha says I should talk about it. Open up more."

We were approaching a dark tunnel, under a deep railway arch. All light disappeared as we entered it. I could barely see him anymore, only his silhouette, beside me.

"I loved my husband, really loved him. He was a fellow journalist, a war reporter. We met on a job, can you believe that? It was a story about a scandal at an armaments company. Romantic, huh?"

"Nearly as good as pensions," he joked.

"He was witty, and funny, and I thought I had everything. Wonderful job, wonderful husband, wonderful home. I'd cracked it, this awful thing called living."

"I'm not sure any of us ever really manages that," his voice was soft. "What happened?"

We'd reached the middle of the tunnel, and my words echoed slightly against its hollow walls.

"The Gulf War, that's what happened. Christopher went out with the first wave of troops. Embedded they called it. He'd send me long letters home. He was horrified by what he saw. The brutality, the wanton violence …"

He nodded understandingly.

"Then his letters changed. Something had happened to him. He crossed the Rubicon."

"Did he come home?"

"A couple of times, yes. That's when it started …"

Ross stopped and in the dark I felt him put a finger on my lips, as if to seal them. But I wanted to go on.

"The third time I ended up in hospital."

"I'm sorry."

"Don't be. The marriage gave me Philip."

"You didn't lose the baby?"

We were out of the tunnel. In a few moments more, we would be at my flat.

"Thank God, no, at least, not then."

"When you came out of hospital …"

"I started divorce proceedings. It was all very messy. I had to get an injunction. Police were called on two occasions. The last time, they locked him up for a week. I had the baby. I adored him, from the moment I set eyes on him. He made sense of that terrible time. Gave

174

me a reason." I hadn't spoken so candidly about that time to anyone, not even Marsha.

"Children can be life savers," he seemed to understand.

"But then he got sick. His kidneys malfunctioned. They said they'd never developed properly."

"Was it because …?

"I try not to think about it. What would be the point? One morning I went to wake him and he was cold. He'd had a massive brain haemorrhage."

"I'm so sorry," he apologised again.

"I miss him so much," I could feel tears welling up.

"Do you still see your husband?" Ross asked.

"No. He stays away. The injunction hurt his standing over here. He went abroad. I get second and third hand reports of his whereabouts from time to time. As far as I can see he runs from one war-torn hell-hole to the next. I guess he's trying to lose himself in some dark corner."

"Outrun his demons maybe?"

"Maybe …" I suddenly realised I had reached my road. "I live half-way down on the left," I said.

"I'll see you to your door."

When we reached my small front gate, I wasn't sure whether to ask him in or not. He stood there shifting his weight uncertainly from one foot to another.

Suddenly, I knew I didn't want him to go, not yet.

"We didn't get anything to eat." I said. "Come in, I'll fix you something."

He looked at his watch. "No, I must get back."

"For a coffee then, or a cocoa."

"Better not."

"OK …" I smiled, understandingly. "Goodnight"

I leant towards him, and kissed him on the cheek.

"Goodnight," he said, staring at me with a strange look in his eye, I couldn't construe.

"Goodnight then," I repeated, and turned to walk up the path, when his voice called after me.

"Julia, I've had an idea. You don't have to answer now, think about it. I've a cottage up north. Why don't you come up for the weekend? We've both been working hard. We could get away for a few days. I'll ask my mother to keep the children. She won't mind."

"I'm not sure." This was all rather sudden. Only a few hours ago, we had been screaming at each other.

"I could meet you at the airport Friday evening. If the weather's good, we could take the boat out."

"I don't know," I repeated.

"On second thoughts, don't think about it, just come. Sort out your flight tomorrow and let me know what time to meet you."

I smiled, as if in surrender.

"OK Sandy," I called him by his Christian name for the first time.

"Great," he leaned towards me, kissing me goodnight again, this time lightly on the lips.

I watched him disappear down the road, this great puzzle of a man, before putting my key in the door and going in alone.

Chapter Thirty-four

10.30am Tuesday, November 6, Whitechapel

Before I had a chance to sort out my flight the next morning, Ludgate called.

"We're in trouble. Cameron's lawyers have been on the phone. They are not at all happy with you."

My stomach lurched.

"They've taken out an injunction against you," he continued.

"They've taken an injunction out against me?" I repeated, flabbergasted.

"They claim you've been harassing one of their retired employees, whose health is vulnerable."

"Patterson. How do they know I've been to see him?"

"I don't know how they know. Presumably he's complained, or they have someone watching him. You're not to go anywhere near him again. Understood?"

"He's material to the investigation."

"Do you want to go to jail?"

It was brutal, but I got the message.

"OK," I acquiesced.

"Do you have any Cameron papers in your possession?"

"Only stuff that was downloaded off the internet." This was a lie. I had the Cameron papers Jamie had faxed me, which I had faxed to the office.

"Good, we have no papers here either. So there's nothing to hand over." He knew I was lying, and I knew he was lying, but who knew who was listening in.

"Right," his voice relaxed, slightly. "What are you filing for me today?"

"Not sure yet."

"OK. Keep at it. Let me know."

"I will."

"And be careful. The heat is on," he said, before putting the phone down.

I wanted to call Omar for advice, but remembered he was in court. I'd have to shred those papers. But without them, we couldn't defend our story. On the other hand, we could never hand them over as evidence, because they could be traced back to Jamie. If he had signed a confidentiality agreement, he could be in big trouble.

Jamie, I needed to see Jamie. The phone rang, it was Poitu.

"What do you want?"

"You know what I want." He was back to the buffoon act.

"Can't you give it a rest. We've got Cameron's lawyers after us now."

He laughed loudly at the other end of the line.

"It's not funny."

"Not in your position, I can see that. Don't tell me you're surprised?"

"I haven't written a word about them."

"Forgive me, if I'm imagining this, but I thought your great scoop was tantamount to calling them organised criminals."

"I didn't mention them by name."

"Thorn-in-my-side, if only I had your gift for ignoring the bloody obvious …"

"What d'you mean?"

"Every other story you've ever written on this so-called scandal of yours, named Cameron as advisers. Do you never use the internet? Did you entirely miss the links to those stories at the bottom of your 'big exclusive' about the transfers."

"The internet doesn't count. It's not covered by any laws."

"Have it your own way, anyway what's cooking?"

"Tom Kelly. He's got a nightclub in Glasgow."

"Well done, Lightweight."

"Be serious for a moment. Is it respectable?"

"Is it respectable?"

"Yes, is it respectable?"

"It's a nightclub in Glasgow."

"So, is it legit?"

His phone rang, and he put me on hold.

"I've got to go," he said, when he came back. His mood had darkened. "Anything else I should know?"

"Not really, only, Sandy Ross has asked me to go away with him for a weekend."

He snorted.

"So, it's Sandy now, is it?" and with that he hung up.

At 11.30am, I picked up my bag, and headed out to Whitehall. When I reached his office, I asked for Jamie at reception. He came straight down.

"Julia, what brings you here?" He seemed surprised.

"I was passing and wondered if I could treat you to a quick spot of lunch."

"I do have a lunch appointment," he said, eyeing me quizzically. "Can it wait?" I shook my head.

He dialled his mobile and asked a colleague to cancel his lunch. Then, with a hand at my back, he steered me out through revolving doors. We retired to a sandwich bar along the road. I ordered two sandwiches and coffees, and we retreated to a small round table in the furthest corner from the street.

"Julia, you don't look great," he said, "What is it?"

I told him about Cameron's lawyers.

"You shred your copy, and I'll keep mine."

I sighed with relief. "That's what I hoped you'd say. But Jamie, it could get nasty."

"From what I can see, it already is. If you need those papers, I'll have them, don't you worry."

I felt calmer when I left him, and arrived back at the office.

There was an email there from Sandy's secretary:

'Mr Ross has asked me to book a flight for you for Friday. Here is the confirmation. I hope the times suit. He suggested this flight would be

best. He'll be waiting for you.'

In the panic over Cameron I'd forgotten all about weekend. How kind that he took care of it for me. At least, I thought he was being kind.

Chapter Thirty-five

8.45pm Friday, November 9, Glasgow airport

As good as his word, Sandy was waiting for me in the luggage hall at Glasgow airport. The flight was surprisingly quiet for a Friday evening. He had already fished my suitcase off the turntable.

"It was the only yellow suitcase. It had to be yours." He greeted me with a kiss. It was the first time I had seen him not wearing a suit. Casual dress suited him, made him look younger. He wore a tan-coloured, short-waisted leather jacket, black t-shirt and light chinos.

"You mean, you read all the labels," I squeezed his arm. "How very romantic."

His car was a short walk from the arrivals door.

"It's going to be a long drive," he said, manoeuvring his black Mercedes estate onto the M8.

The stresses of the week combined with the Friday evening dash to the airport, were beginning to take their toll. He switched on some music, the soundtrack of the film 'Good Night and Good Luck', largely jazz classics. The film was one of my favourites. It told the story of a bunch of journalists trying to expose the truth behind the McCarthy witch hunts. I wondered if he had chosen it especially.

We soon left the lights of the conurbations behind and headed north. It was a dark, clear night without a cloud in the sky. Sandy accelerated hard into every corner, like he knew every twist and turn of the route.

"Looks like it could be nice tomorrow," my voice was slightly strained. It was a very long time since I had been away with a man.

"If it is, we could take the boat out," he smiled reassuringly, as if he understood.

I gave him a doubtful look about the sailing.

"No seriously," he laughed. "It's the gulf stream. Sometimes the weather on the west coast can be unseasonably warm for this time of the year."

Before long we left the traffic behind, and the road narrowed as we entered the hills. At about 10pm, Sandy called ahead and told someone he was on his way.

"The ferryman," he explained, when he had finished the call. "He's a friend of mine. There's a short bit of water we can cross, takes about an hour off the journey. But we'll not be there for the last ferry."

I smiled. How remarkable to live in a community where friends turn out to do favours, at all hours.

"Are the children OK?" I asked.

"They're fine. If a little puzzled at me going away with a woman."

"You told them?" I was surprised. Surely, a white lie would have sufficed in the circumstances.

"Of course." He reached for the temperature gauge and turned up the fan, to clear the windscreen. It had started to steam up.

"I also told them it was strictly business," he added, as the screen cleared.

"Business ..." I repeated.

"Strictly business." There was a mischievous glint in his eye.

I slept after that, lulled by the motion of the car and the music; a deep sleep, I so seldom enjoyed of late. I even missed the ferry crossing.

I woke when Sandy touched my shoulder to tell me we had arrived. He had pulled up outside a white terraced cottage. I checked my watch. It was midnight, not a soul around. I could see nothing in the pitch black darkness. I would have to wait until the morning to inspect the waterfront. But I could hear the riggings of boats tinkling softly in the wind. A distinct smell of the sea hit me as I stepped out of the car.

Sandy led me directly upstairs to the room I would be sleeping in, pointing out the bathroom on the way. He opened a window to let fresh air in. The cottage smelled musty after being locked up for some time. He looked tired, as he said goodnight and closed the door behind him, leaving me alone.

I woke the next morning, to the sound of waves lapping rhythmically beside the harbour wall, and opened my eyes to find the sun streaming into the bedroom. It was a pretty room, so unlike the work of a man. All floral curtains and quilts, with china knick-knacks, the decor reminded me of Sally and Timmy's home, Wisteria Cottage. There was a wrought iron fireplace and neat marble mantel. At each side of the bed was a small round table, covered by tablecloths in matching floral material, with ruffled skirts in layers.

The bathroom, too, oozed Victoriana. Unmistakeably, this cottage had been decorated by a woman. It wasn't hard to guess by whom. I wondered if they had ever shared the bed I had been sleeping in.

Sandy was already up, and a delicious smell of bacon wafted from the kitchen.

"I take it you can manage a full Scottish breakfast?"

"That rather depends what's included."

"Pretty much the same as an English breakfast, only much, much, tastier."

"Naturally." I laughed and followed him from the kitchen into a tiny dining room at the front of the house. He placed the breakfast on the table at a window looking out onto the harbour. This was my first view of the sea and the cobbled quay.

"It's lovely."

"The view or the breakfast?"

"Both ... and the cottage."

"Glad you like it," he said, raising a fork to his mouth.

An oak fireplace dominated the room, which was again decorated in a pretty cottage-style.

"We bought it 20 years ago. It was madness really. I was qualifying. We had no money. Couldn't afford a place in Edinburgh. Came here and fell in love with it, I suppose."

"You ... and your wife?"

His face darkened slightly, but he nodded and quickly changed the subject.

"I'm hoping to take the boat out later. Not far. Just a quick spin.

Will you join me?"

"I'm no sailor."

"You'll be fine."

"What's she called ... the boat?"

He hesitated before replying, blushing slightly, "True love."

"'High Society'," I referred to the romantic movie.

"It wasn't my idea," he added, shiftily.

"No." I wanted to say 'You must miss her,' or something equally crass, but said instead, "I love old films."

"Me, too," he replied, and we discussed our favourite classics for the rest of the meal.

After breakfast, I strolled round the harbour, while he disappeared to his boat. The sun was hot, although the wind cool, but I was warm enough in my Burberry. The harbour was lined with fishermen's cottages, painted in different colours. Many were white, but some were deep blues and a few pink. Boats bobbed at their moorings, like eager puppies waiting for someone to take them for a run. The fishing fleet was in, its catch long dispatched south, but the quayside remained a muddle of nets, oilskins, baskets, and ropes.

There were a couple of small shops with very little in them, a pub, 'The Kilberry', and a hotel. It had the aura of another world, caught in a different time warp, set apart, remote. As I wandered enjoying the sun, and the lingering smells left by the departed fish, a slight cloud hovered. I couldn't help wondering what I was doing there, and why Sandy had brought me? The cottage, the harbour, the boat; it had been their special place.

Towering above the village, on higher ground, was a church with a striking tower. I climbed up to it and turned the handle. The door opened.

It was starkly beautiful inside, but in a dour sombre way. It was the first time I had entered a Church of Scotland place of worship. It seemed dark and Calvinistic, cold and empty. I thought of Sister Robert's bustling Stella Maris and was glad to step out again into the sunshine.

The water was surprisingly calm as I idled back along the dock, staring out into the middle of Loch Fyne. Such tranquil water, like it had never known a storm.

I heard Sandy's voice as I approached the grocer. He was walking backwards out of it, his arms full of a box of stores. He would have bumped straight into me, had I not averted the crash.

"Goodbye then, Mary," he shouted at the shopkeeper inside, oblivious to the accident he nearly caused. "Ah, there you are, Julia. Lunch." He tapped the side of the box.

I peaked inside. There were sandwiches, a meat pie, scones, cake, and fruit.

"Shall we head off, then?"

I followed him along the quay, until we reached the True Love.

He jumped aboard, put the box down, and reached to help me step aboard. The boat rocked as I did so and he caught my weight, steadying me in his arms. Then he smiled and released me. I saw another figure at the helm, already working on the ropes, a young lad, who looked about 17.

"This is Joe, Julia. Joe, meet Julia. I'll need someone to help me crew, because I can see you won't be much help. Put these on."

He threw me a body warmer, waterproof, and life jacket. They were a struggle to get on. When I'd finished, I sat down on a ledge-bench and leaned over the side. The boat began to move away from its mooring, slowly at first, then gaining pace. Before long we were moving swiftly, the wind behind us, the warm sun on my face. Sandy and Joe worked at the sails. I watched them both switching the steering between them, as they moved to adjust the sails, working together as a team.

And as I watched them, an overwhelming sense of being free and being alive flooded through me. The dark thoughts and worries, which had haunted me for weeks, began to dissolve. Nothing seemed to matter outside this boat and outside this loch. If there was a heaven, this had to be it.

After about half an hour, they slowed the pace and we drifted, slowly and effortlessly.

"Time for lunch I think, don't you?" Sandy said.

"If you don't mind Mr Ross, I'll go downstairs for a snooze." Joe, the soul of discretion, headed for the cabin below.

"Late night?" Sandy grinned.

"Very," said Joe, raising a hand to his head.

Sandy handed me a sandwich and piece of pie.

"It's beautiful," I said dreamily.

"I thought you'd like it. It keeps me sane."

"Your hideaway."

"Exactly."

We ate in silence for a bit.

"I'm glad you could come."

"Me too."

I put my feet up on the bench and leaned back against him. He wrapped two arms around me, holding a sandwich in his left hand, which he bit into intermittently. I felt warm and safe. He began gently stroking my right ear-lobe. Tingles ran through me. We stayed like that, eating our lunch, for perhaps half an hour. No words passed between us, just our bodies close together. His hand moved from my ear, slowly, to touch my neck, and afterwards, to tenderly stroke my hair.

Then, he kissed my head and got up.

"Let's have some coffee and then we can have some fun." He banged the cabin door, and Joe emerged, stuffing a sandwich in his mouth.

The boat was moving again, but not like before. This time it raced furiously across the water. I loved the speed, the excitement, and the sense of danger. Not since I was a child, when I found myself astride a runaway horse, had I screamed and laughed so much, simultaneously. I thought my lungs would burst. There were moments, when the stunts seemed a step too reckless, unless the intention was to tip me into the loch.

The boat bucked and reared on the water, as we flew across the waves, with me clinging for grim life on the sides. Just when I thought I was getting to grips with the speed, Sandy would swing the vessel round on a pinhead and race off in another direction, leaving me winded and clinging on even tighter.

After a while, he handed the steering wheel over to Joe and came and sat beside me again.

"Having fun?" he shouted, above the wind.

"I thought actuaries were supposed to be risk-averse?"

"We are, very cautious people," he laughed. Joe gradually reined the speed in and began turning us around.

"It's getting late," Sandy said, getting up to help him. "It'll be cold when the sun goes. We'd better go back,"

He returned to the wheel and the pace dropped to an easy cruise, leaving me to soak up what was left of the sun. I relaxed, closing my eyes, but, time and again, I found my eyelids peaking open and my gaze drawn towards him. What was it Churchill had said of Russia? 'A riddle, wrapped in a mystery, inside an enigma'. This man was certainly full of surprises.

As we neared the harbour, it became busy with other boats coming and going. A larger boat was making time on us, its wash buffeting us and making it harder for Sandy to stay his course.

As it passed, the crew waved and cheered loud hellos in our direction. I waved back, but Sandy and Joe looked the other way. And then I saw him. Tom Kelly. And I saw the name 'The Sea Witch' blazoned across the bow.

"Did you see, that was Tom Kelly?" I shouted at Sandy.

But it was Joe who yelled back.

"No doubt back from their latest drugs pick up."

I looked from one to the other.

"He moors his boat here too." Sandy's face was a mask, exactly as it had been when Timmy had told him about a visitor to Upton Grey, with a tattoo of a boat called the Sea Witch.

"What do you mean, Joe, about drugs?" I asked.

"It's well known, according to local gossip, anyway."

187

"Sandy?" I turned back to him.

"Who knows." He shrugged, like he didn't care.

"Is this why you brought me here, to see all this?" I felt anger rising. He hadn't wanted my company at all this weekend. He was manipulating me.

"Don't be ridiculous. I brought you here to have a nice weekend, I thought it would do us both good. I should have known it was a mistake."

His words stung, I was confused … hurt. The mood soured.

"What is going on here?" I asked slowly, trying to sound calm.

"You're the award-winning investigative journalist. Work it out yourself." And with those words he went below deck. It might have been the wind, but the door slammed shut after him, with an almighty crash.

Joe brought the boat safely to its moorings. It was getting late, the sun weakening, and the wind gaining strength. A chill shivered down my spine. Sandy did not reappear until we anchored. He came back on deck, handed me the keys, and told me to let myself into the house.

"Joe and I have things to do," he said, helping me ashore. The magic spell was broken.

Chapter Thirty-six

3.30pm Saturday, November 10, Tarbert, Loch Fyne

Back in the cottage, I headed straight for the bath, and submerged myself in an ocean of hot, soapy water. Tom Kelly a drug runner? Could it be true? And if so, why? He didn't need the money. The Kellys were wealthy and he had his own business interests.

But were they wealthy anymore? The brewery had been in decline for years, if Ludgate was to be believed. The accounts I studied confirmed seriously declining fortunes for at least five years. Perhaps the money had all gone, trying to keep the business afloat.

If that was so, where did Tom Kelly get the money to set up his nightclub empire? Was that where the drugs came in? And if Tom Kelly was into drugs, what else was he dabbling in behind the façade of legitimate business. Another thought struck. How much of all this did Poitu know? And what had Ken Strachan known? Strachan's diary had spoken of killing two birds with one stone. Was this what he was referring to?

I tossed these thoughts around, getting nowhere, until I realised the water had cooled. I wrapped a towel round to dry, and stood gazing in the mirror above the taps. Sandy's things were scattered around the sink. I picked up his razor and ran my finger along the long thin handle. I imagined him standing there shaving. A tingle ran down my spine.

"Get a grip," I muttered, leaving the bathroom to finish drying in the bedroom.

Once dressed in fresh blouse and jeans, I headed downstairs and had a scout round the kitchen. Sandy hadn't mentioned dinner, but it seemed unlikely there was anywhere along the harbour capable of producing a decent meal, so I decided I to put supper together. It could be my gesture of appeasement after our cold parting.

I found some fresh steak in the fridge, he must have brought from Edinburgh. There was a very old plait of garlic hanging from the wall. No sweat, garlic keeps, and with the bottle of burgundy I took from the wine rack, I could make a decent sauce.

I was thumbing the steak when my mobile rang.

"How's love's young dream?" it was Poitu.

"Shut it." I might be 400 miles from London, but I could still speak the language.

"Going well is it?"

"That's no business of yours."

"Remember the deal, my business is your business. Anyway, thought you might like to know, I'm coming north myself tomorrow."

"I'm supposed to find that even moderately interesting?"

"That depends. Are you flying straight back?"

"Undecided."

"Humour me with a date."

"Not if you were the last man on earth."

"Hurtful, but faint heart never won fair lady. I was going to offer to take you to Tom Kelly's club on Monday night. There's a little show on there. Hot ticket I'm told."

"Ahh …"

"Thought that would tempt you."

"Poitu, have you heard anything about the Kellys and drugs?"

"One day, along came a beautiful prince and woke sleeping beauty with a kiss."

"You are infuriating."

"OK, call me Monday, babe."

I let the 'babe' go, hit 'call end' without saying goodbye and went back to preparing dinner.

The food was cooking nicely when Sandy finally appeared, looking cold. His face brightened, as he breathed in the aroma of succulent steaks on the hob.

"Hmmmm, something smells good," he said, joining me in the kitchen, but his expression quickly changed when he saw the empty bottle.

"That's my best bottle of burgundy. It cost me …" he gasped.

"The steak will taste all the nicer for it."

He pulled me firmly towards him and for the first time kissed me full on the lips, our earlier exchange, if not forgotten, forgiven.

"I was going to take you out."

"So why did you buy the fillet steak?"

His eyes glinted.

"In case."

"In case of what?"

"In case we wanted to stay in."

He moved away from me.

"I'll go and change," and he left me to finish the meal.

By the time I went through to the dining room to set the table, a wood fire was blazing in the fireplace, as was another in the small lounge. He must have lit them before going upstairs.

I poured myself a glass of wine, and one for Sandy, while I waited for him to return. It wasn't long before I heard his foot on the stairs. He picked up the glass I had poured and stood by the fire.

"Hmmm," he savoured the wine. "It's so nice to get into a bath, and soak away all your …"

"Worries and troubles," I finished for him.

He laughed.

"If only it could do that."

We were quiet for a moment, before he began again.

"Look, about earlier …"

I placed a silencing finger over his lips. "We both have a short fuse." I said.

"We do," he smiled. "I didn't used to. I used to be so easy going."

"It comes with age …"

"And responsibilities," he added.

I nodded. "Hungry? Dinner's nearly ready."

He followed me back into the kitchen.

"Here take these."

I handed him dishes with vegetables and potatoes, while I carried plates of steak through to the dining room. Before sitting down, he put on some music; this time Tchaikovsky's 'Sleeping Beauty'. Surely, he couldn't have spoken to Poitu?

"Poitu called when you were out," I said, as he joined me at the table. "He's invited me to Kelly's club on Monday evening."

His expression flickered. "You be careful ..."

"He said there was a show on. A hot ticket."

"I dread to think," he said drily, wiping his fingers on his serviette.

"About this afternoon ..."

He threw his serviette onto the table.

"Look, I don't want to talk about all this now. For just one evening, I want to forget about it. Is that too much to ask?"

"No, no, of course not." I placed my hand over his.

"I know Tom Kelly keeps his boat here, but so what? Is that good reason for us to stay away?"

"No, no, of course not," I repeated. "It's just ... if what Joe said this afternoon is true... it changes things, doesn't it?"

"Not for me it doesn't."

"I mean, it's not just a cosy, white-collar crime any more, is it?"

"Cosy white-collar crime?" he looked at me in disbelief. "Strachan is dead. Livingstone is dead, a girl is missing. When was this ever a cosy white-collar crime?"

"Strachan is dead. Livingstone is dead ..." I repeated, as a terrifying penny was about to drop. "Jesus, what about you? Are you in any danger?"

His face broke into a reassuring smile. "The only thing I'm in danger of is wringing your neck, which I will do if you don't change the subject."

After dinner we went for a walk around the harbour, stopping for a quick drink in the Kilberry. Half-a-dozen or so of the locals were standing at the bar. Sandy seemed to know them all, and chatted with them easily. I felt several eyes giving me the full scrutiny.

He introduced me to the landlady, Mrs McDonald, a matronly woman, who looked warm and kindly, but not a lady to cross. She looked from me to Sandy in a way which made me think I might possibly be the first woman he had brought here since his divorce.

"We'd better be off," Sandy said draining his glass. "It's good to see you all."

"Come again, soon," Mrs McDonald shouted after us, as we walked though the bar. We were nearly at the door, when it opened and in walked Tom Kelly, his long dark hair flowing freely over his shoulders. He wore a black T-shirt, a tattoo of the Sea Witch clearly exposed on his forearm.

"My, my, my, Ms Lighthorn. What a lovely surprise. And ..." he nodded to Sandy, "I hadn't realised you two were such good ..."

"I wanted to see some of your famous scenery, and Mr Ross kindly offered to show me Tarbert."

"I'm sure he did. He loves it here ... like I do. Our greatest love, wouldn't you say? Never let's you down."

Sandy brushed past him with a curt nod, me close on his heels. As we left, I saw a man with a gold earring, following in behind Kelly ... a gold earring with a small cross at the base. His head was shaved and he had a body like a gorilla. I thought of Mrs Livingstone's description of one of the men who had called for her husband, the night he disappeared.

I started to tremble as we walked back to the cottage, partly from the cold. Sandy put his arm round me and drew me closer to him.

Once back in the cottage he rekindled the fire, and we sat together on the sofa, watching the roaring flames, their burning warmth dispelling the chill. I put my feet up, and leant against his firm body, and, like on the boat, he began gently stroking the back of my ears, and then my neck. I felt him relaxing too, and after a while I asked about Tom Kelly again. This time, he was more forthcoming.

"Black sheep of the family. Wanted nothing to do with the brewing business when he was younger. Kicked out of Fettes. Oh yes, only the best for our Tom. There was some incident involving a local girl, who worked at the school. Depends who you believe ... rape, indecent assault. Whatever it was, Jack paid her off, and the police were kept out of it. Fettes kicked him out though, and he went off to art school.

"There, he met another student, Frankie McSherry. Poor kid. Dragged himself up through the school of hard knocks. East End of Glasgow.

"They dropped out of college, the pair of them. Lived a feral existence for a few years. Then I suppose Jack Kelly put his foot down. They went into business together."

"The nightclub ..."

"And other stuff ... he's got a few clubs, a casino and rumoured to have," he hesitated, "other interests."

"When did all this start?"

"I'm not exactly sure. Not all that long ago. They must have bought the first club about five years ago, I guess."

"Five years ... where'd he get the money?"

"Jack Kelly, I suppose."

"Do they get on?"

"Not particularly, I don't think. Tom's got a reckless streak, too wild for his father. Jack can't understand with all that education how he amounted to so little."

"Thinks he's an idiot?"

"He did when he was younger. I get the impression they've become closer of late."

"You said he started investing in Tom's clubs about five years ago. What if ..."

"Ssssshhhhhh ... enough for now." He silenced me with a long deep kiss, and I felt desire stirring for the first time after a very long absence. He began gently kissing my face, all over my face, as he unbuttoned my blouse. His lips were on my lips again, and I sucked at his breath, as his hands moved up and down my back, a sweet pleasure sweeping over me. And I wanted more. Much more. I had waited so long for this moment. A new desire, stronger now, started to possess me, one I wasn't sure I could control.

Sandy sensed it, and flicked the clasp on my bra loose, lowering his mouth to taste my breasts. At the first touch of his lips, a flame burst through me. But it was too powerful. It frightened me. It was too much … too soon. I panicked. I didn't want to do this anymore. I sat up, pushing him away.

"Julia, what is it?" he looked genuinely concerned.

"I'm sorry. I can't,"

A flash of hurt passed momentarily across his eyes.

"I'm really sorry."

He nodded, but I'm not sure he understood.

"Of course," he got up and left the room. I heard him filling the kettle in the kitchen.

I re-clasped my bra and headed up to bed. Alone.

Chapter Thirty-seven

7.30am Sunday, November 11, the West

It was a long drive back, so we left early the next morning. The weather had turned. Much of the journey was spent in silence, broken only by my occasional raptures over the spectacular scenery, with Sandy adding a few comments or explanations about the places we travelled through. It wasn't as awkward as it could have been, but hardly easy companionship either. Something had come between us.

He dropped me on the outskirts of Glasgow, so I caught a bus to the hotel, and spent the evening having a bath and trying to read. But the weekend had unsettled me, and I couldn't concentrate.

First thing the next morning, I rang Sister Robert to see if she could spare me half-an-hour. I needed to catch up with her. She was coming into the city an hour or so later, so we arranged to have a coffee in the Museum of Religious Art at eleven.

Poitu called at about 10am and said he would meet me at the hotel at 8.30pm, which would still leave the afternoon free.

I bit hard on my thumb nail for a few seconds, and then dialled Mary Kelly's number. Angus answered the telephone. Without consulting his employer, he invited me to Kelly Castle for lunch at 1.30pm.

My heart was heavy as I approached the museum, close to St Mungo's Cathedral. Thoughts of Strachan's funeral came flooding back. I arrived first, so bought two coffees, and was sitting at a table taking my first sips, when Sister Robert arrived.

Her face broke into a sparkling smile as she said hello and sat beside me. There is something magical about people whose smiles literal light up everything around them and give us all courage and hope. Unfortunately, she had not brought anything by way of good news with her. She had asked all the centre's regulars to put feelers out, but there were no new leads indicating what might have happened to the child Roxy.

"We must hope and pray for the poor child, but she hasn't been seen anywhere," Sister Robert said.

"Does anyone have any theories about what might have happened?" I asked.

"Oh yes," Sister Robert replied. "Many young women," she paused, a look of pain flashing momentarily across her eyes, "and girls, illegal immigrants particularly, can find themselves locked up in brothels. If she's alive, almost certainly, that's where she'll be."

Brothels seemed such a strange word to emanate from the lips of a nun, and in a religious museum at that. But sex and religion could become very muddled.

"No one knows where any of these places are?" I asked.

"If they do, they won't tell me or the authorities."

"You'll keep trying?" I asked. She nodded and then, barely stopping to catch breath, she related all the latest news at the Stella Maris. I didn't know anyone who could speak so quickly, and so long, with such few breaths. She spoke of the regulars and newcomers, and always with that sparkle in her eyes.

She drained the last dregs of her coffee and started fishing in her bag, finally pulling out an aerosol, which she placed on the table. It looked like a perfume spray.

"It's for you," she said. "I want you to take it."

"What is it?" I said, picking it up.

"It's a pepper spray, just in case …"

"I don't need this sort of thing, Sister," I said, handing it back to her.

"Of course not. We can trust in God. But it would ease my mind, if you would take it."

"Really, there's no need."

"Julia, there is a need. These people, and the world they inhabit …" she didn't finish.

"Please, for me."

I took one more look at the self-defence spray and put it in my coat pocket. Coffee finished, we said our goodbyes. Before we parted, she turned towards me taking both my hands in hers.

"I'm doing everything I can to find out what has happened. If I hear any whisper, you'll be the first to know. But you must keep trying too, Julia. We must find this child."

We parted and I hailed a cab to take me to Kelly Castle. Mary Kelly stood waiting for me on its wide, stone steps. It wasn't a castle of course, but a folly. In fact, it was all a fake. There was no ancient Kelly clan, and no amount of Rapunzel towers, gothic arches and stained glass could change that. I asked the taxi to wait for me.

I was surprised by how frail she looked. I came expecting a dominatrix, yet was met by a tiny figure, exuding courtesy and charm.

"Ms Lighthorn," she descended the steps. "At last we meet. I trust you had a good journey?" She spoke with a gentle, but crisp enunciation.

I followed her into the grand entrance hall, big enough for a family to live in. Rich, oak panelling rose up to a stunningly white ceiling. Everything was pristine, just like her immaculate white blouse and blue tartan skirt.

"The cornicing dates back to the 19th century," she said, as she caught me staring at the elaborate ceiling. A man servant, dressed in a kilt of the same tartan, announced lunch in the "Laird's Parlour." I recognised his voice immediately.

"You've spoken to Angus," she said, introducing me formally and leading me into the parlour.

Huge windows opened out onto the loch below, edged by hills. Even in the depths of winter, it possessed a rare beauty.

"It was my husband's favourite room," she said.

A light lunch of salad and cold beef had been laid out on small occasional tables in front of the fire. She signalled for me to sit in a rather stiff-looking leather armchair.

"Please," she pointed to the food.

I picked at it to be polite, but I did not plan to stay long.

"I've heard so much about you," Mary Kelly began.

"Not good, I doubt."

"Ah, the menfolk, with their big clumsy feet, trampling over everything." She paused. "I understand and admire you for your concern. It has all been a terrible business. The Strachans."

"Ken and his family."

"We feel for the family. Poor Maggie, Mrs Strachan. We were at school together, a very long time ago now …"

I wasn't sure what to make of this information, but it added another twist.

She paused, as if to catch her breath, and I noticed a slight rasping sound, as she inhaled.

"Did you know there had been bad blood between the families years ago, the Strachans and the Kellys?"

I shook my head.

"Long before we were all born. There was a bishop in the family. He tried to stop people buying our beer and whisky. Led a campaign against Robert's father. Came to nothing."

"Robert?"

"My husband."

"Yet Ken worked for you?"

"We were one of Scotland's biggest companies. Feuds get buried in the past. We learn to let sleeping dogs lie. Close-knit community, live side by side, marry our neighbours, work t'gether and then we …"

She didn't finish her sentence. She didn't say that they died together and were buried together.

"The pension?" I brought us both back to the here and now.

Her expression hardened slightly.

"Aye, you think our family's to blame." She was wheezing again, and I realised for all the polish of her appearance, she was truly frail. "Certainly, the pension has not been our greatest success. Trying times."

"Ken Strachan and others believed the fund had been illegally raided."

"Ken Strachan was as mad as his ancestors. He used to claim lots of

199

things, without a shred of proof."

"In my experience there is seldom smoke without fire," I said.

"The Kellys are not criminals, Ms Lighthorn, whatever Ken Strachan may have tried to persuade you."

The picture of Robert Kelly and Joe Kennedy working together to bust the US Government's prohibition on alcohol came into my mind, followed by Tom Kelly, running drugs on his boat, the Sea Witch.

"My husband, Jack's father, was a good man," she said, as if reading my mind. "He didn't have an easy life."

Her eyes circled the room.

"You look at all this and you think we've got it made. This is the fruit of hard graft and sacrifice. Glasgow was poleaxed by the depression. The great days of the empire were over. People were starving. The rest of Britain forgot about us. We endured 60 years of poverty.

"Ship-building, coal mining, any kind of business went to the wall. But Kelly's stayed alive. The men couldn't find work, not for a few years or for a few decades, but for generations. Fathers, who had never worked, had sons, who bred more sons, all destined for life on the scrap heap.

"Robbie's father took over the brewery when he was 17. You could spit its profits into an egg cup and not splash the sides. Sales were low. The men always wanted more money. Two strikes ... nearly bankrupted us. He wouldn't let them win.

"He fought the men, and he fought the depression and he made this company great. He went out into the world and found new markets, new enterprises. He let nothing stand in his way.

"My Robbie built on his success. He always said while there was breath in his body, they'd ne'er stop Kelly's barrels rolling. And they never did. They rolled through the wars and the dark times. And so they do still, today."

This was becoming too much for me to swallow in silence. "The firm called in the receivers over six months ago," I quietly reminded her.

"Aye, modern times brought new challenges, but we restructured. We've been through bad times before."

"Is that why Jack took money out of the pension fund?"

"Our money, our business," she shot at me.

"So you admit it?"

"I admit nothing. I can assure you, if any money was removed, it was all done legally. We are a reputable company."

"Your workers lost their pensions. Their dreams of a happy old age," my voice was quiet, but firm. A tiny part of me felt sorry for this old woman, whose world had vanished.

"What old age did my Robbie have?" She wouldn't give an inch. "Died at 42 from pneumonia. He kept those miserable ungratefuls in well-paid work, and he paid for it with his life. Jest like his father before him, he went to an early grave. They drove him there. So before you start attacking us, remember the suffering and trials we went through to keep this brewery going. We provided jobs when no one else would. Without us, they would have starved."

"I'm not sure what any of this has to do with pensions," I said politely.

"There is no story here, Ms Lighthorn. There are no secrets. You can dig as much as you like. This company has always acted legally, to the letter of the law. We're all sorry the pension scheme didn't work out. But, as they say, that's life."

"Is that why you asked me here, to tell me that?"

"I wanted you to understand about us. I want you to leave my family alone. We've got a chance of a new start, and I want them to be able to take it. Jack and Tom."

"Tom has his own business affairs. The brewery means nothing to him."

"You are wrong, Ms Lighthorn. The brewery means everything to Tom."

"He refused to join the business."

"He was young. Like all young men, he can be hot headed. Says and does the wrong thing. Still does at times. He doesn't need people bothering and fretting him. He can be …"

"Reckless?"

She opened her lips to reply, but closed them again, distracted by the sound of a car driving on the gravel outside. She had a visitor, and my pulse raced at the thought it could be her son or grandson.

"I must go," I said, standing and thanking her for lunch. I held out my hand to say goodbye.

She picked up the tea pot and poured herself a fresh cup of tea. The message was clear. I could show myself out.

Chapter Thirty-eight

2.30pm Monday, November 12, Kelly Castle

I relaxed, when I saw a district nurse getting out of her car on the drive. I wouldn't have to face either of the Kellys, at least, not yet. My taxi was still waiting and drove me back to the hotel. I spent the rest of the afternoon and early evening going over the encounters with the two women, Sister Robert and Mary Kelly; both strong female characters, but so different. I thought, too, of Margaret Strachan and her childhood friendship with Mary Kelly.

Poitu arrived on the dot of eight-thirty.

"Unusual habit for a plod," I said, as I emerged from the stairs and pushed my way through the swing doors onto the street outside. "I thought the filth had perfected the art of being late, as in arriving after the event."

"Unlike gutter hacks," he snapped back. "You arrive before a crime is even a twinkle in a villain's eye, and what hasn't happened you make up."

"I suppose it's being so funny keeps you going," I retorted, adding "Where's the car?" There was no vehicle in sight.

"I thought I'd take you on an adventure. If you can risk your life on the high seas with an actuary, walking through Glasgow with a copper won't stir a hair on your pretty little head."

The club was at the other end of Sauchiehall Street. We passed through modern shopping precincts, followed by the small yet significant financial quarter. Then scenes of affluence gave way to the shabby end of town, largely populated by students. We continued beyond this, too, and reached the streets too rough, even for the adventurous young.

The exterior of the club was a deep blue, and the letters of 'The Sea Witch' shone in silver neon against the dark background. There were four bouncers on the door. They were dressed in sharp suits, but their faces looked like they'd been hit by a lorry. Poitu handed over our tickets. We were waved inside.

We walked down a dimly-lit corridor, with a plush, but stained, red carpet. The walls were a deep scarlet. It was airless. Before long, I would be struggling to breathe.

"Do you need to powder your nose?" he asked, pausing at the ladies toilet for a moment. There was mischief in his eyes.

"I'm fine thanks."

At the bottom of the corridor, double doors opened into an explosion of spinning lights and throbbing music. The room was packed with sweaty bodies. Though it was early by normal nightclub standards, this audience was already hyped up by the prospect of the spectacle ahead. And then I saw it, high on a platform in the middle of the arena. The cage.

Poitu seemed to relish the slow dawning of what I had let myself in for.

"It's called cage war," he shouted, through the pounding beats. "You lock two Neanderthals in a cage and watch them kill each other."

My gaze circled the huge arena. There had to be nearly a thousand people here, maybe more. The hammering music was piercing my eardrums, and the flashing lights made me nauseous. There was a massive screen on a far wall, playing out previous fights.

"What on earth makes anyone come to a place like this," I shouted to Poitu, above the noise.

"Our desire to kill each other. Bloody and brutal, ain't we? Want a drink?"

I grabbed his arm.

"Don't leave me," I said, pathetically. He looked down at my grasp and smirked.

"How touching. You see, I do have my appeal."

This was too much, so I let my arm drop. "I'll have a soft drink, lemonade, orange. I'll be sitting there." I pointed to a table against the back wall. "Don't be long."

From a door across the room, I watched as two fighters entered the club and approached the cage. The crowd broke into an almighty roar, a primeval, atavistic sound, savage and ferocious.

A strobe light followed the fighters, flashing on them menacingly. Both their heads were shaved and one had a vicious scar running the length of one side of his face. I had seen one of them before, just the other night at the Kilberry. He was the man with the gold earring.

I followed their progress as they mounted the steps to the central arena. And then I saw him, Tom Kelly, on the opposite side of the cage. He was talking to another man, dressed in a classic three-piece suit.

"Heard of Frankie McSherry?" Poitu said, sitting beside me.

"No, thanks to you."

"That's him." He pointed to the man Kelly was talking to. I had been wondering as much. He had clean-cut hair, different from Kelly's, whose dark locks were once again tied back in a ponytail.

"You see this fighter?" I replied. "I saw him with Kelly when we were up at Tarbert."

"And?"

"He wears a gold earring, with a cross. Exactly the type Mrs Livingstone said one of the men her husband disappeared with, was wearing."

"You saw this character with Kelly?"

"Yes."

"That's what I wanted to hear."

The fighters entered the cage, which was locked behind them and the sport began. The crowd's roar increased in violence, as they punched and kicked at each others' body and face. It did not take long for one man to be knocked down onto the floor. It was the one with the earring. His opponent, scar-face, smashed his head down repeatedly onto the cage floor. With each crashing blow, the crowd roared approval.

"My god, he's going to kill him." Even, from a distance, I could see blood gushing from his ears and nose.

"No, they'll stop it, before he's actually dead."

"Can't you stop it, Poitu?"

"All perfectly legal, m'dear."

"His brains will burst open." I stood up. "I can't stand this. I've got to go."

He followed me out, the thunderous roar of the crowd still hammering in my ears. Once back in the fresh air, I leant over the kerb and retched.

"Those tickets cost me £45 each. Dinner's going to have to be on you."

Sympathy was never his strong suit.

"I couldn't eat a thing."

"Come on, I'll buy you a drink."

"I want to get away from here."

"OK, OK … We'll go somewhere else."

A cab passed, he hailed it, and within minutes, we were back in the Merchant City, outside the restaurant we had visited after the inquest.

"Come on, let's revisit our scenes of crime, eh? You'll be safe in a prison."

I was past caring where we went. The table we had last eaten at was free, so he asked if we could sit there. I ordered camomile tea, to settle my stomach. He asked for a pint of beer, and began studying the menu, finally, ordering steak, rare, chips, and all the trimmings.

"Sure you don't want anything?" he asked, as he finished ordering. I shook my head. The tea calmed my nerves. It wasn't long before his meal arrived too.

"That club. Is it legal?"

"The fight is legal."

"It's barbaric, disgusting."

"Of course, but what a money spinner at £45 a ticket."

I watched him cut into his thick steak. Blood oozed all over his plate. What a barbaric species we are.

"Were you casing the joint?" I knew these words sounded like something out of a cheap cop drama, but I couldn't think of a better way to put it.

"I wanted to have a good look around."

"So the club isn't legal?"

"It's fully licensed. I guess that makes it legal."

"What everything?"

"Ahhh," he said, concentrating harder than ever on cutting his steak. "I didn't say everything going on under that roof was legal."

That reminded me of my afternoon visit to Kelly Castle.

"I went to see Mary Kelly this afternoon," I said.

"The grand dame, what did she say? 'My family are innocent, we worked hard for every penny.'"

"How did you guess? She was impressive though. This city had a hard time for decades. In London, we recovered from the depression quickly. I don't think they did here, not until recently."

"Explains a lot. But don't start going soft on the Kellys. It doesn't suit you, and I don't think I could stomach it."

"It puts things into perspective sometimes, that's all. Two sides to every story and all that."

"We are talking about the Kellys here." He was wiping the last trace of juices off his plate with a piece of bread, when his phone rang. "Ah..huh … right … Gallow Terrace … I'm on my way."

He clicked off the phone and stood up.

"I've got to go."

"Where to?"

"Job,"

"Can I come?"

"No. Not the press." Seeing my face fall, he relented, "Oh, come on then. It's nothing you've never seen before."

As he moved away from the table, he pointed back at it.

"Three tenners should do it."

I threw the money down.

He had parked a car around the corner, one from the police fleet, I guessed, and punched an address into the Sat Nav. We seemed to be headed out Black Top way, but it was dark so I couldn't be sure. After about 20 minutes, he pulled up outside a rundown tenement.

Three police cars were already there. We arrived as two men were being manhandled into the back of one of them.

"You're so fond of the Kellys. Come and see their handy work."

Poitu jumped out, slammed the door, walked over to one of the cars and spoke to the officers. I got out too, and waited. I didn't catch what they were discussing. The car sped away with the prisoners inside. Poitu produced his ID for the cop on the door. We were both waved into the block.

The inspector raced up the stairs two at a time. They were dark, dank and smelt of urine. One naked bulb at the top lit the whole stairwell.

The fifth floor was a buzz of activity. More officers at the door. For the second time that evening, I felt my stomach heave into my mouth. The stench of filth and decay hit me full force as I crossed the threshold of a depressing little apartment. The walls were marked with what looked like blood and excrement. I looked into the kitchen. Rotting rubbish was piled in a corner. Three mice scampered over the leftovers. I followed Poitu into the lounge.

There were four young women there. Another brothel. Two women officers were attempting to interview them with the help of interpreters. They spoke no English.

"Seen enough," Poitu came back to me, and spoke in a low voice. But I hadn't. Not yet. I approached the scantily-dressed girls.

"I'm looking for a girl called Roxy. About thirteen years old? Do you know where I might find her?"

Their expressions were blank, as they either shrugged their shoulders or shook their heads. I couldn't tell if they didn't understand what I was asking, or they didn't know the answer.

"You shouldn't be here. You've no right to question witnesses," one of the women officers said.

"Come on, we'd better go," Poitu pulled my elbow. I followed him out. He drove me back to my hotel. When the car stopped, I didn't move. He leaned across and opened the door.

"I think this is your stop."

I made no attempt to get out.

"Do you want me to come in with you?"

It was piteous I know, but I nodded.

"I suppose, I could use a coffee."

"No sugar for me," he said, a few minutes later, sitting on my bed. "I'm sweet enough as I am."

"How can you make gags after that." My temper was ragged. "Poitu, that house ... you said the Kellys' work. Are the Kellys behind it?"

"We've taken a couple of their goons into custody. Let's wait to hear what they have to say."

"You've held out on me all the way. Be straight with me now ... please."

"Me, keep Lightbulb in the dark? I've not kept things from you. But there's no point passing on theories I can't prove."

"Such as?"

"Think about London. You know the London Clubs, and some of their famous owners. What do a lot of them have in common?"

"They're often fronts for more serious criminal activity."

"Such as?"

"Drugs, prostitution, what you guys call vice, I think. This is all way out of my area."

"Exactly."

"The Kellys are different," I shook my head. "They have a respectable business. How could the brewery fit into this, or the pension, come to that?"

"It could be connected. We just have to find the connection."

"Had Ken Strachan found a connection?"

"It's possible."

"The girls."

"Illegal immigrants. Tricked into a new life in a new world, thousands of miles from home."

"Sex slaves."

"They reckon there are 10,000 in the UK, and Glasgow has the highest number after London …"

"Why don't they just run away? Go to the police?"

"Run where? They've nowhere to go. No money, no papers. You can bet they've already learnt what a good beating feels like."

"And the police are up to their eyes in all this?"

"I don't know about up to their eyes. There's rotten apples in every barrel. I've got a good team here, men I can trust. We'll root them out."

"When?"

"All in good time, Lightship."

I thought of the grand dinner I had attended at Kelly Castle; of Jack Kelly, a respected figure of the community, politicians at his elbow. And then I thought of Patterson, and his quiet, conservative life in Hampshire. And finally, I thought of the stench in that flat, and the mice crawling over the garbage.

Poitu looked at his watch, stood, and placed his cup on the coffee-making tray.

"I'm tired. I'm going back to my hotel. I suggest you catch the next flight back to London." He opened the door, before pausing to add.

"Make sure you keep this well locked." He closed the door behind him.

If only I had followed his advice.

Chapter Thirty-nine

12.30am Tuesday, November 13, Glasgow

My phone rang about half-an hour after the inspector left. It was a man's voice. "Are you looking for a girl called Roxy?"

"Who are you?"

"I have the information you are looking for."

"What information?"

"Meet me in an hour."

"Where?"

"The brewery … down by the vats. No one will trouble us there."

The phone clicked dead. I was unsure what to do next. A small voice of caution warned me to be careful. But what if the call were genuine? It was perfectly possible mine, or Sister Robert's, inquiries had ferreted out a source. This might be my last chance to help the poor child and solve the connection between her disappearance and the death of the Strachans, if indeed they were connected.

I looked out the window. The street below was deserted; the glitter of premature Christmas lights, banging in the wind, eerie rather than cheery. Sleet rain had begun to fall, mingling with a few flakes of snow. Freezing hail looked on its way. It was going to be a bitter night. I could call Poitu; ask him what to do, but be would probably dismiss the call as another hoax.

I caught a cab at the Queen Street rank and asked the driver to drop me half-a-mile away from the factory, so I wouldn't be spotted slipping in. The wind and sleet bit into my face. With each step, the stench of the brewery grew more nauseous. There was a light on in security, but no one was there. The site seemed deserted. A strategically-positioned lamp lit a signpost, giving directions to specific parts of the site. It was simple enough to follow.

I found my way easily to the wells, and on to the brew house. There were brass plaques on each of the chambers identifying their functions. The brew house was stifling; hotter than a sauna, and the smell of mashed hops stewing in huge coppers was overpowering. I wondered whether I could make it through without being sick. Would you ever get used to the rancid smell, I wondered, even after a lifetime working there.

The brew house led through to another dank chamber, where the temperature eased slightly. It was snaked with massive pipe-works leading to even bigger tanks, where I suppose the boiled mixture was cooled.

Another door at the far end opened onto narrow steps leading down to an underground cellar. Here the temperature suddenly froze, taking my breath away. This was the cavern of the vats, the appointed meeting place. It was bitterly cold. I was the first to arrive. There was no one there. A dim light glowed, but the rest of this underground chamber was in total darkness. I waited for five minutes, then another five. My legs began to stiffen. I tried to keep warm by moving, but that seemed to make it worse.

A dull burning sensation crept into my bones, as I waited another five minutes. I couldn't survive this temperature much longer. At last, I heard footsteps at the other end of the long cellar.

"Hello," I shouted. "Who's there?"

Gradually, out of the darkness, an outline of a male figure emerged. It was Frankie McSherry, Tom Kelly's business partner.

"It's kinda cool down here, don't you agree?" he said, as he loosened the button on his jacket, the same classic suit he had been wearing earlier that evening, at the club. This was not what I had expected, not at all. I waited for him to speak, unsure what would happen next.

"It's good of you to come," he sneered.

"I'm looking for a missing girl. Do you know where I can find her?" My tone was confident, but my courage was ebbing fast.

"There's only one girl I know anything about, and it's a nosey parker journalist, persecuting an innocent family."

"Look, I'm cold and tired."

"They are the least of your worries." He moved close to me now and spoke into my face, his breath as putrid as the smell of soured malt.

"I've got a message for you. Leave the Kelly family alone." Then he turned and shouted back into the dark end of the cellar.

"She's all yours."

A group of thugs emerged from the shadows. I recognised two immediately as the cage-fighters; scarface and the man with the gold earring. The kaleidoscope had twisted again. I heard a terrifying cheer, half animal, and saw a mouthful of gold teeth sparkling in the dark.

I began to run. But my legs were too cold. I stumbled and felt two arms grab me, and I knew what was coming next. My mind flashed back to the beatings I'd endured at the hands of my husband. Something inside me snapped. No, not without a fight. I reached into my pocket for the spray Sister Robert had handed me that morning and sprayed it full into the face of the brute holding me. He pitched back. I re-aimed the spray again and zapped two others lurching towards me. They, too, fell back. As he staggered, the one with the earring knocked the spray out of my hand.

But I was free and I ran as hard as I could. I made it to the stairs and was half way up, when they caught up with me again, and started grabbing my legs, with fists as hard as rocks. Adrenaline kept me going. I kicked and kicked, viciously into their faces. It wasn't easy, but I made it to the top. My heart was pounding fit to burst as I raced through the snake room, and out to the brew house. I had made it this far. I was ahead. I could see a security light. Once outside, I could run for it, and call for help.

But then, I couldn't see the light any more. The exit was blocked. A huge figure stood grinning before me. There must have been a shortcut. I was trapped. I could hear the rest clamouring up behind.

"We like a woman with a bit of spirit, don't we boys" the scarred-face crumpled into an ugly grin, and again the gold teeth glistened. "She goes that mile further before passing out."

He walked towards me and with one swift kick felled me. My arm seared with pain as it hit one of the scalding tanks. I was on fire, from the burn, the heat and the terror. Four of them pinned me down. My trousers and pants were ripped off. I closed my eyes, and braced myself for the pain to begin.

But then everything stopped, and my world swung into slow motion. I heard shouting. My legs were gripped hard and then released. There was noise everywhere, all around. Footsteps were running past. I started to cry uncontrollably. I couldn't catch my breath. Sobbing like a frightened child.

My clothes were pulled tenderly back over me; a blanket wrapped round me. I heard low voices mumbling. There were people around me. Kind people.

"Let's get you out of here." It was Poitu. I tried to speak.

"No, don't say anything. You've had a bad fright." His voice was gentle, but his face was black. He lifted me up and half-carried me outside, where I was blinded by the flashing lights of countless police cars. He stopped at an ambulance.

"I don't need an ambulance," I said feebly, still trembling.

"Do as you are told for once."

I got inside and sat down. The doors banged shut.

Paramedics started to get busy, taking my blood pressure, and checking pulse and pupils.

"You've had a bad shock," said one, as he injected something into my arm.

The vehicle began moving. I felt drowsy. My legs were lifted onto a bed, and I started to drown in sleep.

Chapter Forty

4pm Wednesday, November 14, Glasgow

The first thing I saw when I opened my eyes, was Marsha. She was sitting at my bedside holding my hand. I didn't know how long she or I had been there. I hoped not too long.

"Omar says he can't believe the lengths you'll go to, to get out of a court hearing." She smiled, smoothing my hair back from my face.

I tried to smile and sit up, but a bolt of pain shot like lightning through me.

"Jeees …" I yelped.

"Hurts, huh?"

I grimaced. Every muscle seemed to ache. Then it all came flashing back; McSherry, his thugs, the cellar, the attack. I could see, as well as feel, my body was covered in scarlet bruises. There was a large bandage on my arm. That must have been where I hit the boiling copper.

"At least your face is OK." Marsha squeezed my hand.

"What time is it?"

"It's about 4 o'clock. They'll bring you tea soon. You've had a good long sleep."

"When did you arrive?"

"As soon as I could."

"How long can you stay?"

"Until you're ready to come home."

"Today?"

"I doubt that, maybe tomorrow."

"Marsha, how did they know … the police?"

"I don't know, doll."

"Did they catch …" I began.

"Shush … let's not talk about last night. You need to rest, gather your strength. Would you like me to read to you for a bit? I found this in the hospital library."

She held up a copy of 'Huckleberry Finn', which she knew to be one of my favourites. I smiled, feeling tears prick behind my eyes. She was right, I was exhausted. She started to read. The familiar words felt good:

'He told the truth mainly. There was things, which he stretched but mainly he told the truth. That is nothing. I've never seen anybody but lied one time or another.'

Her voice lulled me into a dozing, happy nowhere-land, drifting on the edge of sleep. My dreams were interrupted by someone clearing his voice at the foot of the bed. I opened my eyes to find Poitu. I tried to sit up.

"Are you up to talking?" he asked. I looked at Marsha.

"If she must," she threw Poitu a poisonous glance. "I'll be waiting outside … don't be long."

"Did you get them?" I asked, when she had left.

He shook his head, picking up the charts at the foot of my bed and pretending to peruse them.

"That place's a rabbit warren," he said, flicking over bits of paper. "Stairs, exits, cellars, underground passages … good choice for a rendezvous, that's for sure. We did our best, but they had an escape exit planned."

"Were they just trying to frighten me, or would they really …" I petered out.

"I don't think you should think about that."

"How did you know I was there?"

"You were being tailed, thank God."

"I knew you were following me."

"Don't be silly, on police budgets."

"Who then?"

"I don't know. We got an anonymous call. More to the point, what were you doing there? I told you to stay in your hotel room and lock the door?"

"A man called, said he had information."

"And you didn't think to call me?"

"No … Yes …" I corrected myself. "I made a mistake."

Poitu shook his head, but his eyes were smiling. "You're going to have to sharpen your act up, Lightwit, if you want to stay partners with me."

I couldn't help but smile.

"It was too good a chance to miss."

"So you charge off into the night." His voice softened, but the look he threw me was deadly serious. "Do you realise how lucky you are?"

"OK, you've made your point."

"Another thing, where did you get that pepper spray? They're illegal?"

"I didn't know … you won't believe who gave it to me."

"Try me."

"Sister Robert."

"That I believe."

"Shouldn't you be out catching these thugs instead of persecuting me?"

"I'll try, if you help me."

I pieced together what I could remember, but it had all happened so quickly. I began with the appearance of Frankie McSherry and the threats of what would happen to me if I didn't back off from the Kelly story.

"You're 100 per cent sure it was Frankie McSherry."

"It was the man you pointed out as McSherry talking to Tom Kelly in the club."

"Can you describe anyone else?"

"I'm sure two of them were the fighters in the cage. One had a big scar and another that gold earring. You pick them up. I'll pick them out of a line-up."

"I wouldn't hold your breath. They'll have vanished by now and McSherry will have a dozen witnesses putting him a hundred miles away."

"What about my statement? And the link with the Kellys?"

"Not worth much. A court would throw it out. A bust-up journo with a grudge against the Kelly family, who is already being hauled into court for lying. Up here too, on Jack's home patch."

I didn't know whether to cry or be sick. His face was impenetrable as I recounted the rest of the story. When I finished, he changed the subject.

"Want some good news?"

I nodded.

"There's been a development on the missing forensics," he said. "We've found the scientist who carried out the report. He's in South Africa working on some forensic development programme with Cape Town University."

"You've spoken to him?"

"I will do. Right now he's in the middle of a desert somewhere blowing up rocks in a quarry."

"No phones."

"Quite."

"This is a mess."

"And she's a mess and needs some rest," Marsha said, coming back into the room.

"OK ...OK. You're one mean lady," Poitu said to Marsha as he left the ward.

"D'you know doll?" she said, after he had disappeared. "I reckon that geezer's a bit of a diamond."

This was more than I could stomach. I closed my eyes, and attempted to drift back into my drug-induced dream world. But the visitors kept coming. I nearly fell out of bed when, after tea, Carlton Crabb turned up. Marsha's eyes whirled like globes on a collision course, when his head popped round the door.

"I heard the news," he said, standing diffidently at the bottom of the bed. "I did worry. Perhaps, if I'd never given you the d..d..d ..." he paused, and tried again. "the d..d..d ..." He stopped and sighed, unable to get the word out.

"The diary ... Mr Crabb?" I supplied for him.

He nodded. "I was only following Mr Strachan's instructions. I had no idea ... and now ... here you are."

"I'm fine, Mr Crabb, honestly." I tried to smile, but it hurt too much. "It's very kind of you to come."

He didn't stay long, and Marsha burst into a fit of uncontrollable giggles, as soon as he left the room.

"The sooner we get home the better, I ain't never met such a bunch a' freaks."

My next visitor crashed through the door just before visiting finished at 7.45pm, carrying a huge bouquet of flowers.

"Sorry, I tried to get here earlier ... my meeting ..." Sandy began, "Over-ran," I finished for him. "I don't think you two have met."

I introduced them. Marsha eyed him suspiciously. Unlike Poitu, here was a foreigner. But she must have seen something she liked, because she got up and took the flowers from him.

"I'll get a vase for this lot. Very pretty they are too," she said, heading for the door.

Sandy sat down and I watched as he ran an eye over my bruises and bandages. He looked tired.

"How are you feeling? I've been so worried," he began.

"I'll mend," I tried, unsuccessfully, to smile.

"You must have been terrified." He reached for my hand. I felt tears welling up in my eyes. I couldn't speak; just nodded.

"I don't know what to say." A look of pain flashed across his eyes.

"There's nothing to say. It's over now."

"I'm so sorry this had to happen."

He stood and kissed me, first on each eyelid and then lovingly on the lips. I groaned inwardly, drowning in his warmth.

"It could be worse," I murmured, as our lips parted.

"Thank God for that private detective," he said. "You were right about being followed."

"Thank God for my pepper spray."

"Yes, that too. Where on earth did you get it, by the way? I thought those things were illegal."

"You wouldn't believe me." When I told him he laughed.

"But you're right. I owe that private detective quiet a lot. My guardian angel. Do you still have her number? I don't even know who she's working for. Poitu says it's not them."

"It was never the police."

"Then who? Do you know?"

"Not for sure, but I always thought it could be Kane. The bank has more to lose than anyone."

"Kane?" I couldn't believe it. "They hate me."

"Julia, bank's don't have emotions."

He stayed a while longer, and we chatted about inconsequential matters, with me drifting in and out of sleep. Finally, I felt him pressing my hand, and heard him say, "I have to go now."

"When will I see you again?" I asked.

"I'm not sure. Do you know when you're going home?"

"Marsha says maybe tomorrow. Any plans to come south?"

"Yes … in fact …" He hesitated, as though there were something difficult he wanted to say.

"Julia … the children…"

"Yes," I said, slowly. I wasn't sure I wanted to hear what he had to say next.

"I've asked my mother to take them away for a bit. Just a little holiday. My sister lives in France. She retired early, her and her husband. They've no family of their own. It's a tiny little hamlet outside Poitier."

"Poitu country."

"It's remote. Very few non-locals. I'll join them for Christmas."

I started to feel sick.

"Have you been threatened, Sandy?"

"So we will be in London in a few days before they catch the train. Would you like to meet the children?"

"Have you been threatened, Sandy?" I repeated.

He stroked my hair. "I can look after myself."

"Have the children been threatened?"

He silenced me with another kiss.

"Soon, this is will be over," he whispered into my ear. My heart missed a beat.

Chapter Forty-one

8.45pm Wednesday, November 14, Glasgow

"Didn't think much of him," was Marsha's verdict when she returned. "Too clever by half, if you ask me," she added, with a twinkle in her eye.

"No one did," I said, throwing a pillow in her direction.

"My ... my ... you must be feeling better," she laughed.

The hospital released me the next day. We flew to City airport and took a taxi home. Marsha left me for a meeting she had arranged the previous week with a group of Somali asylum seekers, who were looking for cash to set up an import/export business.

I was glad to be alone in the safety of my own home. I was no longer spooked by the thought of being watched. My shadow turned out to be my saviour. A woman police officer rang from the Met wanting to come and see me. I put her off. She stressed her concern for my welfare. Did I feel I needed any medical or psychological support? She was being kind, but the last thing I needed was to be picked over like a wounded bird.

Instead, I ran a bath. I felt dirty, dirty like I would never be clean. I poured relaxing lavender oil into the water and washed my aching body, painstakingly, gently rubbing away tension and pain. Then I lay back in the suds and closed my eyes. I forced myself to stay like that, soaking my way back to normality. My racing heart began to slow.

I tried not to think about what had happened, but there was one thought I could not chase away. Sandy thought Kane had hired the private detective to follow me, but I struggled to believe that.

The other firms of advisers seemed more likely. I could see their insurers hiring investigators. Insurers used private eyes all the time to check out claims. Cameron, for example, could face a big litigation and compensation bill, if complicity was ever traced to its door. Its insurers would want to keep a close eye on any developments.

My thoughts were disturbed by the door bell. I ignored it at first, but it rang twice more, each time more insistently. Not Poitu, not now, I thought, getting out of the bath. Throwing on a dressing gown, I went to the door.

It was Omar.

"Marsha says I'm not to stay long, I'm not to talk about what happened and I'm not to …" he mused for a moment. "Oh I can't remember," he finished, kissing me on the cheek.

"And this is for you," he handed me a bottle of champagne. "A couple of glasses would nice."

"Celebrating?" I said puzzled, not able to see anything at all worth celebrating.

"I hope so." He sat on the settee, picked up the TV controller and began scanning the channels, while I fetched two glasses from the kitchen.

"To victory," he said, popping the cork on my return, and catching the bubbles in the glasses.

"Yes, I'll always drink to victory, but that's not exactly how it feels to me right …" He held up his hand to cut me short.

"To victory and common sense."

I waited for him to explain.

"Kane has dropped the libel action."

"You're joking," I couldn't believe it.

"OK, it's a joke."

"Omar don't play with me."

"OK, it's not a joke."

"Omar which is it?" I shrieked excitedly.

He shrugged. "I always told you there was no case to answer and it was just a matter of bullyboy tactics."

"Which cost me my job."

"True, but it was a crummy job." He grimaced apologetically, knowing that wasn't quite the case.

"Why?"

"Maybe he's had his fun. He's made his point and pushed it as far as he wants to. He's had you wriggling on a hook, and now he's bored with the game."

"Bastard."

"True. But please don't print that in the newspaper just yet. Let's keep you out of court for a few weeks. And rejoice," he topped up my glass.

Omar was as good as his word. He stayed an hour and we talked only of happy things. I hit the sack shortly after he left. Tomorrow, I wanted to be back in the office early. The truce with KNS meant I could finally contact David Black. He had been the one constant figure in this whole murky pensions business, who had neither disappeared, nor threatened me.

Maybe now we could begin working together. As I drifted off to sleep, I thought a lot about Kane. None of it made any sense. Why launch the case in the first place, and spend a fortune in legal fees, only to withdraw it? And why drop it now?

Chapter Forty-two

7.30am Friday, November 16, Southwark

My first thought when I woke the next morning was to call David Black. I knew exactly where I had left his card. It was in the pocket of my tuxedo.

I headed into the office early, and called around 10am. I cursed when I heard he was away for a long weekend. Did I want to try back on Monday?

"Has he got his mobile with him?" I asked.

"I'm not sure. But there's no reception where he's gone, anyway."

I left my name and number, with a message to get back to me.

Damn. I hadn't long hung up, when the telephone rang. It was Sandy.

"How are you Julia? Did you get home OK?" he asked.

"Yes, and I had some wonderful news waiting for me. Victor Kane has dropped the libel writ."

"That'll help the bruises heal …" he said, sounding genuinely pleased. "And a weight off your mind."

"An enormous weight off my mind," I replied.

"We must celebrate. I'm coming to London tomorrow, with mother and the kids. Would you like to meet up? It's Sarah's birthday. We can have a double celebration."

"All of us?" I asked, tentatively.

"Me and the kids. Mum will probably go off shopping on her own."

In for a penny, in for a pound, I thought.

"OK, I'll see you tomorrow."

"Great … there's something else."

"Uh..huh."

"I'm filing my formal valuation of the Kelly's Brewery Pension fund this afternoon with the regulator."

"That'll be a weight off your mind."

"It will indeed,"

"Can I see it?"

"No."

"Have you found all the money?"

"No … to that as well."

"How much have you found?"

"About a third of it."

"That leaves £2 billion short. Can I write the story?"

"If you feel you have enough to go on."

"Without seeing the report?"

"I can't let you have it. But don't forget, a big chunk of the hole will be markets."

"Dwindling share prices, soaring gilts …"

"Exactly, they hammered the fund."

"We know Kelly took nearly a billion out in those transfers."

"We don't know where it went. We've no evidence they pocketed it themselves."

"They started around the time Tom Kelly bought his first nightclub."

"That's quite a stretch, quite an accusation to make without proof."

"I saw the club. Poitu took me."

"He took you to that cage fight, didn't he? I did wonder."

"You knew about it?"

"Big controversy. Church, politicians, all up in arms. They'll ban it before long."

"He took me to a brothel, too."

"To a what?"

"It was a police raid. Sandy it was awful."

"Yes … Damn," he said, as I heard his mobile go.

"You'd better go …"

I put the phone down, and emailed Ludgate to tell him there was a good story on its way.

'Where the hell have you been?' he replied.

Thank God Poitu had kept it out of the Scottish press. Male editors were prone to panic. Even in this age of equality, they could become very nervous about placing female staff in physical danger. The last thing I needed was to be removed from this story by any old-fashioned sense of chivalry.

Chapter Forty-three

10.30am Saturday, November 17, the London Eye

They were already at the London Eye waiting for me. Sandy was dressed in the same tan leather jacket he had worn at Tarbert. He was bending down, talking to the smallest child, a wisp of his hair flapping loose, as I walked towards them.

"Hi," I called out. He straightened at the sound of my voice. Our eyes locked for just a fraction longer than was respectable, before he came towards me, kissed me on the cheek and then stepped back to introduce the children.

Sarah, the baby, at six, who I could see was besotted by her father, never let go of his hand. In the other, she held a scruffy rabbit. Next was Blair, Philip's age, I guessed. He was the image of Sandy, fair and blue-eyed, and looked full of mischief. His wings had not yet been clipped. Laura, at 12, was the self-appointed mother of the family, while James, a shy, self-conscious 14-year-old, blushed crimson every time I spoke to him.

Sandy had already bought tickets. Holding Sarah's hand tightly, he linked his other arm through mine and we stepped aboard. I relaxed as soon as I felt his touch, and was glad to be with them all, even if the Eye was one of my least favourite attractions. An exhilarating, exciting ride, it is not. It moves tamely and sedately like a barge on the river.

Laura, as the oldest female of the family, decided to befriend me.

"Have you been on the wheel before?" she asked, as we began to move.

"Yes, but not for a while," I replied.

"Oh, I've been on lots. My father has an office in London, we are very frequent visitors, quite a home from home." I smiled at her child-like attempt to impress me.

"Dad, where's that?" Blair asked, racing from one side of the pod to the other. "And where's that?"

I looked across the city I loved. The early mist had not yet cleared the river, so visibility was less than perfect.

"That's the gherkin," his father replied.

"And that?"

"The Post Office tower."

"Which park is that?"

"Regent's."

"That's where the Queen lives, isn't it?"

"That's the one."

I smiled at Sandy's patience with the children.

"We've been to Buckingham Palace, haven't we Dad?" Laura was eager to display her worldly sophistication.

"What do you think, James?" I asked, trying to include him, but he looked right through me.

"Can't hear you," Sandy said, pointing to his ear. Of course, James was plugged into his ipod.

As it always does, the wheel seemed to take an age to complete its journey, and the children's interest was beginning to wane before we were even halfway round. Sarah was sucking her thumb, and her eyes were drooping, tired from the previous evening's journey. I watched her little rabbit slip from her fingers onto the floor. When the wheel stopped, as the crowd moved out, she left it lying there. I picked it up and called after her, but she was leaving the car with her father, and did not turn round when I called, so I slipped it into my bag, for safe-keeping.

Sandy, though, looked back over his shoulder and smiled.

"She'll love you forever for that," he whispered in my ear, as I caught up with them. I hoped so.

"Dad, you said we could go to the Imperial War Museum next." Blair raced behind his father's long strides, taking two for every one.

"Oh no ... I don't want to go to some gory war museum full of dead bodies," Laura objected. Sandy raised his eyes to me as if to say 'help'.

"Actually, it isn't, Laura," I offered. "It's very interesting, and there is a section about women and war. It's more like a history museum, all about families, and how they survived. You'll like it."

"I doubt that."

"Well, if you don't, you and I can leave and go to the Globe, which is nearby. That's Shakespeare's theatre."

"Robbie Burns is better than Shakespeare," Sarah said. "Isn't that right, Dad? My teacher says so."

There was more than a glint of amusement in Sandy's eyes, as they met mine. He, too, was relaxing and enjoying the lazy morning. We wandered along the embankment among the pavement artists, book sellers and street theatre.

"Edinburgh has far better street art than this, doesn't it Dad?" Little Sarah wouldn't give up, and couldn't resist another put-down for my ears.

We sat for a while at a table outside the National Film Theatre. The children had cokes and Sandy and I coffees. The air was chill, but the sun was warming up. River traffic was building. Pleasure craft, tourist boats and tugs glided past. The mist was lifting and a blue sky trying to break.

We finished our drinks and were getting up to leave, when Sarah started to scream, piercingly. Her father crouched down and put his arms comfortingly round her.

"What is it, Sarah, what's wrong?"

"I hate London, I want to go home. I hate it here. I want my mummy," she screamed, opening tearful eyes and looking, pointedly, at me. "I want my mummy, I want my mummy," I watched Sandy's face fall.

"She's lost her rabbit, that's all that's wrong," Blair wasn't having any histrionics from his sister ruin his day.

Laura took charge, pulling chairs out to look under the table for the stuffed animal.

"Silly rabbit," I said, pulling it from my bag, and handing it to the small child. "He got lost."

She stopped crying immediately, and grabbed the battered toy.

Thumb went in and she sucked hard for a few moments, as if contemplating her next move.

Then, she began to scold her beloved friend, "Naughty rabbit … you're a very, very naughty rabbit … naughty rabbit."

But, as we began to walk in the direction of the museum, I felt a little hand creep into mine, and for the rest of the day Sarah didn't let go.

As I predicted, the girls loved the Imperial War Museum as much as their brothers, particularly the scenes of family life in the shelters. The boys were fascinated by the trenches. We grabbed a sandwich at the canteen before heading back to the river, where all the children agreed they wanted to visit the London Dungeons.

Sandy went in first with Blair, followed by Laura and James, with me and Sarah coming up the rear. At first, we were all laughing at the gore displayed in the scenes before us, but I was unprepared for how realistic the suffering quickly became. The museum was packed and we walked through in a tight queue. People squashed up against us, front and behind. It was dark and close, and suddenly I found myself not feeling at all well. A wave of nausea swept over me.

The figures didn't seem like plaster casts any more. They moaned as their torturers whipped and crucified them, tore them in two on racks, or squeezed their thumbs. I couldn't breathe and broke out into an uncomfortable sweat. As soon as I saw the exit, I made a run for it.

I must have looked queer, because Sandy came straight over.

"Are you OK? You look like a ghost," he said.

I tried to nod my head affirmatively.

"I'm not good in dark places. I get claustrophobic."

"I'm sorry, I should have thought. After what happened …"

"No, it's OK, really, I'm OK now," I continued under my breath, so the children wouldn't hear, "Didn't you find all that a bit sick?"

Sarah and Laura came over and each took one of my hands.

"Don't be afraid Julia, it's just make believe" Sarah said, as she gently stroked the back of the hand she was holding. "Don't be afraid, it's just make believe," she repeated.

That evening, we went to see the musical 'Oliver' at the Palladium. At the interval Laura said, "Julia, it must have been awful growing up in London. We're so lucky to live in Edinburgh."

"Did you have to go out stealing, when you were a child?" Sarah asked.

I laughed, explaining that life in London had much improved by the time I was born. As we returned to our seats for the second half, I found myself wondering just how much had truly changed since Dickens' days, and how much hadn't changed at all.

When the show was finished, Sandy asked if I wanted to go back with them, but I declined. This was their last night together as a family for some weeks. They needed time together.

"Tomorrow?" I suggested, gazing deep into his eyes.

"Not really," he said, softly. "I have to get this lot off first thing, and then I'm flying straight back home."

I wanted more than anything to kiss him and the hungry look in his eyes told me he was thinking the same. Our timing was all wrong.

"Thank you for a lovely day," I said.

"Yes, it's been lovely," he smiled.

Had I'd known then, the circumstances which would bring us together again, I would never have let them go.

Chapter Forty-four

10.30am Monday, November 19, Whitechapel

"David Black," the voice said at the other end. "I hear you've been trying to contact me." I was in the office, hoping he would call.

"Ah … Mr Black. It's Julia Lighthorn." I took another deep breath and crossed my fingers. "I wondered if we could meet up … sometime soon … talk."

"Yes, that might be useful. I'm getting very close to having material I would like to share with you. I think we could be of use to each other."

"Sounds promising. When would be convenient?"

"I'm not quite there yet. Various pieces of the jigsaw are coming together. Next week should be good. I'll call you next Monday and sort something out, maybe Tuesday or Wednesday."

"I'll make sure I'm free," I replied, wondering what jigsaw he was putting together, and which pieces were finally slotting into place.

"Good," he replied.

"I'll look forward to hearing from you again," I said, and with that he hung up. My, my, things were getting interesting.

In fact, the week passed uneventfully until Wednesday morning. Marsha was out. I read the newspapers, made a few calls, threw a three-foot high stack of press releases in the bin. Even the phones were unusually quiet, so I flicked on Sky News to see what was happening in the world. An area of Tottenham had been cordoned off by police after a shooting the previous evening. The pound was up, the market was down. A child was killed in Gaza.

I was just fancying a coffee, when, at about 11.30am, I heard the sound of feet thumping up the stairs.

"You've got visitors," Mina shouted from our tiny reception, which puzzled me, as I wasn't expecting anyone. Two heads popped round the door, both wearing Austrian green felt hats with identical feathers.

Sally and Timmy had come to visit.

"Come in, come in," I said, surprise mingling with pleasure. It was a tonic to see them, and they brought with them their own special oasis of sweetness and calm.

"Julia, we hope we're not intruding," Sally was slightly puffed from the climb.

"No, no, not at all, come in, come in."

"Didn't want to bother you," Timmy began.

"But a telephone call seemed ..." Sally shook her head, and tutted.

"And a letter ..." Timmy pulled a disapproving face.

"You said to be your eyes and ears."

"Eyes and ears," Timmy echoed.

"Come and sit down both of you. I'll get us some tea."

The words were hardly out of my lips, when Mina arrived with a tea-tray, her excuse to goggle at our visitors. To this veteran of cardboard city, they were as alien as visitors from Mars.

I poured the tea as Sally and Timmy removed their hats carefully and placed them on the desk in front of them.

"So what brings you both here?"

"Major events," Timmy began.

"Now don't be melodramatic, Septimus," his sister chided. "But there have been developments."

"Developments," Timmy nodded furiously.

"I bumped into Hilda Harris in the post office yesterday," Sally continued. "She was paying a big cheque into her bank account. She says her job is done."

"It must have been severance pay," Timmy pointed out helpfully.

"The divorce has come through, the property has been sold, and it seems," Sally hesitated, as if wanting me to fully appreciate the importance of what she was about the reveal. "According to Mrs Harris ..." she continued.

"Hilda Harris, that is," Timmy helpfully explained

"He has been cleaned right out."

"Taken to the cleaners were her words," Timmy echoed. "Right out.

And we are not talking about the furniture." For once, they were both one step ahead of me.

"Go on," I said.

His sister took up the tale. "She …"

"Edna Patterson … the wife," Timmy interjected.

"Edna, indeed," his sister thanked him. "Anyway, Mrs Patterson got a very smart lawyer, who wrangled all his money off him, poor blighter."

"But surely …"

"Highly unethical in his state," Timmy speculated.

"Oh no," his sister contradicted. "He was given the chance of a legal representative, and was adamant that he didn't want one."

"How convenient," I couldn't resist. It meant Patterson had no assets to claim against, in the unlikely event we were ever able to prove … I still didn't know what, but prove anything.

"What's happened to him?"

"The very worst bit," Timmy shuddered.

"Well, we don't know that for sure, Timmy," his sister cautioned.

"An asylum," Timmy's eyes rolled.

"What?"

"He's gone to St Agatha's. It's a nursing home for people who are …" she hesitated.

"Barking." Timmy winked at me. He was enjoying himself.

"Forgetful," his sister corrected.

We drank more tea, and exchanged pleasantries. Mina admired their hats, although I wasn't entirely sure her compliments were genuine. Then, they headed off to the shops, with plans for catching a matinee before the train home.

"Don't get up to town all that much anymore," Timmy explained. "But we always enjoy it."

"We like to get home again, though, don't we, Timmy?" Sally stood and straightened her hat carefully on her silver hair.

"Yes, we do," he said, also standing. He waited for her to finish with her own hat, and then to position his perfectly on his slightly balding head

"Thank you so much for coming," I showed them out.

"We promised. Eyes and ears." Sally winked.

"Eyes and ears, indeed."

Poitu was the next to call. He was elated.

"I've heard back from Cape Town. They sent some officers out to interview the forensics man."

"What in the middle of the desert?"

"Yes … no … I don't know. Anyway they made contact."

"And?"

"It had been wiped clean."

"What do you mean wiped clean."

"The gun. There were no prints on it."

"Which means?"

"Dead men can't wipe their finger prints off a murder weapon."

"Gloves?"

"No sign."

"Strathclyde must have known."

"They knew alright. He made a full report."

I paused, trying to take in what he was telling me.

"So Ken and his family were murdered."

"It's hard to draw any other conclusion."

"Why wasn't he called to the inquest?"

"Sent abroad shortly after filing the report … presumed it would be put before the inquest. He'd done his job."

"Priceless," I spat. "How many more times do we have to hear of police cover-ups, for anything to change. I never believed those rumours about police statements being changed after that football disaster. Now I'm beginning to wonder. How can you bear working for such a corrupt force?"

"If you're going to insult me, I have better things to do." He slammed down the phone. I immediately redialled his number.

"OK, I'm sorry."

"That's better."

"Did you get anything from those men you arrested in Gallow Terrace? Anything that could lead to the Kellys?"

"Not yet, but they've been charged with brothel keeping and pimping. It's enough to hold them in custody and continue questioning."

"If Ken didn't kill his family, then who did?"

"And who killed Livingstone?" the inspector added.

"Nothing to say they were killed by the same murderer, of course."

"There's nothing to say categorically they were murdered."

"We always come back to the beginning of the circle." I sighed. "What about the suicide note? Did the forensics man know anything about that?"

"Zilch. De nada. I've told you before, there was no note."

"All we do is go round and round in circles."

"Be patient, Hornblower. Softly, softly, we catchy-this-monkey."

Chapter Forty-five

11.30pm Sunday, November 25, Southwark

I decided I wouldn't wait for Black to call, but would telephone him first thing Monday morning, and try and see him the same day. If he had any information to unlock this puzzle, we needed it urgently. All day Sunday, I could hardly think of anything else, sensing I was on the verge of a major breakthrough. I felt it in my bones.

I was getting into bed on Sunday evening, when the phone rang. I wasn't expecting anyone to call, but I got up to answer it, anyway. My blood froze when I heard a digital voice at the other end reciting an eerie computer-generated message.

'Dead men tell no tales, geddit? Dead men tell no tales, geddit? Dead men tell no tales, geddit? Dead men tell no tales, geddit?'

I slammed the phone down, and stood shaking in shock. It rang again, and on impulse, I stupidly picked up.

'Dead men tell no tales, geddit? Dead men tell no tales, geddit? Dead men tell no tales, geddit? Dead men tell no tales, geddit?' the sick mantra repeated.

I slammed the phoned down. Almost immediately, it rang again. This time I didn't pick up, but the poisonous loop rang out from my answer machine.

'Dead men tell no tales, geddit? Dead men tell no tales, geddit? Dead men tell no tales, geddit? Dead men tell no tales, geddit.'

I lifted the receiver and slammed it down, to shut it up. But it rang again straight away.

"Julia, pick up, pick up." It was Poitu.

"Julia. Black is dead."

I couldn't understand him.

"Black?"

"The banker, Kane's man."

"He can't be dead, I'm seeing him tomorrow."

"He's dead alright."

"How? What happened?"

"Shot dead."

"By whom?"

"We don't know, a lone gunman."

"Jesus Christ."

"I know, I know," even Poitu was starting to sound rattled.

"Where are you now?"

"In the car, on my way. It's a good drive from Glasgow. His house is in a remote spot in Perthshire. Apparently, the family were watching TV. Door bell rang. He went to open it and bang, bang, he's dead."

"Black lives in Farnham. It can't be him."

"His wife is Scottish. They have a second home up north."

"Jesus."

In that instance, I saw it all. His house in Perthshire; the wife coming to the door, her hands flying to her head as she began to scream hysterically. I saw the children running out behind her, to see their father lying blood-splattered on the hall carpet.

"He told me, what did he say …" I paused, "something about a jigsaw and the pieces coming together. Is it possible he was on to something? The reward, you said it would flush something out. What if Black was behind it?"

"And what if he was screwing the postmistress, and an angry boyfriend lost his rag. There's no evidence any of this is connected with the Kellys."

I told him about the threatening calls.

"I see," his voice was grim. "It'll be on an automatic timer, probably trying to get through now. I'll get it checked out. Unplug the phone when I hang up. They'll only run it for a short time to avoid being traced."

"That poor family," I said.

"Indeed … and I'll see them soon,"

"Heaven help you. Dear God, what have we got ourselves involved with?"

"I'll let you know as soon as I get some concrete news. Be careful. Don't answer the door to anyone and make sure you …"

"Lock the doors and windows, I know."

Poitu shut down the line, and I unplugged the phone, as he instructed.

Sleep was now out of the question. Flicking on News 24, I caught the first reports of a shooting coming in from Perthshire. Details were sketchy. The news crews didn't know he was a banker, nor would they until much later the next day. They had no theories to offer about precisely who had been killed, or why. I checked my watch. I could just make the next morning's last edition. I called the office and was told to file a few brief paragraphs. I didn't add much to the news broadcasts, other than the name and profession, but it meant we had a bit of a scoop.

Finally, I climbed into bed, where I lay tossing and turning. I had been so sure that seeing David Black would provide the breakthrough I had longed for. Now it was another dead end. Literally.

Chapter Forty-six

11am Monday, November 26, Whitechapel

I couldn't bear the thought of being cooped up in the flat the next day, so went to the office as usual, and spent much of it glued to the television coverage of David Black's murder, as if hypnotised by mugshots of his face. It had been a kindly face. I remembered how I had thought at the Mansion House dinner, he had the sort of face I normally warmed to.

His wife gave a short interview to the cameras. I bit my lip so hard watching her quiet dignity, it started to bleed.

Sandy called, and I could tell he was shaken.

"They say a gunman came to the door, shot him at blank range. No motive … no reason," he said.

"He'd been investigating the Kellys."

"Julia, we all knew Kane was Kelly's banker. Nothing explains this. It's insane."

"It has to be connected, Sandy."

"I can't believe it … he paused, then added nervously, "d'you think maybe you should go abroad for a while? A holiday. Just until things blow over."

"I'll go, if you'll come with me," I replied, with a hint of tease.

Despite everything, he laughed, and I knew he was smiling at the other end of the line.

"That's an invitation I plan to accept very soon," he said, his voice thickening slightly, before becoming serious again. "There's nothing more I'd love than to get away now, but it's not possible."

Poitu was as good as his word and kept in regular touch.

"It was a professional job alright. Arrived, bang, and disappeared without trace, probably caught a boat to the continent within an hour."

"That'd be an achievement from Perthshire," I said.

"They've long gone, without a trace," he continued, "deep country all around. Black's home is in the middle of the hills. No witnesses. No one saw anything."

"Interpol?"

"Of course. We're talking to everyone who knew him. We have to find a motive."

"Poitu, we've got the motive, haven't we? He must've been on to something."

"If he was, there's no evidence of it here in his home. No papers, no files. Nothing."

"Have you spoken to the bank?"

"Briefly, they're in a state of shock."

After he hung up, I went back over, again and again, everything that had happened since Ken Strachan and his family were murdered on October 3. They were killed by a gun, which had been wiped clean. He had been investigating a pension scandal and had befriended a girl who had disappeared. His diary hinted at secrets and talked of 'killing both birds with one stone'.

Sandy calculated the pension fund was the best part of £2 billion short, and believed around £1 billion had been channelled directly into Kelly coffers. He could prove monthly withdrawals of £15 million had begun five years ago, but had no evidence of where the money went.

One of the actuaries involved was in a high security mental institution, and another had been fished out of the Clyde.

David Black was Kelly's banker and had launched his own investigation for KNS. He may have been behind the big reward and maybe it had bought him information. But now he was dead.

So many fragments, yet nothing fitted. It was dark outside when I left the office. An early winter night had fallen, the sort which snuffs out the day suddenly and unexpectedly. I used to love the dark, but not any more.

I caught a bus along the embankment and crossed the river on foot. A mist was rising, so the glitter of the lights running along the banks and bridges were faint and fragile.

Even these dimmed, as I cut through deserted back streets. The air was damp, the sort that chilled right through to the bones, and my breath blew cobweb rings. I shivered as I approached a tunnel I had to cross to reach my flat. I thought of Bonfire Night with Sandy. It was in the same dark tunnel, where we had both let our guards down for the first time and finally got close.

It was an old railway bridge. Normally I passed through without a second thought. But I hesitated and looked around, to make sure I was safe. There was no one around. I was completely alone.

My feet clattered on the cobbles, as I walked on faster, the noise amplified yet distorted by the echo in the tunnel. Half-way down I froze. A figure stepped out, blocking my exit. In the shadow of a single street light, a male figure, cigarette in hand, glistening like fresh blood, was waiting for me. My mind flashed back to my ordeal in the brewery. I thought of David Black and of Livingstone. Fear stabbed at my not yet healed bruises.

Adrenaline started to pump through my veins. I was trapped. I heard a rustle to the side, as a rat rushed along the tunnel wall. Turn and run, a voice whispered in my ear. Turn and run. You outran them before, you can do it again.

I started to turn, to make my escape, when a voice boomed towards me. "Don't be afraid." The tunnel acted as a megaphone. My heart raced even faster at his words. I recognised the voice immediately. The man blocking my exit was Victor Kane.

"Don't be afraid, Ms Lighthorn." He held out his hand. "We need to talk."

The shadow lifted from his face gradually as I got nearer. He looked pale, and frailer than when I had seen him before.

"Is there somewhere we could be alone to talk?" He was carrying a box file under his arm.

"About Black?"

He nodded, letting the cigarette stub fall to the ground. I could see the lights of Southwark Cathedral a few yards away. There would be no one there at this time. Evensong congregation would be long gone.

"The cathedral?" I pointed to the building ahead. He nodded and we walked towards it in silence. He didn't stop to stamp out the stub, but left it burning on the kerb.

The church was dimly-lit and empty, so we took a pew in front of the Shakespeare memorial. This was the writers' church, a short walk from the Globe.

Kane took off his round glasses and wiped them with his handkerchief, before replacing them on his nose. Next, he screwed up his brown eyes to look at me. I looked into his face again. He looked sad, but he didn't speak, so I began.

"You dropped the libel case." It was meant to be an icebreaker.

"That's not what I want to talk about. That's history. A sideshow. Over."

"A sideshow? You ruined my career, and made my life a misery."

"You underestimate yourself, my dear," his tone was almost affectionate. "I hadn't thought to bring all that up, but now that you have … what was it you called me?"

My cheeks started to tingle, but I didn't respond.

"'Killer Kane'," he reminded me, "'An archetype among city assassins' … 'Kane but not able' … hardly original that one." His eyes were smiling, as though he had finally got the joke.

A side door opened and an elderly woman entered, moving to the front of the church to pray. I wondered what on earth she was doing out on such a miserable night.

"It wasn't libellous. You over-reacted," I said.

"I have a share price to protect. Every time you published one of your sharp-tongued articles, my share price suffered. That hits the savings of ordinary people and their pensions. Did you never once stop to think about that? I have a duty to protect their interests."

"And your share options," I couldn't resist. "What are you worth now?"

The woman in the pew got up from her knees to light a candle. I guessed it must be an anniversary of the death of someone she loved.

"That's a complete irrelevance. And if I may say so, very tactless in the circumstances."

His jaw quivered slightly. Black's murder had hit him hard.

"I will acknowledge though, Julia," he continued, speaking softly. "May I call you Julia? That the Mainland takeover was not my finest hour. I went too far. Your comments hit home because …"

"They were true …"

"There was an element of truth in them. Shall we agree that, on that occasion, we both went over the top?"

We agreed a truce.

"That's not what's brought me here," he continued.

He opened the box file on his lap, and took out three thick folders. He closed the lid and rested the folders on top.

"The first thing I want to say is we had no knowledge of any of this. We were Kelly's banker. That is all. I want you to believe that."

I nodded.

"When the Strachans were killed, things started to look very wrong. I asked David to find out what was going on. I couldn't allow the bank to be exposed to, potentially, criminal activity. He hired a private investigator."

"Who followed me?"

"From the start, you were out front with all the leads. You were our best source."

"Did Black offer the reward?"

"Yes, he did. And it was money well spent …" he stopped. "Well spent until …" He didn't finish.

I nodded, understandingly.

"With the help of the detective agency, he compiled a dossier. He planned to hand it all over to you, with my blessing, but …"

"He didn't get the chance," I finished for him.

"Do what you will with this, but keep me and the bank out of it," he said, handing me the first file.

I opened it carefully. Inside were bank statements going back almost a decade, every transaction, in and out. Flicking through the pieces of paper, I found Kelly's main corporate accounts, plus a dozen or so off-shore accounts and trust funds.

"You'll need to get a forensic accountant on to these, but you have enough here to show that the money, which came out of the pension fund, went first into a bank in Bermuda, then to another in the Cayman Islands. Then, it was transferred to an account in Singapore, before being used to fund a trust fund in Liechtenstein."

"All places the UK authorities have no reach," I said. It was too much to take in.

"Quite. It is all here, bank details, account numbers and codes. You have bank statements from all relevant accounts, and can trace money in and money out. The sums add up. It's not too difficult to follow."

He handed me a second file.

"These are the full accounts of the pension fund. They show, as your friend Mr Ross has already told you, that Patterson authorised £15 million monthly withdrawals, beginning five years ago. Thanks to Cameron valuations, £360 million was withdrawn and the company enjoyed a payment holiday."

"Kelly put nothing in and took everything out."

"Exactly. A further £540 million came out via these monthly withdrawals under Sherlock, before the scheme collapsed. Tell your Mr Ross to look at the pages documenting changes on February last year and August 1999."

My eye whizzed down the fifth page. "Crikey, in February, the scheme raised the pension age to 70."

"Yes."

I flicked back several pages. "And in August 1999 to 67. And shortly after those two dates, a further £200 million was removed. The staff, the unions, knew nothing about this. And what about the trustees …"

"Quite. The main board was not informed either."

"David Black …"

"Knew nothing, I can assure you, until much later."

"By increasing the retirement age, the liabilities dropped, so technically further withdrawals were legal."

"So it could be argued in court, if everything was conducted legally and according to the protocols."

"But it wasn't, was it. Ken was right all along. Kelly stole their pensions."

"As I say, your Mr Ross will know what to do with all this."

He handed me the third file.

"This one, I think you will find the most interesting of all. It is the assets held by the Liechtenstein Trust Fund."

"How did you get this stuff?"

"David was one of my best men. You will see the trust owns Tom Kelly's nightclubs and a range of other property. With the help of the private detective, David did what he could to find out what activities were going on at these premises."

I flicked through the dossier. It was full of addresses, underlined as headings, with detailed briefings on each of them. Information was attributed to five different sources, the recipients of bribe money no doubt.

One address jumped out at me, '13 Gallow Terrace', the brothel I had attended with Poitu. 'Destroyed by fire' was written by another, followed by a short report.

It read:

'24 Crossglen; destroyed in a blaze on November 16 last year. The premises were a textile factory, staffed by illegal immigrants. They all disappeared. A cabin at the back was used as a heroin factory. A chemist brought in from the Ukraine refined the heroin. He was killed in the fire. The cabin was burned to the ground and all trace of his body removed. Fire brigade and police told it was a store room for the textile factory and did not investigate further.'

My hand flew to my mouth.

"The girl that Strachan befriended. Her father was killed in a fire," I said.

Kane simply nodded.

"Clubs … prostitution … drugs," I said, glancing over the pages. "Tom Kelly's empire. But was any of this connected with Kelly's Brewery and the pension fund? With the deaths of the Strachans, Livingstone and Black?"

Kane winced slightly at the last name.

"Read these accounts and reports carefully," he said. "They build a picture of a traditional family business in trouble. A family determined to preserve its position in society. A family looking for more lucrative money-making opportunities."

"Where does the pension fit in?"

"Study the accounts," he repeated. "As the pension scheme shrank, Tom Kelly's empire flourished. You can trace the money out, to the purchase of his properties."

"Would all this stand up in court?"

"It might. It'd need a water-tight case, probably confessions. Start with Patterson." He opened the bank statement file again.

"Look here," he pointed to a payment of £1.2 million. "He received this ex gratia payment for his services. What services? Cameron was already well-paid."

"It was a bribe to agree those transfers?"

"Go and see him. I think you'll find he's ready to be helpful."

I mulled this over.

"Have you seen him?"

"I think you'll find he's ready to be helpful," he repeated.

"Why are you doing this? Why are you helping me?"

"One of my senior staff is dead."

"Aren't you afraid?" I asked.

"They wouldn't dare. Anyway, I'm well protected."

"Why not take it straight to the police?"

He took off his glasses and began cleaning them again. He seemed miles away as he spoke.

"We are bankers. We must respect the confidentiality of our clients. Our clients don't like it, if they see us turning over details of other customers' finances to the police."

248

"Even of murderers?"

"It is a breach of our terms and conditions."

"Why choose me?"

"This may sound strange, but I admire your work. You're like me. You never give up."

"So, Omar was right about the libel action. You just wanted to frighten me."

"We saved you from a brutal attack. And these papers will build you a far more glittering career than the one you claim I destroyed. That makes us quits, doesn't it?"

We got up to leave, and walked together, slowly down the cathedral aisle to the exit.

"It all started with Patterson, didn't it?" I said.

"They needed money desperately, and he found a way for them to get it."

"Why? He was at the top of his profession."

"Weak. Patterson was weak ... and arrogant. Convinced himself it was all above board."

"Do you think he's genuinely ill?"

"Guilt can do strange things to people."

And with those words we parted. I watched him walk back towards the river, disappearing gradually into the mist.

Chapter Forty-seven

8.15pm Monday, November 26, Southwark

I ran the hundred or so yards to my flat, dropped the box-file onto the table and dialled Poitu's number. I had to tell him about the addresses in these files. If Black's dossier was correct, it was possible Roxy was being held at one of these properties.

His mobile clicked onto answer phone. I left a message, remembering he was in the wilds of Perthshire, so there was no knowing when it would get through to him. I tried his office at the Met, and was assured they would try and get a message through to him. Finally, I called Strathclyde, and spoke to a duty officer who said 'No," he wasn't sure where he was, but 'Yes," he would try and contact him.

I flicked the switch on the kettle, took off my coat and made myself a cup of coffee, before dialling Sandy and asking him to come south the next day.

"That's going to be difficult, Julia."

"Please, Sandy."

"Are you OK?"

"Yes, fine. I can't go into details now, but trust me. It's urgent."

"Well … it'll be awkward, but I could cancel my meetings tomorrow and fly down."

"Fly into Southampton, will you?"

He paused for a moment, as if trying to work out what I was up to.

"Fine," he gave up, with a sigh. "If that's what you want. Meet me, I'll text you the time."

I spent the evening analysing the documents Kane had given me. The Liechtenstein Trust dossier made the most interesting reading. There were 34 addresses in all, scattered around Scotland's major cities, from Dundee to Perth, Inverness to Stirling. Most though were in Glasgow, with a few in Edinburgh. I copied Sandy a set of the papers, to hand him the next day. For the time being, I didn't want anything traceable on email. Who knew what spies were lurking on my computer?

Then, I copied another set for me to take and two more. One copy, I placed in an envelope for my brother in Australia, and addressed another to Carlton Crabb. He had proved himself strangely trustworthy from the start. I thought about ringing Omar, but his being a lawyer, my lawyer, complicated everything. There was still an injunction out prohibiting me from interviewing Patterson. He would insist I let Sandy go alone.

Poitu had not returned my call, when it was time to go to bed, so I tried him again. Nothing. The next morning, I posted the packages before hitting the road to Southampton.

Sandy's flight was on time, so I pulled into the designated pick-up area to wait. I turned on the radio to catch the 10 o'clock news. But I soon stopped listening, when I saw a tall man, with a Trilby atop iron-grey hair, walk through the airport doors and get into a black limousine, parked illegally right outside. I would know Jack Kelly, anywhere.

The car pulled off seconds before Sandy emerged and walked over to the prescribed pick up area.

"I hope this is going to be good," he leaned across the car and greeted me with a kiss. I was too preoccupied to respond. "Could have been better," he teased, as he pulled his seat belt on.

"Sandy, we need to see Patterson, urgently." I swung the car round the roundabout and headed back to the M27, at top speed.

"What's the urgency?"

"It's a long story." I threw his set of documents onto his lap. "Did you see anyone on your flight?"

"Lots of people, why?"

"Look back on the inside lane. We've just passed Jack Kelly. He came out of the airport before you."

"What's he doing here?" Sandy turned back to face the road ahead.

"My guess is, he's going to exactly same place we are."

As I checked my mirror, I saw the limousine pull over to a service station.

"They're stopping for petrol, or breakfast. Good. He didn't see me. That leaves us a fighting chance."

"A fighting chance of what? Julia please stop speaking in riddles."

"A fighting chance of getting to Patterson first."

But Sandy had stopped listening. He was working his way through the documents, shaking his head thoughtfully, as though it confirmed much of what he already suspected.

Patterson's nursing home was deep in the New Forest. I knew the way. It was a crisp south coast winter's day; strong sun, and cloudless blue sky. The leafless trees stood ramrod straight, like ghostly, silver sentinels.

Sandy winced as he reached the dossier on the trust fund, with the addresses, and briefing notes. The forest was deserted, our only companions the wild forest ponies and deer.

"Where did you get this stuff?" he asked, when he finally looked up. I told him about the previous evening's encounter with Kane.

"So, he thinks Patterson will confess," he said.

I nodded. "He said that would clinch it."

"Yeah and a few others. But how?"

"I dunno … from the way Kane was speaking …"

"They've already done a deal."

"I dunno," I repeated. "Something must be going on. What's Kelly doing here? I wonder if Patterson knows about Black and Livingstone? Maybe we should play up the danger he's in."

"I don't think there's anything to play up, Julia," he looked at me, wryly.

St Agatha's, formerly the ancestral home of a military family, was at the end of a long lane, with a statue of a general on a horse in the centre of the front lawn. Today, all fight had gone out of this place. It was inhabited by patients, who had surrendered in that great battle called life.

"I can't be myself," I said, as I moved to get out of the car. Sandy raised his eyebrows. "The injunction, remember. I'm not allowed to be here."

"OK, let's play it by ear," he replied.

A bruiser of a man, more nightclub bouncer than Florence Nightingale, stood at the front entrance.

"Can I help you?" he said.

"We have come to visit Mr Patterson."

"Visitors are only allowed by prior appointment. Do you have appointments?"

"No, but as we are old family friends, holidaying in the area, we thought we should pop in for a few moments, with Christmas coming."

"Hardly Christmas yet," he muttered, turning and pointing inside. "Try reception, they may be able to help."

We followed his directions to the incongruously-named 'Welcome Desk'.

"This place is like a prison," I muttered to Sandy.

"Quite."

We gave our details at the reception, claiming again to be close family friends. The girl on reception was chatty, if none too bright. I crossed my fingers, hoping our luck might be in.

"Mr Patterson is popular. Had a very important-looking visitor a few days ago, and expecting another at noon. And now you turn up."

The clock above the desk said 11.35am. I felt my pulse quicken. We had to get in and out before Kelly arrived.

The receptionist picked up a phone and dialled a number. "I'll let Mr Patterson's ward know you are here. You're supposed to make an appointment," she winked, "but as it's nearly Christmas ..."

Someone answered, and she said, "I'll show them through ... Yes, of course, I'll run the security."

She put the receiver down, pushed a book in our direction, and asked for identification. Sandy filled it in as Mr and Mrs Ross and handed over his ID. She seemed happy with this, and didn't question us further.

"We'll have to get away within ten minutes or so, if we want to avoid Kelly," I whispered to Sandy.

Patterson was sitting at a small round table, waiting for us, when we were led from the elegant hall to a back sitting room. He was still dressed pristinely in pin-stripe suit and red bow tie. Other patients sat at tables, or in wide-winged armchairs, some staring blankly into space, others muttering to themselves. A few had visitors.

"How are you?" Sandy stretched out his hand to the frail figure, who stood to greet us.

"Very much better, since I saw you last, very much better …" So, he knew who we were.

There were three exits from this room, besides the one we had entered, with guards on each door. This was a place from which there would be no easy escape.

The furnishings and décor were luxurious. The off-white carpet was soft as velvet under foot; the armchairs around Patterson's table a neat, bucket-shaped velveteen. Sandy neared a powder blue one, I picked the salmon-pink and Patterson sat again in a white seat.

"Would you like some tea?" he asked, as we sat. We nodded, at which he called one of the attendants and courteously asked if some tea could be brought. The 'nurse' looked like he could put four squaddies through a plate glass shop front with one hand.

"It's been an interesting couple of weeks," Patterson sighed. I wasn't sure if he was referring to his incarceration here or the deaths north of the Border.

"Are you comfortable? Do they look after you well?" Sandy asked kindly. I was quiet, as if suffering from lock jaw.

"Ah …" Patterson sighed again. He looked down, shaking his head. We watched him in silence for a few moments. When he looked up again, I swear there were tears in his eyes.

Patterson composed himself as the 'nurse' placed a tea tray on the table between us.

"Thank you, Ronnie," he said, handing us a cup each, "Sugar?"

"No, thank you," Sandy answered for us both. We sipped for a few minutes in silence. Fine rain had begun falling in delicate sheets. I looked out the vast windows and noticed how late the last golden fall had come this far south. Soon all the trees in the forest would be naked.

"We wanted to see you about the Kelly pension," Sandy began.

Patterson was silent, sipping his tea thoughtfully, as if savouring the last few moments of a perfect world, a world about to shatter. He made no attempt this time to deny recollection.

"You must make a statement," Sandy continued.

"If I thought …" Patterson began.

"Mr Patterson. We could get you out of here." I had found my voice.

He raised his eyes to the four doors, taking in the guards, as if doubting my statement.

"You could be in danger." Sandy's voice was low. "I have to warn you, Livingstone is dead. He worked for Sherlock, took over the account after Cameron. That leaves only you, who knows what went on."

Patterson listened, saying nothing. His right hand began to tremble. His cup and saucer tinkled as it shook.

"A banker has been killed." Sandy continued. "I have been threatened. My children, too. Ms Lighthorn here was attacked, and might have been killed."

"Jack Kelly is on his way to see you now," I continued. "He will never leave you alone, Mr Patterson. You or your family. Unless we put him behind bars."

At that moment, a woman in a white coat entered the room and marched across to us. She seemed agitated. She did not look at us, but focussed on Patterson.

"Mr Patterson, I wonder if we could have a quiet word."

He looked at her resigned, as if he knew what was coming.

"Mr Patterson," she repeated.

"I will come and see you directly my guests leave, doctor." His attempt at firmness was feeble.

"We must speak immediately. You have another visitor due soon."

She reached across and grabbed both his hands. "You are not well. I cannot allow this. It is too much."

She signalled to the heavies to approach, and then turned to us with a diplomatic smile. "I'm very sorry, I must ask you to leave."

Sandy looked at his watch. I already knew it was 11.50am. "We have to go anyway," he said, standing. "Mr Patterson, if I can help you any time, you call me."

There was no arguing. The heavies moved closer. Leaving was the only dignified course of action left. We were frogmarched across the lounge. As we reached the door, I looked back. Patterson was being marched out another exit. As I stared at him, so he looked back at me. His eyes had the look of an old dog, who knows its days are numbered.

I let out a stream of expletives once back out on the drive and kicked the gravel in frustration. Sandy walked straight for the car and waited until I joined him, rain splashing off his shoulders.

A limousine swept into the drive. Jack Kelly had arrived. There was no point trying to hide. His car pulled up beside ours. I waited for him to get out.

"Ross," he nodded a brusque acknowledgement to Sandy, before turning to me. "You'll never learn will you, Red."

"Learn what Mr Kelly?"

"What a very dangerous person you are." He flashed that sinister white smile.

"Me, dangerous?" I said, slowly.

"Think about it, Red," he said, before rushing in out of the rain.

I climbed back behind the wheel and started to drive. Sandy didn't say anything, but his face was taut. He was as angry as me, but he was trained not to show his emotions.

"Do you want to head back?" I asked, pulling out of the drive.

"No, I could do with a drink and something to eat."

I remembered a watering hole at Buckler's Hard, I had discovered, when I'd been sacked and had run away to the New Forest to hide. It was barely half a mile. I knew the way, the food was good and it would be quiet at this time of day. I headed in that direction. A slight mist was creeping off the Solent, as we parked outside the Master Builders. On the clearest of days, this waterfront was a place of ghosts. Nelson's Victory fleet had been built in the old shipyard, and a flotilla of small craft had mustered here before setting off for Dunkirk.

A roaring log fire was burning in the grate to welcome us into the Master Builders, the home of Nelson's master shipbuilders. Sandy ordered two drinks and a shepherd's pie lunch for himself. I couldn't face food. Gradually, the colour returned to his face.

"We were so close," he said, licking the froth from his pint off his lips.

"I wonder if Kelly rang ahead, and got us turfed out."

He shrugged. "Maybe."

"Dreadful place. Do you think it's legal?"

"Private hospitals aren't regulated, Julia. They can do as they please."

"Those guards were scary. You know, I almost felt sorry for him."

"Don't waste your time."

His lunch arrived.

"Another drink?" I asked, emptying my glass. "I'll go to the bar."

"Half please."

There was no one else at the bar. The weather had kept both locals and tourists at home. The bar man was lonely. He wanted to talk.

"Nasty weather this. Far to go?" he asked, in the soft burr of Hampshire.

"I've to get back to London tonight, but my friend's heading for Edinburgh."

"Not flying, I hope. Southampton's shut. Fog-bound. Nothing'll take off t'nite"

"Oh dear."

"Weather's been terrible for days. Yacht went down yesterday rounding the Needles. One of them city types. More money'n sense. Buys a boat for half-a-million, takes it out and holes it on its maiden voyage."

"Uh..huh," I grunted, wondering how Sandy would get home.

"Lifeboat crew had to go out. Helicopter 'n all. Were a close call."

"But they got them off?"

"They did. But it makes me mad."

"Uh..huh."

"Boat wore smashed to smithereens. Serves 'm right. Hope the insurance refuses to pay up. Bloody fools. It's the crews, I worry about. These playboys risk the lives of men worth a hundred times their salt."

I returned to the table in front of the fire.

"Barman says Southampton flights are cancelled because of the fog. What will you do?"

"Do they have rooms here? I could always stay for the night." He looked at me. I knew what his eyes were asking.

"I'll check with the airport. If you can't get back tonight, we might as well stay here. You can fly out first thing, when the mist lifts."

I opened my bag to get out my phone, and saw it immediately. A large white envelope, which I certainly hadn't put there. I took it out carefully. It was addressed to 'Mr Alexander Ross'.

Without speaking, I threw the envelope on the table. He picked it up and turned it over in his fingers.

"Where did this come …"

"I've no idea. Someone must have slipped it into my bag. It's nothing to do with me."

We stared at each other.

"It's addressed to you."

My heart pounded as I watched him tear open the white paper, and unfold a piece of A4 paper, covered in spidery writing. He started reading intensely. Sweat broke out in my palms, as I held my breath. As he read, his face relaxed, and then, very gradually, broke into a smile.

"We've done it," he said, when he reached the end. "Julia, we've done it." He pulled me to him and plonked a big kiss firmly on my lips. Then, he was laughing, laughing, as though his wildest dream had just come true.

"Read," he said, pushing the letter into my hands. It was dated a few days ago.

'November 25

Dear Mr Ross,

I am aware that you are acting as independent actuary in the case of the collapsed Kelly pension fund. You recently visited me to ask me a number of questions in connection. I am afraid I have been unwell in recent months, and suffered lapses in memory.

However, I was recently admitted to a psychiatric hospital where, under treatment, my condition has improved. I would now like to offer you the following information.

I was the appointed actuary to the Kelly's Superannuation Pension Scheme during the period you raised with me. Jack Kelly, managing director, approached me because the company was in difficulty. He needed cash to make investments both in the company and elsewhere.

He asked to make significant withdrawals from the pension fund, which I told him I could not legitimately approve. He offered me a £1.25 million fee, if I could devise a way it could legally be done.

I devised a scheme for making regular withdrawals. However, these depended for their legality on my valuing the fund in a way which would normally be considered a contravention of the high standards of our profession and in violation of my obligation to protect the public interest.

I am profoundly sorry for the action that I took, and now wish to set the record straight.

Yours'

I folded the letter and placed it on the table.

"He must have slipped it into my bag. But why give it to us? And why now?"

"He's scared. Livingstone would have shaken him, but Black's murder must have petrified him. Kelly was on his way down to see him. He's scared out of his wits."

"There was that other important visitor the girl mentioned. That had to be Kane. Do you think he offered him some kind of deal?"

"It's possible. Implicate Kelly, or my bank will freeze every penny you and your precious Edna possess."

"And he could. Maybe the illness was a cover all along? Edna takes the money, goes abroad, he recovers and joins her once it's all died down and the band wagon's moved on."

"Maybe ..."

"This gives you what you need though, doesn't it ... to go after the professional insurers? Cameron's too?"

"Maybe ..." he repeated. "Let's wait and see what the lawyers say. But first ..." His face broke into an enormous smile, as he placed his arm round me and pulled me closer. "Let's see if we can get a room."

Chapter Forty-eight

7pm Tuesday, November 27, Buckler's Hard

When it came to it, we booked two rooms. I guess I bottled it again. Sandy raised his eyes to heaven as I ordered two singles, but said nothing. We parted to go to our separate rooms. We both had work to do. We agreed to meet at 7pm in the bar, and, unless the weather had worsened, take a stroll around the tiny harbour, before eating.

I kept trying to call Poitu. I was desperate to reach him. It was hopeless.

Sandy was already waiting when I appeared at the bar. He gulped down the last dregs of his glass, and pulled on his jacket. Outside, it was dark, but the mist was thinning, making it possible to glimpse a couple of stars through the haze.

"It'll be clear in the morning," I said, as we walked slowly along the water's edge.

"I hope so," he replied. "I need to get back."

"Me, too."

"I need to speak to the lawyers immediately."

We walked towards the marina, and I could hear the distant tinkle of the riggings, like fairy bells in the wind. He took my hand. He felt warm and protective. I wished we could stay there forever.

"What a long time ago it all began," Sandy muttered.

"Yes … a financial scandal, Strachan's death …" I left the list unfinished.

"We've learnt a lot," he said.

"A lot, but not enough," I replied, thinking of the girl.

"It's never enough." There was a distance in his voice.

We walked on a while further. The wind was whipping up.

"We should be turning back," Sandy said, but I wasn't ready yet. I was enjoying the walk and wanted it to last a while longer.

"Not yet. Look there's an old boathouse up there, let's take a look inside."

We opened the door and stepped into a Tardis. From the outside it looked like a glorified shed, but inside was enormous. Sandy switched on an electric light, which glowed brightly enough through multiple layers of cobwebs and dust.

There were four boats in different states of repair, a work bench, and desk. Sandy was fascinated. He left me to walk around the boathouse, studying each vessel in detail and commenting on different aspects of shape and design. It was all lost on me. But as I watched him, I wanted to know more about boats and the sea, to share his passion. I so wanted to be part of his life.

When he came back to me, he slowly, deliberately, took me in his arms and kissed me with every fibre of his being. His fire burnt right through me. We skipped dinner for an early night, and didn't need those two rooms, after all. Don't ask me how many times we made love. I have no idea. I only remember it was the most wonderful night of my life.

Chapter Forty-nine

7am Wednesday, November 28, New Forest

After that night, events began to move rapidly, beyond my control, beyond the control of any of us.

We rose early. The mist had lifted. But while we breakfasted in my room, Sandy's phone rang. It was Joe from Tarbert. His cottage had been broken into over night.

"My car's at the airport. I'll drive straight up." We set off for the airport soon afterwards.

"I could do with a couple of days peace and quiet, to go through these documents properly," he said, kissing me farewell at the airport. "We have to have absolutely everything buttoned down."

"I'll miss you," I said, kissing him back.

"Let's get through the next few days," his voice softened. "Then, maybe, we can get on with the rest of our lives."

Poitu called as I was rounding the M25, so I turned off at the next exit, pulled in at a service station and called him straight back.

"Where've you been? I've been frantic."

"Some of us have more important things to do than entertain elderly colonels in Tunbridge Wells. What's so urgent anyway?"

I recounted, as succinctly as I could, the encounter with Kane and the Liechtenstein Trust Fund dossier, with the list of addresses.

"I need to see this," he said.

"I'm concerned about security … email … fax," I replied.

"Where are you?"

"'Bout ten minutes from Heathrow."

"Excellent. Get the next flight to Glasgow. I'll meet you."

With that instruction he hung up. I didn't hesitate, but started the car and head for terminal one. I picked up a standby, taking off within the hour.

I decided not to call Sandy and let him know I was coming north. He had enough to deal with and didn't need me as a distraction.

Chapter Fifty

1pm Wednesday, November 28, Glasgow airport

Poitu was waiting for me on the road directly outside the airport. Although he drove an unmarked BMW, I guessed he must have police authorisation to park so close. We drove straight to Strathclyde HQ. Poitu entered the premises like he owned them. No longer an outsider.

"She's with me," he said to the officer on the main desk, as he swung through security, and into a small windowless interview room, with the word 'Press' on the door.

We sat at a table, and I lined up three documents in front of him, the bank statements, the pensions accounts, and the Liechtenstein dossier.

"We won't be disturbed here … shoot."

"These relate to the financial fraud," I said, pushing the first two slightly to one side. "This is the one I think will interest you."

He picked up the Liechtenstein Trust dossier.

"So the Kellys own all these premises?"

"According to Black and his sources. Did you see?" I said, pointing to Gallow Terrace.

"This still doesn't prove they were running that brothel," he said.

"And look at the entry for Crossglen."

"Heroin refinery," he sighed. "It figures."

"See, there was a fire and some one was killed."

"It could have been the girl's father." He sucked on one of his teeth. "Again, it doesn't prove anything."

"But the other addresses …"

He read on in silence for a few moments, before closing the dossier and turning his chair to face me directly.

"Great stuff. Well done. But what happens next is police work. You have to leave it to me."

"Oh no. This is my script. You're not writing me out."

"You can't come with us. You can break the story. I'll give you everything and make sure you're ahead of your competition all along the way. But you have to leave the rest to me."

"I want to come with you. How can I tell the story, if I don't see it first hand?"

"You can't be in a hundred places at once. Leave me to do what I do best and I'll do everything I can to help you do what you do best. It was the deal, remember. What we agreed at the very start."

I hesitated.

"Why should I trust you?"

"Because if you don't, I'll lock you up in a cell for obstructing police inquiries … and throw away the key."

"You wouldn't dare …"

"Do we have a deal?" he asked again, grinning.

I nodded.

"Good. I have a lot to do first. Where will you be?"

"I'll stay at the Clanachan … until I hear from you."

"Don't worry, it won't be long." He opened the interview room door and called a junior officer to show me out.

Chapter Fifty-one

9pm Thursday, November 29, Glasgow

I didn't hear from Poitu until 9pm the following evening. I was watching a film in my hotel room, when my mobile rang.

"Can you get over here now? Things could start kicking off soon."

I didn't bother to reply, but grabbed my coat and left the hotel room without even switching off the television.

A sergeant was waiting for me at the front desk.

"Julia Lighthorn?" he opened security doors to let me pass. "I'm Sergeant Brown, we spoke on the phone a month or so ago, when the body was found in the Clyde."

"You cracked the joke about actuaries at the bottom of the sea."

He blushed, slightly. "A good start," he said, "but a very bad joke."

"In the circumstances," I replied.

"We'd better start again. We've a long night ahead."

I followed him down a twisty corridor and up three flights of stairs before he stopped, to unlock a door.

"This is my office, and we're going to share it tonight."

There were two desks, one piled high, the other empty. He moved towards the cluttered one, and pointed for me to sit at the other. "You should have everything you need there to work through the night. If you need anything else let me know. Coffee?"

I nodded, and he left the room.

The desk had a PC, telephone, notepads and pens. I was already logged on and everything seemed to be working fine.

When Brown returned with the coffee, Poitu was with him.

"Good girl," he said, pulling up a chair beside me. He was wired. "Sergeant Brown will be with you all night. We're starting to go in at midnight."

"Going in?"

"We're starting with the clubs. I want to pick up Tom Kelly and McSherry before they get any warning. Shortly after, we'll begin raiding every address on the dossier."

"You've checked them out."

"To the extent that we can, in such a short space of time."

"Any sign of the girl?"

"Not so far."

"What do you want me to do?"

"I'd like something in the morning's newspapers. What's the latest deadline you can file to?"

"I can produce a holding story for early editions tomorrow, not much more. But I can file updates through the night for the later editions and the website."

"Good."

"What about the competition?"

Poitu raised a questioning eyebrow.

"My competition," I repeated for emphasis. I didn't want any photo finishes. I'd worked hard for this story and deserved the gold cup.

"I'm not saying anything to anyone but you, and I don't want you talking, is that clear, Hornblower? I don't want hoards of hacks, and TV crews getting in our way. I promise the story is all yours."

"Ross?"

"Anybody," he looked at his watch. "I have to go. Get busy."

As soon as he had gone I called Ludgate on his mobile.

"There's a big story about to break. The police are raiding about 30 premises owned by a vice ring they believe the Kellys have been running."

"Jeez, where are you?"

"Right now, I'm in Strathclyde head office. They've given me my own little desk."

"The police head-quarters?" he sounded dumb-founded.

"That's right. We've got the story to ourselves."

"You haven't gone native have you?"

"No chance."

"Good." I could hear him thinking. "First edition will be hitting the streets soon. File the best holding story you can, then update for the later editions, and file after that for the web as often as possible. It's the best we can do. We'll cross-ref the web material in the paper, so it will all be well flagged up. I'll send you some web ID and access codes. You can edit it remotely. Any problems, let me know."

When I hung up, Brown came over and sat in the chair Poitu had pulled up, pushing it a little further from me. My briefing began.

"The whole operation will be synchronised. Teams are going into the three clubs at midnight, with others hitting all the addresses on this list. Until we go in, there's no knowing what we will find. Your first story must be filed in absolute secrecy. There must be no leaks. And it has to be general."

"Police last night planning raids at Glasgow top night clubs plus addresses throughout Scotland, believed to be involved in criminal activity … that sort of thing?" I questioned.

"Sounds perfect."

"Can I name the clubs?"

"Yes."

"The addresses?"

"No."

I began to type, and played with the story for half-an-hour or so, before showing it to Brown.

"And they say there's no censorship in the UK," I said, emailing it across to where he sat only a few yards away.

"That looks fine," he said, as he read. "But we want a guarantee of no leaks before I can let you send it."

I called Ludgate again. "Send it direct to Bob Jones. He's running the night desk. I'll call him. That way no one else will have access. It'll go straight into a secure page for the later editions."

I filed the story at 10pm, and there was nothing to do but wait. Brown took me down to the canteen at 11pm, for fish and chips. Then we returned to his office to wait out the night.

To Poitu's credit, once the action began, the calls came in fast and furious. Every team had someone designated to report back to us.

The first report came from the Sea Witch club. Poitu had taken twelve men into custody, including Frankie McSherry. Similar news came from the other clubs.

Across the country, reports were coming in of arrests at brothels, and the seizure of drugs, from heroin to crack cocaine and dope.

I filed stories through the night, updating as fast as I could with the latest information. Wave after wave of vans arrived at the station, filled with suspects picked up at various addresses. The air was alive with a medley of shouting and doors slamming. Similar scenes, I guessed, were taking place at nicks all over Scotland.

By 4am, the local radio news were on to the story. They had little to go on and were mainly lifting reports from our latest web bulletin. Through it all, there was no news of Tom Kelly or Roxy.

At 6am, Poitu walked into the office. He looked grim.

"I think we've found your girl." By his tone, it was not good news. "McSherry's singing like a canary. He's determined not to take the rap for everything."

"Tom Kelly?"

"Disappeared."

"The girl?"

"McSherry says Kelly ran children out of houses in the Black Top housing scheme."

"Near the Stella Maris?"

He nodded.

"The properties were empty when we got there. Looks like they'd cleared the girls out."

"Jack Kelly?"

"We've picked him up, but he's saying nothing."

"So we're no closer then. How do you know there were children there?"

"They left their things behind, clothes, shoes ..." his throat caught, "tiny ... there were even a few toys."

"And now?"

"Go back to the hotel and get some sleep. There'll be more work to be done later."

"The press conference …" Brown had already told me there was a press conference planned for 9.30am.

"They'll be told nothing you don't already know."

I got up, picked up my coat and headed for the door. I was so tired, I couldn't see straight.

"You need to rest too," I said, as I brushed past him.

"Don't you worry about me," he said, "I'll be fine."

Chapter Fifty-two

Noon Friday, November 30, Glasgow

I slept fitfully, troubled by dreams of Mary Kelly, Margaret Strachan, and their ancient feuds feeding through to the next generation of Ken and Jack. I awoke to the sound of my phone ringing. It was Sandy. I saw I had several missed calls.

"I've been trying to get you. What the hell's been going on?"

"Where are you?"

"I'm still in Tarbert. Where are you?"

"I'm in Glasgow."

"I guessed from your stories."

"Sandy, they've got dozens in custody. McSherry among them. Poitu says he's singing like a canary."

"The Kellys?"

"Tom's disappeared."

"No, he hasn't, he was here. I saw him this morning, on his boat."

"Jesus. I must tell Poitu."

"I already have."

"Where is he now? Kelly?"

"I've no idea. The boat's gone."

"What did Poitu say?"

"He said he hoped he wouldn't do something stupid."

"I'd better go," I said, dialling the inspector's mobile the second I hung up.

He was already one step ahead of me.

"I'm heading to Tarbert. D'you want to come?"

"It's a three or four hour drive," I said.

"Be downstairs in ten minutes," he replied. The line went dead.

I switched on Sky News as I dragged on some jeans and a sweater and splashed water over my face. Fighting had broken out on the Lebanon border with Israel, and there were food riots in Zimbabwe. This was followed by a four minute package about a co-ordinated series of raids on clubs and brothels in Glasgow.

Poitu was waiting outside the Clanachan.

"Get in," he pointed to the back seat of the BMW. His driver nodded a silent hello, and we sped away.

Poitu turned back to me. "Apparently, the fastest way to get there is up the Clyde. I've been told we can do it in an hour-and-a-half."

The car weaved its way towards Glasgow's modern quay, where derelict wharves stood side by side with modern hotels, offices, and conference halls.

As we neared the quayside, I could see a boat waiting, with half-a-dozen officers in life jackets waiting to embark.

My phone rang. It was Sandy again.

"Are you with the inspector?" he guessed right. "Let me speak to him."

I handed the phone over, and watched the gulls diving for fish, hundreds of them, cawing noisily. Poitu listened poker faced.

"I see," he said. "We'll be there as soon as we can."

He handed my mobile back.

"Bad news?"

"The boat's gone. It's been seen on Islay. Thinks we could catch up with him off one of the islands,"

He threw me waterproofs and a life jacket, which hit me hard in the face. "Here, get into these. And get a move on."

It was a struggle getting into the gear with trembling fingers. I wasn't sure whether it was the ice wind, or nerves, which turned my fingers into bendy straws, that could move, but not in the direction you wanted. As I wrestled, I remembered Sandy's words the first time I met him. "The Kellys have property all over the islands."

At least the weather looked promising, if chilly.

"What kind of boat is this?" I asked the pilot, as he helped me aboard.

"They're called ribs … rigid inflatables. Very fast …"

Sure enough, the boat took off with a kick like a stallion. I was unprepared for the speed with which she tore across the waves.

"How fast?" I asked Poitu, who sat beside me. He shouted the question to the pilot.

"We're aiming for 42 to 43 knots," came the reply.

"Fast," Poitu said, handing me a set of goggles. I didn't have to wait long, before we hit a shower and I needed them. The rain slashed against my face, as the boat crashed over the waves. Raindrops, innocent enough on land, sliced like splinters of glass into the skin at this speed.

Fortunately, it didn't last. The sun came out again, visibility improved, and the goggles came off. We passed old abandoned dockyards, others still working, and sped through Holy Loch, where the US naval fleet used to dock.

"It's huge, isn't it? The Clyde."

"Vast," Poitu replied.

"Bigger than the Thames?"

"No way," he grinned, but I wasn't so sure.

The shower resumed, and we journeyed on in silence. But it brightened up again as we headed towards the Highlands. By the time we reached the Isle of Bute, it was brilliant sunshine. The water glistened below green mountains.

The pilot pulled into a narrow water inlet between Bute and a neighbouring island, to give us a break. He turned off the engines, handed us each a bottle of water, and let the boat gently drift.

Poitu stood up to speak to the pilot.

"How much longer?"

"Less than an hour, hopefully … unless the weather turns."

"This weather is good?" Poitu sounded surprised.

"Remarkable, very unseasonal, never known it so mild."

"I wouldn't call it mild," I whispered to Poitu, as he sat down.

The pilot restarted the engine.

The scenery became more dramatic as we flew across the waves past Arran and Mull of Kintyre, racing towards who knew what. And yet I felt strangely happy. I was intoxicated with the sunshine and beauty unravelling before me. And soon I would see Sandy.

Chapter Fifty-three

4pm Friday, November 30, Tarbert

As we neared our destination, the sky fused into a melange of yellows, oranges, reds and ochres, bewitching, like a glorious dawn; but strangely out of place so close to dusk. Clouds distorted, constantly changing shape and colour.

"Have you ever seen anything so beautiful?" I said.

Poitu wrinkled his brow as he stared, puzzled, at the horizon. He looked worried.

"Weird," he said, "the birds have gone." He was right. The gulls, whose cawing had accompanied us up the Clyde, had disappeared. I thought of Strachan's funeral and the flocks heading inland to escape a storm.

I forgot the sky, though, when I saw Sandy standing on the quay waiting for us. He wore a powder blue jumper, the colour of his eyes. My heart soared. He waved, as the boat pulled up at the harbour wall. He reached to help me ashore, and held me in his arms for a few minutes, while Poitu took a call from one of his officers.

"They've been trying to get us. No reception till now," he said, coming ashore. Sandy released me from his arms.

"McSherry's spilling more. Reckons Kelly's panicked and is fleeing abroad," Poitu added.

"So, we're too late?" I asked.

"Not necessarily." He shook his head.

"He could still be somewhere in the islands," Sandy said.

"Exactly," Poitu agreed. "First sight and we'll get him."

A rumble of thunder echoed in the distance. Sandy looked at the sky, and bit his lip.

"I don't like the look of this weather," he muttered. "There's a wind getting up."

The warmth from a fire burning in the grate hit me as I entered the cottage.

"That's wonderful I said," collapsing on the settee, and closing my eyes. Sleep overwhelmed me, and I drifted straight off.

"And more wonderful still," I added, when Sandy woke me, handing me a steaming mug of coffee and a plate of sandwiches.

"How long have I been out?" I asked, yawning

"Couple of hours. You must've been up half the night."

"I was," I grimaced. "But I slept a bit this morning. My body clock's out of synch."

Sandy laughed

"D'you think Tom Kelly will get away, make it out of the country?" I asked, sipping my coffee.

"Not in this weather, he'd be crazy to try," he shook his head.

"Why take the girls with him? Why not just run?"

"Tom's an adventurer. He doesn't stop to think."

"Why risk the girls?" I asked again.

"Family honour."

"Honour? The Kellys?"

"You don't understand, Julia. In this part of the world, even now, the Kelly name means something. Sure, it operates in a different world to the one we're used to; legitimate business, shored up, when times are tough, by dubious activities. Folk round here can accept that. Drugs, booze, what's the difference? Illegal sweat shops? Well, the immigrants wanted to come. Prostitution? Willing adults, whose business is it?"

"The girls are children."

"Exactly. The Kellys could never survive an association with child abuse. The West of Scotland is deeply religious. Children are sacrosanct."

"That doesn't explain …"

"He'll have panicked. He'll have been terrified of the reaction of his father and grandmother."

"Jack wouldn't have known?"

"The clubs, the drugs, the prostitution? Probably. But the children

..." he shook his head.

There was a knock at the door. Sandy got up to open it. A gust of wind momentarily iced the room. It was Joe.

"The Sea Witch has been spotted off Jura. Poitu is going out and asking for volunteers."

"What about the rescue services?" Sandy asked.

"They're already out," Joe said. "Ship's goin' down out west, Russian, heading for Belfast."

"How bad is it?"

"Not too bad right now, but anything up to gale ten winds forecast for later."

"What about the other rescue boats?"

"Fishing fleet's not docked, they can't be spared."

"Not on a bunch of trafficked kids ..." Sandy muttered under his breath, adding "Sure, sure, give me a minute."

He closed the door and came over to the settee. He sat beside me for a moment, gently stroking my hair.

"I have to go, they're only children ..."

"I'm coming too."

"Julia, you're no sailor. This won't be a punt in the park."

"I'm coming and you won't stop me." To his credit he didn't try.

He locked the cottage door. Great gusts of wind battered us as we made our way to the quayside. A deep scarlet washed the sky. Sandy banged on a door as we passed the row of cottages, where Joe lived.

Along the harbour, groups of women huddled together, gazing out to sea, hoping for some news of the fishing fleet. A few muttered prayers, like spells. Old sailors shook their heads, as they looked from sky to sea.

The True Love was moored close to the rib. Poitu looked relieved to see us.

"We've got her," he shouted through the wind. "She's heading back to Jura, looks like he lost his nerve."

"If Kelly's in trouble, it must be bad out there." Sandy looked grim.

"Bad. It'd be mad to take a boat out given the forecast," the pilot of the rib chipped in.

"For Christ's sake," Poitu's strain was starting to tell. "We'll be signing those girls' death certificates, if we don't."

Sandy nodded in agreement.

"Are we ready then?" Joe jumped aboard the True Love.

"OK, we go," the pilot agreed, as if against his better judgment. There were no other volunteers. The rib and the True Love would be going alone.

Thunder cracked over head, like a hammer splintering the skull of the world. Sweeping gusts of rain pounded the waterfront. We leapt back as a twenty foot wave crashed onto the quay. Small boats, anchored in the harbour, lurched like crazy drunks. One smashed on the sea wall.

"Come on, we'd better get moving." Sandy said, jumping aboard before turning to help me climb into the boat. We hastily pulled on waterproofs and life jackets.

"I'll steer under power to get us started, but we'll need those sails for when we clear the harbour Joe," Sandy shouted to Joe, as we began to motor out of the harbour. The True Love couldn't match the rib for speed. It soon left us behind.

Joe pulled on some ropes in the cock pit, and the sails began to unfurl. I heard a screeching sound, like an animal in pain. It was the wind straining the mainsail.

"Here, clip on this harness," Sandy said. "It's going to get rough out here."

The three of us huddled together in the cockpit, as the last light of day leaked out of the sky. The sea had moved into the driving seat and was propelling us forward.

"The winds getting up." Joe shouted across the gusts. "I've never seen it build so quickly." They exchanged a glance, which I only partly understood.

"At least it's veered to North West," Sandy shouted above the clamour of the wind.

"What does that mean?" I asked.

"It's behind us, pushing us along, working with us," he tried to reassure me.

It didn't feel like it was working for us. Lightning split the dark and a crack of thunder broke overhead. Waves pummelled the boat relentlessly, as we pitched and rolled. I prayed that Sandy and Joe's knowledge of these waters would keep us safe.

There was no sign of the rib anywhere, but it could outrun the True Love by miles. Nor did we see a shadow of the Sea Witch.

Next came the big shock. The craft began to vibrate as a mighty wave rumbled beneath, before exploding, spewing us up out of the water. I was thrown violently across the cockpit. Straps on my harness winded me, as I hurtled through the air, slamming into a winch. I heard a thunderous bellowing at my side, as my crew mates, like me, landed with a crash, just as, thank God, the True Love righted herself.

Sandy wrapped his arms round me and kissed my face, while Joe struggled with the steering.

"Are you OK?" he spoke, gently into my ear.

"We have to go back," I pulled away from him. "This is madness. We'll all be killed."

"Soon," he said, releasing me and turning to scan the waters for signs of life. I heard him say something about a knockdown to Joe. I didn't know what it meant, but I knew it was serious.

I looked towards Joe.

"Joe, tell me the truth. How bad is it?"

"Very bad, in a boat like this."

The arm, which had hit the winch, the same one injured that night in the brewery, started to throb in agony. I wondered if I had broken it. Lightning flashed overhead again. The boat reeled. I felt panic rising, when Sandy pointed excitedly into the darkness.

"They're there, I can see them."

"Where? Sandy, where?" I shouted, adrenaline pumping renewed energy through me at any prospect of finding them.

"They're there, I can see them." He pointed into the darkness.

"Where? Sandy, where?" I repeated as rain lashed into my face, water seeping down my neck. I was soaked.

"There, look, there ... the life raft. See the strobe ..."

Joe wrestled with the boat, swinging it across in the direction Sandy was pointing. I couldn't see anything. I looked and looked, but I couldn't see it.

"Sure you can see it?" I asked.

"It's there." He handed me the binoculars. At first I couldn't see anything for spray and rain, but at last I saw it, a tiny yellow capsule, floating like a lost buttercup, its fragile light winking on top. As quickly as it surged into view, its light disappeared again.

"Jesus Christ, they'll never survive this," I said, as I lost them again.

"They're OK ... be patient," he said, before turning to Joe, and yelling "heave to."

His jaw set hard, and without warning, we accelerated aggressively past the raft, then spun violently into a sharp u-turn. Now we were heading directly into the wind. It blasted viciously into our faces, screeching in our ears. Sails flapped furiously. Noise-levels went suddenly ballistic. This was truly terrifying.

But Sandy stayed calm, as he steered alongside the raft.

"We need to tie a line," he called to Joe, edging closer. But we were drifting fast.

"We're going to hit them," I shrieked in panic.

"No, we're not," he replied, soberly. "You have to trust me. But we have to act quickly. We'll only get one shot at this."

"If we're lucky," I didn't like the tone in Joe's voice.

Sandy handed me a megaphone.

"Shout," he ordered.

I couldn't imagine how they would hear me over the driving winds and slashing rain.

"Shout," he commanded, and I could see in his eyes that his patience was running thin, with the wind, with the sea and with me.

"Can you hear me," I cried, but even I could barely hear my own voice.

"Louder," Sandy insisted.

"Can you hear me?" I bellowed.

Only the screeching of the demented squall replied. I mustered every ounce of energy and this time screamed with all my being.

"Can you hear me?"

A red flare went up from the life raft. It lit the sky long enough to see one young girl, hanging half out of the raft, sending the signal. Then the deep rose up, and the little boat disappeared under a huge wall of sea. I thought we had lost them.

"They're sunk," I screamed at Sandy.

He shook his head. "Those rafts are stable. They take a lot."

He was right. The sea spat them out again, and we watched with relief as the yellow capsule righted itself.

Joe took the megaphone from me.

"We've got to get you off," he yelled. "We'll throw a rope. You need to tie it on."

He threw a coil across to them, but the gods of the sea weren't ready to finish their terrible game. As Joe hurled the lifeline, the little raft lifted all over again, high on a wave.

"Try again," Sandy shouted, and after two more attempts the girl half-hanging out caught the line, and managed to tie it to the ring on the side.

"We have to get them into the water," Sandy said to Joe.

My blood froze. "They can't jump." I screamed above the waters' roar. "They won't have a chance."

"It's their only chance," Sandy replied, as thunder cracked again above us. "They're wearing life jackets. We'll throw them survival rings, and pull them across to the transom ladder. But they have to do this now, or we'll all drown. Tell them … tell them now."

"How many of these rings do we have," I asked, taking the megaphone from Joe.

"Two," Joe got ready to throw them. "They can come two at a time."

I took a deep breath and screeched across at them.

"We'll throw across two life rings. You have to get into the water and we'll pull you in."

Time was running out. None of us could take much more of this. We were taking on oceans of water. Another huge clap of thunder shook the skies followed almost immediately by a series of electric lightning streaks. Sandy shook his head hopelessly.

"Jump now," I shouted, through the megaphone, as the sea subsided for an instant.

It was like a slow torture watching first one and then a second girl climb out of the raft and land with a huge splash in the water. Both managed to clutch the horse-shoe shaped survival rings, and wrestle them under their arms. Joe hauled them towards the ladder, and I helped them climb safely aboard. The waves lurched again, but despite the buffeting, both the True Love and the life raft stayed steady.

At the next brief calming of the wind, I called to the two remaining girls.

"Jump, now, jump."

"It has to be now," Sandy bawled, as Joe threw the two rings back into the water again.

A third girl slid from the raft, as the final smaller child began to emerge from the opening. Once in the water, the third girl deftly reached for the ring nearest her, and wriggled to get inside it. As she did, lightening ripped across the sky unleashing a deafening boom of thunder. A huge wave flung her up, tossing her far out of the ring, ripping the line right out of the True Love. Our survival line was lost, and she was adrift in the water.

Even above the screeching wind, I could hear the shrieking of terror from the girls standing by me. The fourth small child disappeared in horror back into the raft.

"Sandy," I screamed. Strain was etched on his face.

"We've still got one ring," Joe said. "We can get them off."

Miraculously, the deep lifted her up again, washing her towards the remaining ring which was still intact. She seized it for dear life.

Joe pulled her in. I reached down to help her aboard. She was coughing, spluttering and shaking with the cold, and looked badly shocked. But there was no time to attend to her further.

"We need to get the little one off," Sandy said. "Our time is up. The boat's taking too much water. We have to get her back."

But the last girl had vanished. Traumatised by the previously disastrous rescue attempt, she had disappeared back inside the raft.

"Call her, get her out now."

"You have to jump now," I shouted through the megaphone.

"The water's rising," Jo said, with a worried look. I looked down. My feet were drenched.

"You must come out," I screamed again. "You have nothing to fear."

Jo threw the lifeline again, and we waited for the figure to emerge. Nothing happened.

"You must make her jump." One of the rescued girls ran towards me, pulling at my arm. A pain shot up to my shoulder. "She's my sister. Save her, please, save her."

She turned back to the raft and screeched something in a foreign language, I couldn't understand. But I understood the name alright, which she shrieked over and over through the wind.

"Roxy, Roxy, Roxy …"

So this was Ken's Roxy. A little head appeared. She looked out at us, then stared down at the pitching waves, and froze. She was paralysed with fear.

"We'll have to get her," Joe said

"No, it's too dangerous," Sandy replied.

"I'll go," her sister pleaded.

"No," Sandy said. "It's too risky."

"We can't leave her," I looked across at the child, unclasping my harness. "Joe get ready with that ring."

"Julia … No." But Sandy was too late. I hit the water with an almighty crash. It was cold, like ice. I sank beneath a brutal wave, but pulled myself up again, as it subsided. I heard the ring smash into the water beside me. I grabbed it, with my sore arm, and used my good one to try to swim across to the raft. It was hopeless. The swell kept dashing me back. But then I realised, if I stopped fighting it, and deferred to its rhythm, the water would do the work. And so it carried me across. It took a while, but I got to the raft. I hung onto the side with one hand, grasping the ring firmly in the other, and looked into the raft. A teenager, small for her years, sat motionless, staring.

"Come with me now," I said, as the waves buffeted me about. She didn't move.

"Please, your sister is waiting," She shook her head, without looking at me.

"If you don't come, we will all die. The other girls will die. Your sister will drown." She turned to me now, and I saw tears of terror streaming down her face. "Don't be afraid. I'll help you," I shouted through the wind.

Slowly, she began to move towards the opening. I let go of the raft and took one of her hands as she crumpled into the water. She instinctively grabbed the ring with her other hand, and we began swimming together towards the steps.

We hadn't got far when a huge wave smashed down on us. Roxy let go of both my hand and the ring. The sea hurled her high up on the water, and threw her a distance from me. She began to drift away. I tried swimming towards her, but the tide was too strong and my hurt arm too weak to make much progress. Roxy didn't try at all; just drifted slowly away from us. The terror had gone from her eyes, now. They looked only resigned to their fate.

So this is how it ends, I thought. What had I expected? To find the child, and give her the happy ending the Strachan's had been denied? I don't know what I had expected, but not this. Not another pointless young death.

I watched her drift for what seemed like a lifetime, but was probably only a moment or so before the water rose up again, and washed her little body back near my grasp. I seized it with every ounce of strength left in me. Pain seared through my left arm, but I clung to the child, hugging her tightly.

"Pull us in," I shouted, and they reeled us up.

Sandy was waiting at the ladder to help us. Roxy's sister rushed to her young sibling, while Sandy wrapped me in his arms, without saying a word.

"Shall I take them below?" I asked wearily, when he let go.

He nodded. "We can't keep them all in the cockpit. Be careful. It'll be dangerous below."

We went down, and I saw what he meant. The contents of the cabin lay scattered like it'd been hit by a tornado. With the girls, I collected up the lose items and locked them away. When they were safely settled, I went back upstairs.

Sandy looked drained, but he placed an arm round me, and held me tight. I realised I was shaking with the cold and exhaustion.

"Hold on. It won't be long now. Weather front's passed, wind's backing off to the west."

I tried to say something, but my words wouldn't come out.

I don't remember much about the return journey. We huddled together in the cockpit. I remember my arm hurting like hell; I think I drifted in and out of a dreamlike subconsciousness. I remember Sandy's arm around me, when Joe was at the wheel. I remember his voice in my ear, but not what his words meant, his precious words.

And I remember the motion of the boat, pitching and rolling, but now the sea was using its strength to speed us homeward. Before long, the lights of the harbour glistened in the distance.

We had made it. Sandy had landed us safely. We were home and dry … Roxy, the girls, Sandy, and Joe.

Chapter Fifty-four

2am Saturday, December 1, Tarbert

A crowd waited at the harbour. Sandy helped me out of the boat, then he and Joe got the girls on dry land. We were told to go to the Kilberry for hot refreshments. A doctor was also there to see to the injured.

A blast of heat hit me as we entered the pub. My knees went weak and I slumped against Sandy. My arm was hurting like hell.

"Doctor," I heard him call to a man in the bar, "I think she's shattered her arm."

Someone eased me into an armchair, and began gently feeling my arm. Sandy took the girls over to the fire, and then went to the bar to get hot drinks for us all.

"The other girls?" I asked, trying to sit up.

"Don't you worry," the doctor replied. "The Rib's been back. It landed five girls."

Sandy handed me a cup of sweet tea. The doctor paused for me to take a sip, I handed the cup back to him.

"This is for the pain," I felt a pin prick in my arm. "It'll make you drowsy, but I need to manipulate this arm and strap it up, until we can get you to a hospital."

The room started to swirl before my eyes.

Joe came across to us, to speak to Sandy.

"We need to get back out there." I heard him say, "the Sea Witch is floundering. There are still girls aboard."

I tried to speak to Sandy to stop him going out again. He had done enough. But I couldn't move my tongue. I tried to call his name, but nothing came out. I watched helplessly, as he walked out of the door. Then, for me, the lights went out.

I don't remember how long I was unconscious; only the terrifying nightmares of a delirious brain. I was running for my life, chased by demented characters. I outran my first husband, knowing the next beating would be my last. I dreamt of Kane in the tunnel at Southwark; only he didn't smile when I approached. He raised a gun. And I dreamt of the thugs in the brewery. I ran from them for what seemed like hours, but they always emerged in front of me to block my path.

But it was when I awoke, that the real nightmare began. It was getting light. I was in a warm, comfortable bed, my arm numb, strapped up as the doctor had said. My first thought was for Sandy. Had he and Joe landed safely?

I manoeuvred myself out of the bed and went down to the bar. It was buzzing with people, waiting for news. The nine young girls huddled together by the fire.

"Couldn't get them to go to bed," Mrs McDonald explained. "Not without their pals, they said. Poor wee mites."

"The others?" I asked.

"No sign so far, but the wind's dropped. They'll be back soon. Don't you fret."

The heat and the crowd were stifling, so I went outside to wait. Before long, I could see two boats in the distance. My heart leapt. They were coming back. Please God, they were safe, the girls, the inspector, Sandy and the crews.

My excitement grew as the boats got bigger. I could see the rib clearly. It was moving slowly, keeping pace with the True Love. Soon they would be ashore. Warmth rushed over me. It was as though Sandy were standing on the harbour beside me, holding me in his arms. I felt his kiss on my lips.

A slight unease began to stir, as the boats drew nearer. I could see Poitu. There were three more girls in his boat, plus a couple of men I recognised as the Sea Witch crew. There was no sign of Tom Kelly.

As they pulled closer, I wondered why the rib was going so slowly. It could outrun the True Love by miles. I could distinguish Joe, but I couldn't see Sandy. I ran along the quay shouting his name. Still he didn't appear. I called over and over again, and, even at this distance, I could see a flash of anxiety on Poitu's face.

Poitu was the first to disembark.

"We'll take him straight to his cottage," he said.

Four of them carried him on a stretcher, Joe nestling his head. Poitu walked beside me. When we reached the cottage, Joe took him in his arms, carried him upstairs, and laid him on his bed. I followed them up. After making his captain comfortable, Joe left us alone. Sandy was already cold. I kissed the gash across his forehead; I kissed his face, every inch of it; I kissed his hands through my tears. And then, I sat there with him, holding his hand.

I sat there until the sun went down again. Poitu came in from time to time, and spoke to me. I didn't hear what he said. I wouldn't budge, though. Not for him, not for the doctor, not for Joe or Mrs McDonald. I sat there all through the day, and the following night. This was our last time together, and no one could take it from me.

I sat on at my post the next morning. Sometime during the following day, Marsha arrived. She kissed Sandy, and held his hand. Then she kissed me and took my hand. I remember her voice, but even now I don't remember what she said. And in the end she took me away.

Chapter Fifty-five

11am Friday, December 7, Tarbert

It was a few days before I could piece together the events of the night that took Sandy from me. Poitu gave me an outline, but he refused to discuss what happened in any detail.

"Ross, three girls and two crewmen are dead. What else do you need to know?" and with that the subject was closed, as far as he was concerned.

It was Joe, who helped me understand. The general opinion was Tom Kelly had panicked. He didn't want the Kelly name dragged through the mud of child abuse, so he tried to hide the girls on the islands. After he was spotted, first here in Tarbert, and then in Islay, he made a run for the continent.

"He must have known the risks. He was an experienced sailor. The weather was deteriorating," Joe said. "I guess he gambled he could outrun the storm, but it caught up with him, so he turned back. The Sea Witch was taking in a lot of water, so he put some of the wee girls in two lifeboats."

He pronounced girls like curls, as the Scots do.

"It was a death sentence," I said.

He shook his head.

"It gave them a chance. Poitu picked up one of the life boats and we brought the other in. When we got back out there, the Sea Witch was breaking up."

He swallowed hard, as he recalled what happened next.

"They started to jump."

"It was their only hope?"

"The Sea Witch was going down. Life jackets kept them afloat for a while. We managed to pull a few aboard. It was hard slow work, but he wouldn't give up, the captain. He wanted to save everyone, even when there was no point going on."

"Kelly?"

"He went down with the boat. He'd never leave it. That boat was probably the only thing he loved. He took three girls and a crewman with him."

I stared into the fire, thinking of those young lives cut short.

"Sandy?" I gently urged him to continue.

"He wouldn't give up while there was any hope left. We were close to the rib by this time, working together on the rescue. After a wee while, we couldn't hear their cries or whistles anymore. They had been in the water too long. We knew it was over. The rescue was called off."

"So you started to come back?"

"The sea was quietening now, the storm blowing itself out. On the way home, one last surge smashed into us. We all but capsized. The boat righted itself, amazing that boat. But the captain fell badly … smashed his head on the deck. I rushed to him, and sat him up, tried to make him comfortable. He just stared, his eyes …" Jo looked wretched. "They were lifeless and I knew …"

I stayed on for the funeral, Marsha with me. It was held in the small church on the hill. It was a dark, unforgiving place, and seemed to have nothing to do with the warm, funny, brilliant man I had known.

Poitu spoke of his courage and bravery that night, and how he had made the ultimate sacrifice, risking his life for others. The inspector never seemed to smile or laugh any more. He looked grey. He hated the fact that Tom Kelly had escaped justice. A watery grave was better than he deserved, many said. He had stayed on with me for a bit, boarding at the Kilberry, but he needed to go home, back to the smoke.

I knew his officers had been busy. Jack Kelly was charged with employing illegal immigrants, a holding charge. Patterson was hauled out of the nursing home and into Winchester nick for questioning. Three Strathclyde police officers were arrested and held, without bail, for conspiracy. Interpol picked up two men in Oslo, who were being questioned for the murders of Livingstone and Black. McSherry had told the police where they could be found.

Sister Robert was at the funeral with the girls. The police discharged them into her care, with support from local social services.

After Poitu spoke, the eulogies fell thick and fast. Fellow professionals, family, friends. I didn't listen to their words. It was all I could do to hold myself together and not crack before the service was over. Marsha stood by my side, singing loudly, as though her lungs were fit to burst.

I couldn't take my eyes off the children in the front pew. Those sweet children. James, Laura, Blair and little Sarah; even here, she clung to her little rabbit. Throughout the service, they stood straight and stared ahead of them. While tears flowed freely throughout the rest of the congregation, they remained dry-eyed. How Sandy would have been proud of them. If they could get through this without a tear, then so could I.

The sun came out as we began the short walk to the graveyard. It was mild for the time of year, a blue cloudless sky. Gulls cawed, as they swooped across the loch. I looked down at the water, lapping gently below. Sandy had loved it here. Whatever had happened on that terrible night, this was the place he loved. He would be able to rest here in peace.

The prayers finished, the body was lowered, and the family cast their dust into the grave. I had to get away. I wanted to be alone. Sensing my distress, Marsha slipped her arm into my good arm and we walked away from the crowd, down the hill towards the harbour and the cottage. Christmas lights twinkled around the quay.

At the bottom, a woman was waiting, holding Sarah by the hand.

"Julia," she said, walking towards us. "I wanted to meet you. Are you joining us for the wake?"

Sandy's family had arranged some food and drink at the Kilberry, but I couldn't face company.

"No," I said, in a faltering voice, unsure who I was talking to. "Thank you, but it's for the family."

"Could we have a few moments together, then?" she said, quietly. "I'm Laura, I'm Sandy's first wife."

I hadn't even known she was at the funeral. I could see her daughter Laura in her; conscientious, kindly Laura. I could see why he had loved her.

Marsha took Sarah by the hand and led her in the direction of the Kilberry. Laura and I walked along the quay in silence for a bit, before she spoke again.

"He loved you very much," she said, and I saw little Laura again; Laura wanting everyone to be happy.

"I wanted to thank you for setting us free …" She hesitated, "There had been so much bitterness. But we were talking again, like rational adults."

"I'm glad," I said, and I was glad, for all of them, that he had not died with bitterness unresolved.

"I so wanted our marriage to work. He was so brilliant, so hardworking, driven," she continued. "But I wasn't enough for him. I knew that from the start. He needed someone, who was witty, clever and driven like him. Someone like you."

I felt tears slide down my cheeks. Now the children were gone, I could let go. She placed a hand over mine.

"I loved him enough to be able to tell you that."

I started to sob uncontrollably.

We continued walking, mainly in silence. Laura told me she and her new husband were taking the children. Out of this terrible loss, some good had come. Finally, we walked back to the Kilberry together.

I didn't go in. Marsha was waiting outside, so we returned to the cottage, only to find Carlton Crabb on the doorstep.

"Ah, I've caught you, I was af..ff..fraid …"

"Were you at the funeral?" I hadn't seen him and he wasn't in his usual morning suit.

"No, no. Terribly sad, but Mr Ross wasn't a client."

"Question of the wee fee, I suppose," Marsha said, rolling her eyes.

"Question of a letter," he said, handing me an envelope.

"We'd better go indoors," Marsha said, leading the way and disappearing into the kitchen to make some tea.

Crabb sat down on the settee and cleared his voice, before beginning.

"Mary Kelly died last night," he said. "She deposited this letter with me a couple of weeks ago. She said she wanted you to have it, when the end came."

I turned the envelope over. I really didn't care any more about Mary Kelly.

"A heart attack," Crabb said, as though I had asked. "She had c..c..cancer, been ill a long time."

I thought about our meeting, her frail figure, her wheezing. I could see, now, she was dying.

"So, she knew …"

"That the end was c..coming? Oh yes, had for some time."

I handed it back to him.

"Would you like me to open it?" he asked

I shrugged. It was immaterial to me.

"I'm afraid there will be a fee," he said seriously, but then his eyes twinkled. Heavens above, I do believe Crabb had cracked yet another joke. Despite my heavy heart, and aching arm, now plastered below the elbow, I smiled.

"Do you want me to read it?" he repeated. I nodded. He took out a silver envelope opener from his case and carefully slit the seal. An inscrutable hood fell over his eyes as he read. When he finished, he handed the letter to me.

I read:

'Dear Ms Lighthorn,

I am glad we had the chance to meet before my end. Oh yes, I know I am going to die soon, and I welcome the time coming. I have been too much alone since my beloved Robert passed.

Before I die, I need to make certain facts known, to make sure suspicion does not fall elsewhere in my family.

Your friend Strachan was murdered. I was the one who arranged the contract to silence him and to make it look like suicide.

Strachan was getting close. He had to be silenced. It was easy to arrange. We thought to catch him alone. The assassins were disturbed. All witnesses had to be silenced. This is my confession. I murdered the Strachan family.

Mary Kelly.'

"Do you believe it?" I asked Crabb, looking up.

"It is not the job of solicitors, or dare I say it, journalists, to believe or disbelieve. That will be up to the police and the courts."

He was right. "I must tell Poitu," I said.

"Indeed you must," he replied, as Marsha appeared with the tea.

Chapter Fifty-six

4.30pm Friday, December 7, Tarbert

I didn't have to wait long. Poitu called round about tea-time. I showed him Mary Kelly's letter. He shrugged.

"D'you think she could have been behind it all along?" I asked, noticing again how tired he looked. He sat beside me on the settee with Marsha in an armchair at his other side.

"I'm sure she wasn't." He locked his fingers together and stretched them, until his knuckles cracked. "Kelly's started to talk now, as well as McSherry. Both desperate not to go down for the murders."

"Who was behind it all?" Marsha asked.

"It all started a long time ago, didn't it?" I said.

"That's right," he nodded. "The brewery was in serious decline ..."

"Mary Kelly said it had always been a struggle," I said.

"Jack would have done anything to save it while his mother was alive?" Marsha speculated.

"Exactly, he needed a lucrative side-line. Tom and McSherry had been badgering him for some money to open a night club. He decided to give them a whirl."

"With the first tranche of money out of the pension fund?" I suggested.

"It looks that way. He probably hoped to put the money back in time."

"The club was a success?"

"Hugely, Marsha. More than any of them had expected. So it made sense to continue investing in them."

"While developing other side-lines in drugs and prostitution?" I said.

"Both legal in other countries. Jack probably justified it on the grounds that his ancestors had worked one prohibition. It was only a matter of time, before these were legalised in Scotland. Where was the harm?"

"And business boomed," Marsha said.

"Indeed. Before long, it was the brewery, not the entertainments empire, which was the sideline."

"And they never put the money back," I said.

"What about the trafficking?" Marsha asked. "How did they get involved with that?"

Poitu cracked his knuckles again. "Just a natural progression. They needed girls for prostitution, and there was a never-ending supply of people desperate to enter the country."

"How deep was Jack in all this?" I asked.

"He admits only to raiding the pension fund, and making loans available to his son. Nothing else."

"The murders? The Strachan family? Livingstone? Black?"

"Both Jack and McSherry are adamant that was all the work of Tom. They say a red mist of rage descended, the minute the empire started to be threatened ..."

"By Strachan?"

He nodded.

"Do you buy it?"

"I doubt we'll ever prove otherwise."

"Why the Strachan children?"

Poitu cleared his throat.

"You were right, Almost certainly an accident. Tom probably ordered the killing, thinking the family were away. Do you remember they returned home early? Local muscle entered the house, killed Strachan, then panicked, when they found they were not alone."

"You picked them up in Oslo, didn't you? What are they saying?" I asked.

"Nothing. But McSherry is fingering them for this, Livingstone and Black, and your attack in the brewery. The Norwegian authorities are being very co-operative. We're bringing them back in a few days and putting them before an identity parade. I'm certain Mrs Livingstone will identify them as the two men who came to the door posing as police officers."

"Will I have to take part?" I asked.

"Not at this stage." Something in his tone told me he had sought to spare me the ordeal of confronting my attackers.

Yet it still didn't all add up … not for me.

"It doesn't make sense," I said. "Why kill Ken in the first place? He couldn't prove anything. Yes, he was an annoying thorn in their side, but no one was listening to him."

Poitu walked towards the fire, standing with his back to us for a few moments. His trousers were uncharacteristically creased, long overdue a good press.

"I spoke to Sister Robert earlier. She thinks Ken was on to something and getting dangerously close to blowing the whistle. The girl, Roxy, holds the key. I'm going to interview her tomorrow. Do you want to sit in?"

I hesitated, unsure, before nodding slowly.

"Sure you're up to it?

Poitu stayed for supper. He asked for fried egg and chips, and cheered up as Marsha fussed over him. We didn't speak of the case any more, and they talked mainly of London. They were both ready to go home.

After the meal, I left them and wandered up the hill to Sandy's fresh grave. I wanted some time alone together, to say goodbye.

Next morning, Poitu sent a police car to drive us back to Glasgow. It was hard saying farewell to the harbour and to Tarbert. Joe appeared as Marsha and I were getting into the car. I felt tears prick my eyes, as he squeezed my hand firmly in his big fist.

The journey was along the same road Sandy and I had taken that first weekend I visited the cottage with him. We stopped for some lunch at a country hotel, an hour or so from the city. The dining-room was immaculately laid, with white tablecloths and best silver. Life continued normally elsewhere. The world kept turning.

We approached the Stella Maris from the north, its outline visible at a distance.

"You won't need me," Marsha said, as we got out the car. "I'll take a look at the church, while I'm here."

Poitu had already arrived.

"Good journey?" he asked. I nodded.

The receptionist led us to Sister Robert's office. She was waiting with Roxy and her sister. The child's face broke into a smile, as though pleased to see us, but her eyes were brimming with tears. Her sister held her hand fast.

"It's OK if I stay with the girls?" Sister Robert asked.

"Of course," said Poitu, pulling a chair up opposite them. I sat further away, merely an observer.

Poitu got stuck straight in. His questions were direct, although his voice was softer than usual.

"Roxy, we want you to tell us everything you can, that you think might be useful in our investigations. Everything about your time here, your relationship with Ken Strachan, and with the people you came into contact with."

She did her best, falteringly, stopping often to bite her lip, or look at her sister or Sister Robert for confirmation, or support. But it was her story and she was determined to tell it.

She began with her father, love shining from her eyes.

"He was a brilliant chemist, wasn't he Marietta?" Her sister nodded. After their mother died, there was nothing to keep them in the Ukraine. He had no future professionally. He had upset too many people with his criticism of the slow pace of reform. He saw Russia's influence growing again, and it frightened him.

"He wanted to get us away," Marietta said, "A new start."

"So, he started to investigate emigrating to another country," Roxy took up the tale. "He grabbed the offer to come to the UK all expenses paid. He had to work for two years for the people who arranged our trip. But that would soon pass, he said."

"It's what he always said," Marietta chimed in. "He would hold our hands and smile and say, 'this will soon pass'."

Roxy took up the tale again.

"Marietta and I worked in the sewing factory, when we arrived, and he worked in a workshop behind. He never spoke of what he did, but I knew it made him unhappy. He always said this will soon pass and a happy life was waiting for us.

"Then there was an accident. We never saw him again. Marietta was taken away from me. I was put to work in another factory, near the church."

"That's where you met Ken Strachan?" Poitu asked, gently.

"Yes. We became friends. I told him about my family, about the factory and my father's death. He made some enquiries and said he believed those behind what had happened were involved in another matter he was investigating. He showed me a photograph of someone and asked if I had ever seen him near the factory."

"Did you recognise the picture?" Poitu interrupted.

"Immediately. I'd never mistake that face or the long, dark ponytail. He was often at the factory, telling the manager what to do. He was the boss."

"What happened next?"

"Ken said he needed proof. He gave me a camera, and asked me to take pictures, when he came again. I did and I gave the camera to Ken. He was very excited and told me not to worry. He wanted to download the pictures and then, he said, he had the proof he needed. We took a picture of ourselves, me and Ken together, to mark the occasion."

"But they weren't over," Marietta shook her head.

Roxy bit her lip. "I saw Ken the next day, and he gave me the camera back. I don't know why. We neither of us thought much about it. But it was a digital camera. The pictures were still there. The camera disappeared from my bag. Someone had found it. Next thing I knew, I was moved to the new house. The one with locks ..." A blank look shut down her eyes, as her voice tailed off.

Sister Robert placed a protective arm around her shoulder.

"I think that's enough for the time being, Inspector."

For once he had nothing to say.

Chapter Fifty-seven

3pm Monday, December 24, the New Forest

Christmas arrived with what felt like indecent haste. I decided I wanted to spend it alone. Marsha always loved the big East End knees-up with her enormous family. Though the Khans were Muslim, you wouldn't know it at Christmas time. They, too, loved any excuse for a big family get together.

I couldn't face any of that. I opted instead for a quiet few days in the New Forest, on the river Beaulieu, staying in Buckler's Hard. It had been my retreat in times of trouble before.

Not that recent events were viewed as trouble by everyone. Ludgate was over the moon. We had out-scooped the world, with some of my follow-ups. There was talk of a top journalism prize.

Poitu cheered up significantly once he returned south, and was charging anyone he could pin anything on. Jim Sugden was jubilant and already pressing the new trustees for a law suit against Cameron.

My own suspicion was the rejoicing would be short-lived. It would take years before any of it came to court. There would be appeal after appeal. I could see Patterson doing a deal and being pronounced 'unfit' to stand trial. He'd be sunning himself on a beach with his beloved Edna before long.

Jack Kelly would take the rap for the pension fraud, but nothing much else. In the unlikely event he actually went down, the most he would serve was a couple of years.

It would be very hard to pin much on Cameron. Their insurers would hire the best lawyers. A few scalps would be sacrificed. They would survive.

McSherry would serve time, but for nothing like what he deserved. The killers, the hired hands, would get the stiffest sentences.

But the scandal had forced the Government to put together a financial rescue package for the pensioners, which is what Ken had wanted all along. They would get most, but not all their money.

"Well done, Jules," Omar said, yawning as he leaned back on the chair in my office, after taking me and Marsha out for a pre-Christmas curry lunch. "You got them their money in the end. And you always said it couldn't be done."

"But not enough, Omar."

"It was never going to be enough, Julia."

I arrived at the Master Builders after lunch and checked in. The sun came out, so I took a stroll along the waterfront. The water shimmered silver. The rigs tinkled their fairy bells on the boats moored along the way. I followed the path Sandy and I had taken that last evening we spent here together. The boathouse was unlocked and deserted, just as it had been. I opened the door, and there he was, Sandy. I saw him all over again, walking towards me, smiling, as he had done that night, before taking me into his arms. I was about to step inside, but something stopped me. I stood at the door, I don't know for how long. And then I closed it, and turned to walk back.

As I neared the hotel, I saw a figure standing waiting for me. He waved as I drew closer. It was Poitu.

"Marsha told me you were here," he said, smiling. "Had to come and buy my partner a drink on Christmas Eve."

"Long way to come, inspector," I said.

"It's been a long way for us all, Julia." It was the first time he had called me by my name.

"He was killed for the pictures, wasn't he?" I said, as we walked back towards the hotel.

"Looks that way. We never found them. I looked again. No trace on his computer."

"Wiped?"

"Who knows," he shrugged.

"And who cares," he added. "It's Christmas. Let's celebrate. And this time," he said, opening the door for me to enter. "I'm paying, the drinks are on me."

I laughed.

Postscript

Two years after the Financial Assistance Scheme was established in 2005, the credit crunch struck, along with a global banking crisis. The financial sector in general, but banks specifically, were blamed for triggering the most severe depression for a hundred years. Bank bosses were knocked off their pedestals. Their hubristic days as the untouchables were over.